A Heart for the Homeless

SISTERS OF STELLA MARE BOOK 1

ANNIE M. BALLARD

DEVON STATION BOOKS

Published by Devon Station Books, Fredericton, NB, Canada E3A 2Z8

Contents

A Heart for the Homeless

Chapter 1

Dorie tossed her keys into the basket as she ran through the kitchen into the living room.

"Dad! Dad, where are you? I'm on the news!"

Scrambling for the remote, she clicked the TV on. Someone was moving around upstairs. "Come on, Dad, you're gonna miss it!"

She threw herself on the old, overstuffed couch and tuned into the six o'clock news. Yes, there it was.

"Today in New Brunswick, another case of animal cruelty. We join our reporter Jeannette Sirois on the scene."

"Thanks, Harry," said the slim, well-groomed brunette on the screen. Dorie turned to see her father stomping down the stairs.

"What's all the fuss, Dore?" he asked, sounding irritable. "I was taking a nap."

Dorie frowned at him. "Hush. Watch this."

Jeanette Sirois had been talking. "...isn't the first instance of dog hoarding we've heard of in this community. The RCMP have been called out to three homes in the last month, where the occupants were suspected of either hoarding animals or raising them in unsafe conditions for sale. The people gathered here include both interested neighbours and some activists. I had a chance to speak with a couple of them earlier." A new picture arose, of Dorie and a shaggy-looking man of about forty.

"Hey, kiddo! That's you on TV!"

"Yeah, Dad, that's what I've been telling you. I got interviewed by the MNN reporter while at the scene."

"Yeah, I bet you were at the scene," James muttered, but he settled on the sofa beside her to watch.

"Mike Maybee is the director of County Animal Rescue. Mike, tell us what you know about this situation."

Mike spoke directly to the camera. Though sitting in her living room, Dorie felt his gaze and his words intensely. "Hi, Jeannette. This is our fourth call this month about extreme cruelty to dogs. Our agency received a tip which we passed on to law enforcement. Many of these situations are due to mental health problems, or even well-intended individuals who take on more animals than they can care for."

The reporter questioned, "What does County Rescue do, Mike?"

"We work with other agencies and the police. Animal Control will seize the dogs for their safety. The RCMP will determine if there are charges to be laid. If the owners can't keep their dogs, County Rescue will foster and rehabilitate those that we can, and we help them to find new homes."

"We're also joined by Dorie Madison. Dorie, what's your interest in dog welfare?"

Dorie elbowed her father. "Look!" On the couch, staring at herself on the screen, she hoped she didn't come off like an idiot.

"You look a little nervous, there," James opined.

"Well, I never was on the news before, was I? Listen."

"Well, I love dogs. Dogs are better people than a lot of people. They're my best friends. I can't bear to hear about dogs being hurt, stuck inside, tied up for weeks, anything like that. So I volunteer with Mike at County Rescue and try to help. And I even..."

"Thank you, Dorie. Mike, would you say that County Rescue needs volunteers?"

"Jeannette, we can use all the help we can get. We appreciate donations, too, from community members who want to support safety for dogs here in Stella Mare."

Jeannette Sirois turned to a well-coiffed blonde woman in heels. "And here is Andrea Chase, of local canine welfare agency, BARC. Andrea, what's your interest in this situation?"

Andrea looked into the camera with a winning smile. "Jeannette, my organization, Better Activity and Regulations for Canines, works hard to encourage our government to protect dogs from unscrupulous breeders, to prevent cruelty, and protect them from neglect. We're always at work in the capital to make our province a better place for dogs. Situations like this, well, they just remind us that there is always more we can do for our best canine friends."

Jeannette Sirois turned a toothy smile to the camera. "There you have it, Harry. Dog hoarding may be criminal or not, but County Rescue is there to help out the dogs."

The film cut away, back to the live feed where Dorie could see the RCMP taking away the yellow police tape and the crowds had dispersed.

"Wait!" Dorie was incensed. "Hey, she cut part of it out. Oh, man..." She turned to James on the couch.

"Well, that was my fifteen minutes of fame, and most of it got edited out. I was telling her about the business, you know. I thought it would be good for the Pampered Pooch to have a little free advertising." She turned back and clicked off the remote. *Darn it.*

James leaned back on the couch and grinned at her. "Nice try, daughter. Your business isn't news."

Dorie scowled. “Yeah, I know. But I figured dog lovers would be watching the story. Worth a try anyway, right?”

James shook his head. “Dorie, there's no shortcut out of hard work. What were you doing down there anyway? How can you get customers if you're never in the shop? You've got bills to pay, right? You're not growing a business by hanging around watching the police work. Or by helping Mike take care of dogs.”

Dorie sighed. This again. “Yeah, yeah. Mike called me and asked me to come, and it wasn't like I had anyone scheduled. There were twelve dogs in that place.”

“Customers pay the bills. Volunteering is for retired people, Dorie. Work! You don't build a business without work. Work is how you build a life.”

Dorie stifled a sigh.

The kitchen door creaked open. “Ahoy, the house!”

“Hi, Corinne,” Dorie called. “We're in here.” Thank goodness her aunt was here. Maybe this would keep James from delivering a well-worn lecture.

When her aunt entered, Dorie jumped up from the couch to deliver a hug. “Hey. I was on the news.”

“What? Just now, you mean?” Corinne sat in the rocking chair near the couch. Dorie sank back down, avoiding her father's gaze.

“Hi, Corinne,” he said shortly.

“Dad's about to give me a lecture,” Dorie said. “I'm pretty sure it's a rerun.”

Corinne raised her perfect eyebrows. “Some people need repetition.”

“Not you, too.” Dorie sighed. “Do I really need so many people to keep me on ‘the proper path,’” she said, offering air quotes. “It’s crap being the youngest forever, you know? Everyone knows everything better than you.”

“Well, is it true?”

"Heck, don't know. I don't know how I'm supposed to get people to come to a dog spa in this town and get them to pay money for something they think is frivolous. You can't change people's minds. It isn't my fault."

Corinne looked at James, who shook his head. He looked at Dorie and said, "It's not the people in town, honey. Six dollars for coffee is frivolous but some people pay it daily. You must show them that they can depend on you. You say you're available for walk-in appointments but you're never there. People need to know you're reliable. You have to treat this like a real business to be taken seriously. You're not a kid anymore and it's not a hobby."

It was an effort, but Dorie refrained from rolling her eyes. "I've heard it all before, Dad. Honest. I do listen."

"You listen but you don't hear. Nothing changes, little girl. Yes, I get it." Her father leaned over and tugged on her ponytail. "Okay. I've said my piece. You were on the news to stand up for dogs, and now that's over. What about dinner? Corinne, you here for dinner?"

"Is that an invitation? I really just stopped by talk to Dorie about a work problem, but if you have dinner, I could eat." She waved a manila envelope.

"You want to talk to me about your work? Really?"

"Yes, it's a dog thing. But food, are you really offering food?"

"Yah, well. Dinner at the moment is pretty hypothetical," Dorie admitted. "If you want to eat, you might have to have some ideas."

Corinne laughed. "Well, I can get that level of dinner at my own house. Another time, guys. You all take care, okay?" Leaning down, she kissed James on the cheek. He patted her shoulder.

"Walk me to the door, Dorie. It'll only take a minute. See you later, James."

Curious, Dorie followed her aunt into the kitchen. "So, what's this work thing?"

Pulling on her coat, Corinne said, "You know I love social work, most of the time, but working with seniors can be hard."

Dorie nodded. "I bet. But what's that got to do with me? And dogs?"

"A lot of the people I work with have dogs and there's no real plan for the animals when their people have to leave home. I had another one today. Her fluffy mutt was the love of her life, her best friend. I must've spent half my day trying to find a setting where she could take her dog. She really can't take care of a dog, not without help. I was wondering, with all the volunteering you do for Mike at County Rescue, have you heard of anything that could help? It's one thing if relatives will take the dog, and I guess that's what most people do, but otherwise...well, it's heartbreaking."

"Is this actually a rescue situation?"

Corinne shrugged. "It depends, I guess. I have worked with Mike once in a while, but we need a real solution for this problem. Just because you can't take care of yourself and your dog, you don't stop loving them and wanting to spend time with them. But most residences don't permit dogs, and they don't have staff to take care of dogs as well as the people."

"I really don't know what to say, Corinne."

"I didn't expect you to have a solution for me," Corinne smiled as she turned up her collar. "I figured I'd get you to put your brain to work on it, and you'll probably come up with something."

"What? Me? The kid who never gets anything right?"

"Yes, you." Corinne leaned into a hug. "Now go make food for my brother-in-law."

"Right, dinner. Bye, Corinne."

Dorie headed back into the living room.

"Corinne looks so much like your mother." James sounded wistful.

She plopped herself back on the couch beside James. "Yeah. Even I can see it. And she's what, twelve years younger? More?"

She looked at her father's eyes, now distant. *How does he keep on going?* It had been almost three years since her mother Aggie died—since the heart of their family was cut out. *And we just keep on doing what we do. Like argue about who makes dinner.* She heard her stomach growl. With a sigh, she forced energy into her legs and jumped back up.

"We were talking about dinner. Right. I'll make you a deal. I'll come up with something if you take the dogs out. Or I can take them if you want to cook?" She looked at him hopefully.

Wistfulness gone, James laughed. "Little girl, you're always negotiating about something."

"Yep. That's how you know it's me and not some alien taking over my body. If I ever just agree about everything, you'll know I've been invaded by a body snatcher."

"All right, then, it's the dogs for me," James said. Pushing up from the couch, he headed to the kitchen. "I can recognize the better of two bad options."

"Well, then, it probably will be hot dogs for the both of us," Dorie threatened, but he scoffed and grabbed several leashes where they hung near the door. The jangle of leash hardware brought a huge burst of activity from the sun porch beyond the living room. Custard and Mallow each had massive dog beds that took up nearly all the floor space. Often oblivious to human events, they came alive in a single burst with certain key sounds: the leash hardware, the opening of the big tub of kibble, or any sound made by their food bowls.

They gamboled into the kitchen wide awake with excited pleasure.

Dorie gave them an irritated glance. "What's with these guys? I came home and they didn't even bother to say hi. Corinne was here and left and they didn't move. You jangle the leashes and suddenly you're the Chosen One. Huh."

"Man's best friend, Dorie." James grinned. "You're missing the man part."

"Ugh, Dad. Get out of here. I have a dinner to invent."

Chad didn't bother watching the news most days. Being his job, it was old hat and, right now, he was on vacation. Not working, supposedly. But Jeannette had called and asked very prettily if he would help her out. A sucker, he said yes. There was a tiny part of him that thought if he said yes and was the good guy once again for Jeannette, she would have a drink with him. A date? No, that was impossible. But maybe a drink.

When he proposed it to her after they wrapped the story, she all but laughed at him.

"Oh, Chad, is that what you think this is?" Her silvery laugh sent a chill down his spine. "Oh, no, thanks. No drink. Thanks for helping." She flipped him a backhanded goodbye wave and was off in her shiny red convertible before he even realized what hit him.

Oh, man, will I ever learn? Of course, she just needed a cameraman for this story. *I'm supposed to be on vacation. Or what passes for vacation in my life.* He climbed heavily into his old black truck, driving back out of town to his grandmother's place. Turning on the radio, he caught a bit of the local news as he was sliding toward his favourite music station. It was that woman, he realized, from the interview.

"Dogs are better people than a lot of people. They're my best friends. I can't bear to hear about dogs being hurt, stuck inside, tied up for weeks, anything like that. So I volunteer with Mike at County Rescue and try to help."

He shook his head at the sentiment. Dogs were dogs. They weren't people, although he could agree that he liked some dogs better than he liked some people. Like his grandmother's dog,

Frou-Frou. Annoying little animal, but nicer than Jeannette, his inner self growled.

The little snippet on the radio made him think about the interview. Mike was a pro at talking to media, but he really didn't care about making an impression. He was cool, calm, collected. But the other one, Dorie, she appeared different. Chad found himself warming a bit as he thought about her. She looked pretty uncomfortable, smiled too much (but she did have a cute smile), and talked a lot. Really a lot, and very fast. Most of it got sliced up in Jeannette's edit, but she had said a few things about dogs and people, and about her work. She had a beauty salon or something like that. Only for dogs. It sounded weird. Dogs liked to hunt. They rolled in mud and went swimming in lakes to retrieve ducks that their owners shot down. Or they were watchdogs, protecting people and property. He didn't think much of a pooch who needed a beauty salon. Although Frou-Frou, well, he might like a little salon time.

As he thought about the day and Dorie's smile, Jeannette's tinkling laugh and his own humiliation faded. *What time is it? Maybe I can get home to see the six o'clock news.* He stepped on the gas.

"Hey, Nan, I'm home," he called, entering the old farmhouse. "You need a motion light out that back door," he added, coming into the living room. "It's dangerous in the dark."

His grandmother smiled at him but shook her head. "Oh, Chaddie, always telling people what they need. That's a bad habit. I've lived here sixty years without a motion light and that's twice as long as you've been alive. You don't need to tell me what I need."

"I think it would be safer," he said seriously and dropped onto the old Chesterfield by her side. "You're not as, um..."

Alice raised her eyebrows at him. "Yes? I'm waiting for you to finish that thought. Not as what?"

"Never mind." He grinned. "I should know better. Let's watch the news. I want to see the story I was on today."

Watching the news at his grandmother's house was like being dropped back into the 1990s. The TV was old, big, and boxy. He had no idea how it was still working. There was a remote control, but it was enormous, so large it stayed on the coffee table.

"Much better." She grinned at him. "What were you working on?"

"Dog story. Hoarding or some such." Frou-Frou, Nan's mid-sized poodle, yipped. Chad scoffed but Nan was sure Frou could understand human talk.

"Don't worry, Frou. I might be old but I'm not getting dozens of dogs."

"That dog," Chad said, giving Frou-Frou the side-eye. "He's too nosy for his own good."

"Oh, Frou is a good boy, Chaddie. Look. Your story is up next."

Sitting on the uncomfortable ancient Chesterfield put him next to Alice. Little Nan, just about half his size, he thought, looking at her, fragile in appearance but tough as nails. Like that darned dog. Frou-Frou was all fluff, but the thing would defend either of them to the death and had tried, when squirrels attempted an invasion of the back porch where Nan stored a basket of apples.

"Oh, look, here it is!"

"Oh, there's that Mike Maybee. He's a hard worker, that one. And look at those poor dogs!"

"I think Animal Control is taking care of them, Nan."

"Oh, but...Chad. Who is that?"

Chad looked up to see Dorie's slightly nervous smile. Less than a sentence later, Jeannette's face filled the screen.

"Chad. She is cute. Who is that?"

"Doris, Dorie, something like that. I can look it up for you. Why?"

Nan shrugged. "Well, you don't seem to be meeting anybody out there in Saint Jacques. Might be a nice girl from Stella Mare would keep you home here. That Jeannette, she called you to come help. Even on your vacation. Do you like her?"

"Man, there is no privacy here, is there?" He gave Nan a sideways glance.

"Privacy? This is family. I'm only looking out for my favourite grandson, you know. If you won't do it, I might have to."

"Yeah, well, I kind of did like Jeannette, and so when she called me, I thought possibly, but she kind of blew me off. She's pretty, but she's pretty self-involved too."

"Don't you worry," Nan said stoutly as she patted his knee. "You don't need that."

"It really wasn't a big deal, Nan. I'm here to visit you, anyway, not to try to find a woman."

Nan pursed her lips as she gazed at him.

Chad's face warmed under her look. "Nan, come on. I'm good. I have a good job, a decent apartment, some friends, and I've even been able to collaborate on a film recently. You don't need to worry about me."

"I don't worry about you, dear. Don't you think that. I worry about me not getting to see you enough."

"Ahh, I get it. It's all about you, Nan, right?"

She nodded. "Yes, that's right, Chaddie. All about me. I don't worry about you one bit. Except you are a little bossy."

"Bossy! Me? I wonder where I got that from?"

"Don't you start. You need to watch out for that know-everything attitude. Puts some people right off. Even if you're right."

"Nan. I am right. I don't say anything that doesn't have a solid basis in fact."

Alice shook her head. "Do you ever sound like your father. Now that was a man who thought he was right."

Chad leaned in. "And?"

"Well, he was, most of the time. But he didn't make a lot of friends that way."

"I remember that no matter what I did, he had a better way."

Alice looked at him, a question in her eyes.

"Yeah, Nan, I didn't love that when I was a kid, but now I realize he was right."

"He was right about stuff, but was he right about how to relate to a little boy? Think about that, Chaddie, when you feel like you have to be right."

He remembered feeling small and awkward and always wrong-footed in the presence of his larger-than-life father. "I wish he was still here. I'd like him to know that things turned out, well, okay."

Alice patted his cheek. "I wish he was too. And I think you turned out more than okay. He wanted to be a good dad, but he just couldn't let any detail go."

"Yeah." Chad felt his chest tighten a bit. Did he do that to other people? Hmm.

"Enough of that though," Alice went on. "No point in rehashing what's over. Let's have some supper."

Chad looked up. "There's always a point to supper."

"I made your favourite. Fish chowder and cheese biscuits."

"Everything you make is my favourite. That sounds great. You make it so nice to be here every time I come, Nan."

"Now you know my motives. They're no longer secret." Alice got up from the Chesterfield and Frou-Frou followed. "No secrets here, grandson. Everything is all about me. Now let's eat."

Chapter 2

Chad woke up to the good smells of coffee and French toast. He really should visit his Nan more often. She took good care of him when he came for a visit. After pulling on clothes, he headed for the kitchen.

Alice sat at the table, sipping from her mug, with the newspaper folded in front of her. Chad smiled as he saw it. Stella Mare's local paper, still read daily by the older generation.

"Good morning. Now I see where Dad learned to fold the paper." Chad bent over her at the table for a quick hug.

"Hello, grandson," Alice smiled. "Breakfast?"

"I could smell it," Chad noted. "You sit. I can serve myself. I live alone, remember?"

"Don't keep reminding me. By the way, I found your girl here in the paper."

"My girl? What are you talking about?" Chad carried his plate of French toast, dripping with butter and maple syrup, to the table. Getting up again, he went in search of cutlery and a mug.

Alice tapped the page. "That girl on the news. About the dogs. Turns out she's James Madison's youngest. Lots of girls in that family. Too bad about Aggie, you know. You know who I mean?"

Chad, sitting, shook his head. "Nope. Should I?"

Alice tsked. "You did grow up here, grandson. Let me think. Maybe you knew Evie Madison? She was ahead of you in school by a couple of years. She'd be Dorie's next sister."

He shook his head. "No. I don't really remember many people from here. Well, the guys I played hockey with, I guess. And Jeannette, but I didn't get to know her until university."

"Hmph. Well, those Madison girls are pretty nice, I think. The oldest one turned out to be a big deal lawyer in Ottawa or something, and then Loretta is a nurse in Saint Jacques. I never did know much about the little one, there, the one on your news show, but I do know that Aggie was a good woman and a good mother and it was a shame what happened to her."

A shadow crossed Alice's face. Chad felt his own forehead wrinkle along with her. Nan looked a little older and frail when her face got sad like that. He didn't like it.

He tried to shift the mood. "What are you doing today?"

She lifted her gaze and her face lightened. "I hope you've planned something for yourself because I've got a full day. Bridge this morning, helping at the soup kitchen from eleven to two, then coffee with a friend, and I'll get home in time to make dinner for my favourite grandson. Unless he has a date?" she added hopefully.

Chad sighed. Once Alice was on a roll, it wasn't easy to get her off it. "No date, Nan. But let me cook for you tonight. Is there anything you need me to work on around here? I'm at your disposal. Getting the house ready for winter or something?"

"Well, yes, you know there's always a list for the house. But I really need your help with Frou-Frou." The dog lifted his head from where it was resting on Alice's foot. Chad could almost hear him saying, "Me? You want Chad to do something with me?"

"You want me to do something with Frou?" Chad asked. Dog and man both gazed at Alice in surprise.

Nan busied herself with gathering her dishes and cutlery. Walking to the sink, she said offhandedly, "Yes, please. Can you take him out with you? He's going to be stuck here in the house all day. Oh, and by the way"—she gave Chad an arch look over her shoulder— "maybe you could take him to his appointment?"

Frou-Frou glared at Chad. Chad glared back. "What appointment, Nan? Finally getting him neutered?" Frou-Frou growled very quietly.

"Chad, really. You don't need to be openly hostile." Alice switched to a whisper. "Besides, that was done years ago."

He laughed. "He's not really listening, Nan. Besides, he probably knows what happened to him. What kind of appointment?"

Alice turned back to the sink, but Chad continued to look in her direction. *What's going on? She's acting a little strange.*

"I made an appointment for him to get groomed. At the new place. I wrote down the address. Can you take him?"

Chad sighed. "Of course, Nan. I'm here to do whatever you need me to do." He gave Frou-Frou a resigned look. He could swear the poodle smirked.

Alice returned to the table with a smile. "Thank you, Chad. Aren't we lucky to have Chad here, Frou?" She scratched the dog behind his ears.

How smug could one medium poodle get? Well, I guess he's the center of her life now that the rest of the family is gone and I'm in Saint Jacques. I should be glad she's got him to love. "Do you ever think about getting a real dog, Nan?"

"Real dog? Frou's a real dog."

"Man, those ribbons in his ear hair. How can he have any self-respect?"

Frou bared his teeth from his place beside Alice.

"He knows his worth. I don't think he lacks self-respect. He's not worried about being manly, or dogly, or whatever it is you're thinking." She leaned down toward the dog's head and murmured, "He's a sweet baby, isn't he?"

"Well, he does seem to run things around here," Chad agreed. "I guess he knows what he's doing."

"Of course he does. Don't let those ribbons and the name fool you. Frou-Frou is a force," Alice said firmly.

"Gotcha. No more complaining." Man and dog had an uneasy truce, most of the time, but his Nan seemed determined to make him like the darned dog. Or to make the dog like him. He chuckled internally. If Nan wanted him to spend the day with Frou, so be it. But Frou-Frou had to come along on Chad's terms.

"Okay, Nan, I got it. You go ahead and get ready for bridge. I'll clean up here and get the list started. I'll take Frou to his appointment. Whether he likes it or not." Chad gave the dog a hard look. Frou hoisted his leg and started licking his privates. *Oh, you little snot. We'll see how this day goes.*

"Okay. I can depend on you." Nan gave him a nod. "Thank you."

"Mmm.

Dorie was behind the little desk in her workspace, hair untidily piled on top of her head, her light-blue coverall smock damp and adorned with curly black dog hair. Holding the phone on her shoulder, she said, "Yes, hold on. Just a minute. Let me see what I can do."

She pulled the appointment book toward her. *I'll have to get a website and let people book online. Either that or hire a receptionist. This is ridiculous. There's no business at all and then when I have work to do, the phone keeps ringing.*

"Yes, Mrs. Corrigan, I can take her on Saturday morning at ten. Thank you for calling. What? Oh, yes. You can leave her for the morning, but I close at one p.m. on Saturday, so please pick her up before then... Okay, yes. Thank you."

The bell on the door jangled. "Hi. Welcome."

The man gave an irritable tug on the leash. "Come on, Frou. You'll probably like it here." He looked up to lock eyes with Dorie. Deep brown eyes behind glasses, dark curly hair, broad shoulders all registered immediately, and he gave her a warm but diffident smile. The dog sat stolidly outside the door and the man's smile disappeared into a grim glare at the poodle.

Oh, that was a nice smile, but where did it go? Who is this guy that doesn't like his dog? She came out from behind the counter, hand extended. "I'm Dorie."

He tugged his poodle through the door, but the dog practically needed to be dragged. Dorie put her hand behind her back and hid her grin.

"Oh, hi," he said, looking and sounding flustered. "Yes, hi, Dorie. Is this your place?" He looked around the storefront room as the door banged behind the dog.

"Yes, it's mine," she said. "Do I know you? I mean, have we met? You look..."

"Yeah, well, not exactly." He shoved his glasses up his nose and peered imploringly at her. "Ah, this ornery beast is Frou-Frou. He's, um, awkward around new people."

"He is, is he?" *Yeah, I know someone else who is awkward. But points to you, buddy, for turning the attention to the dog. Dogs are good for breaking the ice.* Squatting down, she held out her hand. "Hey, Frou-Frou."

Frou-Frou sniffed her hand and gave it a quick lick. He looked at her face and wagged his whole rear end. "Yeah, you know I have treats, don't you?" She grinned at the dog over her shoulder as she headed back to the counter. "Can he have a treat?" she asked.

"Uh, yeah, I guess so. He's, he's not my dog," the man said.

Dorie's hand stopped in mid-motion. "He's not?" she asked. *That might explain the awkwardness. And the dislike.* "And so why are you here with him?"

Frou-Frou yipped, looking at Dorie. She narrowed her eyes and looked closer at the man.

"Let me start over. That was a bad beginning," he said. "Hi, Dorie, my name is Chad."

Dorie felt a small smile begin. "Hello, Chad."

"Hi. This is Frou-Frou. I'm visiting my grandmother, Alice Simmons, and Frou lives with her. She asked me to bring him here today. She said he had an appointment."

"First things first. Can Frou-Frou have a treat?" Dorie was aware of the expectant look Frou was lavishing on her.

"Yeah, I think so. He gets enough of them at home."

"Great." Dorie brought the treat back toward the pair. Frou's rear obediently hit the floor, and his eyes were pasted on Dorie's face.

"Look at that! He's not like that for me."

Dorie raised her eyebrows at Frou. "Well done. Good." She bent to hand over the treat. Frou delicately lifted it from her fingers.

"He's very well mannered. But not for you, huh?" She stood back up.

Chad shrugged. "Well, we don't get along all that well. I have a hard time respecting a dog with hair bows." Frou shot him a look as he crunched his treat.

Dorie's eyebrows were as far up as they could go. "Hair bows put you off?"

"Well, yeah. On a boy dog, anyway. Besides, dogs are dogs. Hair bows are a people thing. I don't know why people have to pretend their dogs are people."

"I know who you are," she said, pointing her finger at Chad. "You're some guy from the paper coming to write an exposé on dog spas. Why going to the dog spa is a waste of money and a sign of disrespect for the common working dog."

Chad burst out laughing. "You're joking, right? Because that's pretty funny. Do you think someone from Stella Mare would do that?"

Dorie felt a little self-satisfied. She had made him laugh. "Well, I haven't found that this town is especially welcoming to the idea of pampered pooches. It isn't an easy sell. And you've got an opinion about it, apparently."

"But that's not all you do here, is it? Pamper pooches? Is Frou supposed to be here for a spa treatment or something?"

She pulled the appointment book toward her. "I don't see an appointment here for Alice Simmons or Frou-Frou, and he's not been here before. I wonder if there was some kind of mistake."

Chad looked a little miserable.

"It's okay, don't worry. We can call her and find out what she wanted done, right?"

He sighed. "Yes, I guess. I think she got this idea after seeing you on the news last night."

"Really? I was hoping that might happen. Your grandmother saw me on the news and wanted Frou to have an appointment. That is so great. Wow, they even edited out the stuff about the spa. I wonder how she knew all that?" Dorie was jubilant.

Chad just stared at Dorie for a long moment. Then he seemed to come to a decision. "Nan saw you on the news and decided that I should meet you. She thinks she's playing matchmaker."

Dorie tried to show no reaction. It was impossible. She giggled. "I don't know what to say."

"Yeah, me either. That's my Nan. She's got an agenda, at least for me. Also, full disclosure, I almost met you yesterday. I was the cameraman for the dog hoarding story. I told her about the dog spa, because I heard you talking about it."

"Oh. You were there. Behind the camera."

"Yes."

"Were you responsible for cutting out most of what I said so that I looked like a flaming do-gooder without a brain in her head?"

He shook his head. "Nope, I can't take credit for that hack job. That was Jeannette."

"Is she really as nasty as she seems? I didn't really like her. Or I'm just jealous that she gets to wear nice clothes to work." Dorie brushed at the dog hair on her smock.

"You've got good instincts. Jeannette takes good care of Jeannette. You look great. Dog hair is the perfect accessory for the owner of a dog spa." He flashed another one of those shy, disarming smiles.

"Right."

"But that's also why I thought you did other stuff beside pampering pooches."

Dorie shrugged. "I do volunteer with County Rescue, but my father keeps telling me I have to grow up and make a living, that I can't save all the dogs, and that volunteering is for 'rich dilettantes' and I'll never be either rich or a dilettante."

Chad looked puzzled. "I don't even know what that means."

"Yeah, me either. I looked it up. A rich person who can putter at things that interest them. Not like plain old working folk, as my father sees himself. And me, I guess."

"I get it. You can volunteer for the rescue group, but it can't be at the expense of your paid job, because that's what is really important. Yep, that sounds like my Nan, actually."

Dorie nodded. "I know that most people here have lived hand to mouth, as my mother used to say. Stella Mare isn't a rich town, and most people here farm or fish or work in the tourist industry. None of that is easy money."

Chad smiled. "My Nan tells stories about living through the winter on salt fish and boiled turnips and potatoes, and that they were happy to see the dandelions in the spring because they dug up the greens and finally had some fresh food. I guess that's why they have trouble understanding why anyone could do something just for the love of it, even though it doesn't pay the rent."

"Yeah, I just worry about the dogs." Dorie wondered what it was that Chad loved so much it didn't matter if he got paid.

"What did you say your Nan's name is? I wonder if Dad knows her."

"Alice Simmons. She knew your mom," Chad offered.

Dorie's smile dimmed a bit. "My mother had a lot of friends."

Chad's brow furrowed. "Yeah, Nan said she died. Was that recent?"

Dorie nodded, surprised. A man who would ask about her mother. Maybe he wasn't as awkward as she originally thought. Most people just stopped making eye contact and slid away when they heard that her mother died.

"Yeah, it feels recent, even though it was three years ago. She just got sick suddenly, and they said it was pancreatic cancer and then boom, just like that, she was gone." Dorie softened her voice. "Now when I meet new people it's like, oh, yeah, my mom's gone, and it is just so weird that they'll never know her. Thank you for asking about her. That kind of made my day." She gave Chad a deep and genuine smile.

His brown eyes gazed into hers. "I know about losing people," he said. "There's a reason I hang out with my Nan. But let's save that story for another time. Right now, I think we have to figure out what to do about Frou. I'm calling Nan."

Yes, get back to business. No time to get lost in grief today. Dorie squatted to mid-sized poodle height. "Oh, Frou-Frou, what did your mother want me to do for you? Whatever it is, we'll have a good time." The dog licked her chin.

A few days later, Chad called to invite Dorie to dinner. Dorie slipped her phone back in her pocket under her father's curious gaze. "Nice boy who calls instead of texting," he commented. "Not much notice though."

Dorie kept silent. Her life wasn't so exciting that she needed much notice for a dinner date. And besides, it meant nothing. No need to get Dad too excited. This was just a sort of a date with a sort of a customer, no lifetime commitment.

"I guess so," she said briefly. "Now what are you doing tonight, Dad?"

James shrugged. "I guess your sister Evie said something about coming over."

"Ugh." Dorie put her hand over her mouth. *Did I really just say that out loud?* "That's good, you'll have some company."

"Yes. You could be nicer about your sister, Dore. She's not a bad sort."

"Oh, Dad, you have to say that. You're probably right that I could be nicer. I just don't always want to be."

He scoffed. "You kids. Just like when you were little, always squabbling over something."

Dorie leaned over him to kiss his cheek. "Yep, we'll never grow up. See you later."

Dorie walked downtown to meet Chad. He'd suggested meeting at her shop, and she was a little early. Unlocking the door, she stepped in, but left the lights off. Behind the counter, she bent over to do a little tidying of the lower shelves.

She lifted her head at the sound of the door opening. "Dorie?"

"Oh, hi, Chad. I'll just be a minute." She stacked the papers back on the shelf and stood. "Hi, there." She looked at his form silhouetted against the streetlight coming in the front glass. He was bigger than she remembered, but trim. Attractive. Hmm. What was he carrying?

"Hi." His smile warmed her. "I hoped you were here when I found the door unlocked."

Dorie giggled. *Giggling! What's happening to me?* "Well, it is Stella Mare. Not too much bad stuff happens here."

"Is that so?" He looked a little surprised. "What about all that animal cruelty stuff you were talking about?"

"Well, yeah, that. But I meant things like robbery or being mugged, or stuff like might happen in the city where you live."

Chad scoffed. "Saint Jacques is a pretty nice place. Even working for the news station, it seems like a good place to call home. Compared to Toronto, or New York, or some place with a lot of crime."

She slipped from behind the counter. "Are we really talking about relative crime rates?"

He looked abashed. "Well, I guess so. Awkward first date conversation. Sounds like you want to talk about something else."

"Crime isn't my first choice, that's all. Can you tell me what you have in your hand?"

"My hand?" Chad looked down at his hand as if he'd never seen it before. "Oh, this. Yeah. I usually have a camera with me. You never know when you might need video."

Dorie raised her eyebrows. "Really? For what?"

Shoving up his glasses with one finger, he said, "Well, really, it gives me something to do with my hands. I think better with a camera in my hand, and, well... I guess that's why."

"You can't just film people without their permission, you know."

"Oh, I know. I'm careful about privacy. I don't shoot people, usually, but I like settings, and I especially like old places like this building." He turned all the way around, gazing toward the high tin ceiling.

Mollified, Dorie softened. "It's a great shop, isn't it?"

"It sure is. Very early 1900s, right? Do you mind if I shoot a little?"

"Sure, go ahead. I like this building a lot. It's probably cold in the winter, but I've only been here six months, so I don't know for sure."

Chad rotated and then poked into the dim corners of the big room with his camera. "I'll just be a minute. Thanks for indulging me."

"Sure. Better than talking about crime." She tucked away the appointment book and picked up her jacket.

"What? Oh, yeah. I'm better at pictures than I am with words. That's what Nan told me when I was a kid, and I think it's probably still true."

She thought about that while he finished checking out her shop. "That must make first dates a little challenging."

He laughed. "Yes. I try to avoid them. But I don't have a dog, so I couldn't keep dropping in here for services to try to talk to you."

She smiled. "Well, that was nicely put. Not awkward at all."

His face reddened. "Luck, I guess. Uh, well, I made a reservation at La Place in St. Stephen. Do you like French food?"

French food? Like French fries? "Sure, I'm game. None of those little snail things though, okay?"

He laughed. "I promise. Only food you can recognize. And pronounce. Let's go."

Chad pulled his car into the parking space in front of the Pampered Pooch. Dorie turned up her jacket collar and put her hand on the door handle. Stilted dinner conversation plus Chad's advice on her diet was more than she bargained for. *I can't wait for this evening to end.*

Pointing his camera at the door of her shop, Chad pressed record. "The Pampered Pooch. I don't get why you think you can make this pampered thing work," he said, turning toward Dorie. "You seem to have a good understanding of what these people are like. Nobody in this town is going to spend money having their dog's toenails done."

Dorie frowned. "Your grandmother did."

"She's different. She had an agenda."

"Other than Frou-Frou? Really? Tell me." *This guy was nothing but annoying, with his camera and his opinions.*

Chad stammered a little, "Well, she's always, she, well, yes, I guess she did want Frou-Frou to be pampered. But she wants us to get along better."

Dorie was unconvinced. "You and the dog. She's worried about your relationship with the dog."

"Yeah, that. That relationship." Chad said, sounding relieved. "Yeah, Nan thinks she's getting really old, and she might end up leaving me with Frou and I really have no respect for his fluffy little curlicued silliness."

"Silliness." Dorie wondered if her voice reflected how annoyed she was feeling.

"You know, Dorie, nobody really is going to go for this idea you have. Why do you keep on with this business? I'm not even sure you think dogs should be"—Chad added air quotes—"pampered."

"I'm not sure I get your meaning," Dorie said, dangerously calm. "It sounds like you think my whole business idea is unworthy or something."

"No, not unworthy. Just unworkable. Or maybe unworthy of you."

"Excuse me?"

Chad stared out the side window of his car. "I first saw you at a site where you were protecting dogs from cruel treatment. I thought you were passionate about that work."

"I was! I am," she retorted with heat. "But you're acting like my dog spa is silly."

"Not silly. Well, yes, silly, but mostly not likely to get the business you need here in Stella Mare. And besides, how does it help dogs?"

"What?" Dorie spluttered. "How does it help? It makes them feel good, makes them clean and pretty, and I don't know. It helps dogs. It does."

Chad shook his head. "It helps dog owners take care of their dogs, I get that, kind of. At least dogs that need baths and grooming. Rescuing abused animals is real. Pampering, well, it's fluff."

Dorie stuck her chin out. "Grooming is good for every dog."

Chad scoffed. "My uncle's hunting dogs don't need to be groomed."

Dorie sighed. "Well, actually, they do. Dogs in the woods get ticks, their hair gets tangled up and caught in the brush, and they're hanging out in mud and muck a lot of the time. Scratches get infected. Taking care of your dog means taking care of those things, too." She stuck out her chin. "Why are you telling me this stuff? What gives you the right to even have an opinion about my business or how I run it? Or what I even do with my time?"

Chad looked chagrined. "Yeah. You're right. I don't have a right. I hardly know you."

"You hardly do."

"But I like you."

"Oh." *I don't know if I like you.* "Usually when a person likes someone, they don't tell them their whole life's work is silly and useless. At least in my world. It's not a very good way to make friends."

Chad looked concerned. "Your work with the rescue group isn't silly and useless. And maybe dog pampering isn't either, I probably really don't know. Pampering is going to be a hard sell in this town, that's all."

"Yeah, well, thanks for your totally unqualified opinion. I could have stayed home to hear it from my father and my sister. Thanks for dinner. Good night." Getting out, she slammed the door of his truck.

That was that. She stomped down the street toward home.

Chad pulled up alongside her and put down the window. "Dorie. Dorie, I'm sorry. You're right, that was out of line. At least let me drive you the rest of the way home. It's late."

She hesitated. "You're sorry?"

He nodded. "I'm sorry I upset you."

"You're sorry you upset me? Are you sorry you told me how to run my business and my life?" She was incensed.

He looked confused. "I said I'm sorry, didn't I? But I still think my advice is good."

"Oh, oh you... Are you pointing that video camera at me? Go on. Just go." Dorie huffed, pulled up her collar, and stomped off toward home.

The truck followed for a moment, then took off in the other direction, tires squealing.

Good. Don't come back.

Chapter 3

Chad went back to Saint Jacques early Monday morning. The twisty road off the peninsula took a little attention, but when he got to the highway, he lost himself in thinking about where things with Dorie had gone so wrong. He liked her, he really did, but she had crazy ideas. Why did she ever think something like her pampered pooches would fly? Local folks had hunting dogs, working dogs, not pups that needed pampering. He pushed the thought of Frou-Frou out of his mind.

Plus, he had apologized when he made her mad. What else did she want? He hadn't meant to make her mad; in fact, he really wanted her to like him. Helping her out, that was what you did with people you cared about, right?

That girl! She had the sweetest smile, but when she was mad, that went away in a heartbeat. He recalled uncomfortably the grim set of her lips when he gave her his advice about her business.

I thought she'd like to hear the truth. But he knew better. Nan had put it to him plainly. Quit with the advice. Nobody likes to be told that their idea is a bad one. He wondered miserably if Dorie would ever talk to him again. Parking on the street in front of his building, he sighed. *Good one. Nice work. Another nice girl alienated.* He pulled his duffel from the back of the truck and headed upstairs.

Dorie sat at the counter in her shop staring at a pile of envelopes in front of her. Why had she waited so long to pick up her mail at the post office?

Avoidance. That was why. The last batch of mail had held her eviction notice. The building was being sold, she had thirty days to move out, and she had no stomach for more bad news. So she just didn't pick up her mail. Well, until today.

She sorted flyers into the trash can, but stopped when she got to a thick, creamy envelope. Uh-oh, she thought, looking at the return address. The bank.

Grimly she slit the envelope and pulled out the heavy paper. Her eyes widened as she read down the page.

She slid off her stool, letting the paper fall to the floor. "Aargh! Never any good news. What next!" she shouted into the empty room. She stomped across the floor to look out the door. "This is so stupid!"

The midmorning street outside was empty of pedestrians, and only one car carefully traced a path down the lane. Dorie watched until it was out of sight, the distraction only lasting a minute. Stomping back to the counter, she picked up her phone. Who to call?

Before she could decide, the bell on the door jangled. Andrea Chase walked in. *Where did she come from?* The street had been empty.

"Oh, there you are, Dorie," Andrea said in her crisp, authoritative way. "I'm glad you're in. I've got a situation and I need your help."

"What's going on?" She gave the creamy sheet on the floor a despairing glance, then focused on Andrea.

"Another animal hoarding situation, on a farm about twelve kilometres from here. Someone called it in on the tip line over night."

"The tip line? At the County Rescue? I didn't know BARC was involved." Andrea's organization kept pressure on the government to legislate safety for dogs.

Andrea went on. "I was going to investigate, but BARC's policy is that we don't go alone when we're checking things out. I need you to come too."

Dorie felt her forehead wrinkle. "Investigate? Why not Animal Control or County Rescue? Or the police? I didn't know BARC did investigations."

Andrea stood very straight. "We will call the police if we find evidence of a problem. I can't just call in based on an anonymous tip on the phone."

Dorie puzzled over that. *The police followed tips too, so why not let them do their job? But no, Andrea has been in this business for a long time. She knows what she's doing. Besides, checking out a tip is more fun than trying to solve my money problems.*

"Yeah, sure, Andrea. There's nothing happening at the Pampered Pooch this morning. My next appointment is on Thursday," Dorie remarked grimly, flipping pages in her appointment book. "I can go with you." She pushed the offending letter under the counter with her toe, grabbed her jacket, and locked the shop door behind her.

Andrea's car was new and remarkably clean, Dorie thought. The woman herself was the epitome of good grooming. No dog hair anywhere. *My car always smells of dog shampoo, is coated in hair that Custard and Mallow kindly leave behind, and I'm always moving chew toys.* Riding in Andrea's immaculate BMW was like a vacation.

The address left on the tip line sent them into the country. “It's a farm, I think,” Andrea offered as she navigated around a pothole. “Look, there's the house. And there's a barn, too.”

Dorie looked. The house was weathered grey, and some of the windows were boarded over. The barn looked more habitable, with some recent patching of the siding and a clear path to the door. The old barn door was held shut with a heavy plank that looked a lot newer than the door itself.

Andrea parked on a patch of bare ground near the front door. The women got out of the car to a racket of barking.

“That sounds like a whole lot of dogs,” Dorie commented. “Big dogs.” She wasn’t sure heading to the door was a great idea. Andrea forged ahead but looked back over her shoulder.

“We're just here to take a look,” she reminded Dorie. “Just to see if there is anything that seems suspicious. We don't want to get anyone riled up.”

“Okay,” Dorie agreed. *Those dogs sound plenty riled up. I don't want anyone riled up at me. I still think the police should be doing this.*

She followed the older woman up the rickety front steps. Andrea banged on the door with her knuckles and the barking escalated. A moment passed, and she knocked again.

“Shaddup, shaddup! Who is it?” The voice from behind the door was scratchy and irritated.

“Good morning!” Andrea, though shouting over the din, sounded so sweet that Dorie was startled.

The woman in the house shouted over the barking dogs. “Who's there?”

"Hello, there," Andrea chimed musically. "We just want to talk to you for a minute."

"Are you them witness people? I don't want to talk to no religious."

"No, no, we're not. We're animal lovers like you."

"You got something for me? Dog food or something?"

Andrea turned to Dorie. "Go get a bag of dry food in the trunk of my car," she whispered, handing Dorie the key fob.

Dorie jogged off toward the car, keeping an ear cocked to hear what was happening on the front porch. It sounded like this woman would talk to them for a bag of dog food. Where'd she get the idea that anyone would bring her dog food? Dorie opened the trunk to find it full of ten-pound bags of food. Hmm, good idea.

She looked up the driveway to see Mike's County Rescue van pulling in. He slid the van in beside Andrea's BMW as Dorie hugged a bag of dog food and slammed the trunk.

"Hey, Dorie. What are you doing here? I tried to call you."

Dorie nodded toward the house. "Andrea picked me up. She said she got a tip. You?"

"Yeah, us, too. There's a lot of barking going on here, eh?"

"There's like an old lady here and apparently a lot of dogs. Not very welcoming."

"I can imagine. Let me take that bag."

They approached the house as the old woman stepped outside, closing the door behind her. Dorie saw Andrea trying to peer over the woman's shoulder into the house.

Andrea squinted at Mike. "More fun," she said irritably. She extended her hand toward the woman. "I'm Andrea Chase and this is Dorie. Oh, and that's Mike. We love dogs too."

"Yeah, so?" The woman was small and appeared frail, wearing a nightgown and thin wrap, her wispy grey hair pinned messily on the back of her head. She did not take Andrea's hand.

Andrea persisted. "And you are?"

"None of your business. I didn't invite you. What are you doing here?" The racket in the house started to quiet.

"Do you need dog food?" Andrea asked kindly.

"I always need dog food," the woman conceded. "But I don't know why you would be giving it to me. Dog lovers," she scoffed.

Andrea looked at Dorie. "Because we care about dogs and want to make sure they are taken care of."

The woman scowled. "Them dogs are better fed than some people. Now my dogs, that's not the same."

Confused, Dorie spoke for the first time. "The barkers? They're not your dogs?"

"Them are my son's dogs. My dogs are quieter than this bunch. Nicer."

Mike followed up. "You're here taking care of your son's dogs? It sounds like he's got lots of dogs."

"Yeah, lots. Them dogs are valuable, too. Not like my little mutts." She looked sad.

"Where are your dogs?" Dorie asked gently. "I'd like to meet them."

The woman ignored Dorie but reached out to Mike for the bag of food. Mike held on. "Where do you want it? I'll carry it for you," Mike said.

"I don't know what you're doing here, but thanks. My dogs are in the back, where my place is. Now why don't you girls just go on home, get out of here. You too, mister. You can drop off the food and git going. This has nothing to do with you."

Andrea shifted restlessly. Dorie had never seen Andrea look uncomfortable, but here she was suddenly looking like she wanted to be anywhere else.

"Can I meet your dogs?" Dorie persisted. "I really like the little ones."

Andrea was backing away, but Dorie pressed on. "Please."

"Dorie, I have to go..." Andrea started.

Dorie held the old woman's eyes. She looked terribly sad and alone. “We've got more dog food in the car if you need it,” she encouraged. “Right, Mike?”

“Yes, sure. I've got all sorts of stuff in the van.”

Andrea backed down the walk while the old lady considered.

“Okay,” she said finally. “You can see my dogs. You two,” she nodded to Dorie and Mike. “Not that one.” She lifted her chin toward Andrea, who by now was close to her car.

The old lady turned to open the front door, and the barking increased in volume and intensity again. Then she seemed to change her mind. “No, not this way,” she said and pulled the handle tight again. “We’ll walk around back. That's where my place is.”

Andrea called out. “Come on, Dorie. I'm leaving now. Now.” There was no sweetness in her voice anymore. She sounded rough, demanding.

“What? Right now?” Dorie felt caught. Andrea was her ride out here.

Mike said, “Dorie, get half a dozen cans of dog food from the van and find out what's going on with Andrea. I'll take you back to town, no worries.” He followed the lady around the side of the house.

Dorie trotted toward the BMW, shaking her head. “What's up, Andrea? We're not done here, are we?”

Andrea really looked uncomfortable. “I am. I just can't be here. This isn’t what I thought it was. I'm leaving. We gave her some food, so let's just go.”

“No. No, I'm staying.” Dorie was certain. “You go if you have to. Mike will give me a ride home. Guess this really is out of BARC's jurisdiction, huh?”

“Something like that. You don't have to mention that I was here, right? You and Mike did this bit on your own.”

Dorie shrugged. Who would care? “Sure. No problem.”

The BMW sped off, and Dorie opened the back of Mike's well-worn van. Andrea is kind of peculiar, Dorie thought as she pulled out cans of food. *Or maybe, just the situation.* She shrugged off the thoughts. *Being here, that's what's important. There are dogs here, dogs who might need help. That poor old woman.* Jogging around the corner of the house, she caught up with the woman and Mike as they were going into the ell.

A lot of old Maritime farmhouses were built like this one, with an ell added onto the main house for the kitchen. Despite its age, the ell looked marginally better than the main house, with glass in the windows and a couple of potted geraniums on the steps to the old screen door. As she entered, Dorie could hear the deep barking from the front of the house, but now it was a little muffled by walls. The kitchen was old, with a linoleum floor that reminded Dorie of childhood visits to her great-grandparents' house. Except her great-grandparents never had so many small, hairy dogs. And their house never smelled like this. She dumped her armful of cans on the rickety table.

Little dogs suddenly erupted from another room. And kept coming. The old woman was bent over, petting the swirling mass around her ankles. She picked up one of the puffballs and turned to Mike, dog in arms.

"You're Mike? Right?"

"Yep. That's me. What's your name?" Mike asked.

"Sarah. My name is Sarah Smith. This is Greta." She waved one of the dog's paws toward Mike.

Dorie leaned in to look, while a chaos of small dogs continued to surge through the kitchen, sniffing the visitors. In horror, she watched one lift his leg to a kitchen chair. No wonder the smell was overpowering. The dog in Sarah's arms was matted and dirty and smelled of feces. She wondered what was being rubbed off on her jeans by the mass of excited small dogs.

Mike reached over to pet Greta. The dog responded with a growl and show of teeth. Sarah cackled. "She don't like you."

He put his hands in his pockets. "I guess not. How many of these are your dogs?" Pulling out a treat, he held it out to Greta, who seemed to reconsider her original opinion and snapped it up.

Sarah looked down at the mass of canine energy on the kitchen floor. "All of 'em, I guess. My son, he don't like little dogs."

Dorie counted at least eight small dogs of indeterminate breed, mostly long haired and desperately unkempt. The smell was starting to get to her, and she longed for a breath of fresh air.

"So, Sarah, there are more dogs out front, right? The big dogs, you said?" Dorie watched Mike in action, getting information.

"He keeps them in the crates, them dogs. They're valuable, not like these little guys here. These ones are valuable to me." Sarah looked up defensively.

Dorie could relate. "Of course they are, Sarah. They're your companions."

Sarah put her face on Greta's dirty head. "My babies." Dorie felt her stomach turn.

Mike persisted. "Are there dogs in the barn, too?"

Sarah squinted at him. "Why did you say you were here? You animal welfare or something?"

"Not really," Mike assured her. "I work with County Rescue, for dogs that don't have homes. Your dogs do have a home, but we can help. It sounds like you help your son with his dogs, but he doesn't help you with yours." He gestured to the pack in the kitchen, now settling a bit. Dorie got a better count. *Yes, eight.*

"My son's a good boy. He lets me live here if I take care of his dogs. But he don't like it if I feed my guys his dog food. Those big dogs, they get meat."

"Big dogs? The dogs out front are big dogs?" Dorie asked. Mike was doing the interrogation, but she was intensely curious.

Sarah frowned. "I think you better go. You don't have no business here, do you?" She turned as if to push them toward the door. "Richie don't like people coming around, neither."

"Wait," Dorie said. "I only met Greta. I want to meet the rest of your babies. And besides, I can help you. I like little dogs. Please?"

Sarah stepped back. "Yeah, okay, you come over here, and I'll introduce you." She looked back. "You didn't tell me your name," she said directly to Dorie.

"Dorie. I'm Dorie."

Mike added, "Dorie has a dog grooming business. She could probably help you get your dogs bathed and clipped."

Sarah stood to her full height and held Greta close. "Me and my dogs are fine. They don't need no fancy grooming. I changed my mind. I don't need nothing. You better go."

"Okay, okay." Mike held his hand up. "We're going."

Dorie leaned toward Sarah. "Thank you for letting us meet your dogs, Sarah."

"Yeah, yeah. You go now. My son will be coming soon. Get going."

"Can I leave you my card?" Dorie asked. "If you need more food or something, you can call me."

Sarah looked suspiciously at her, but tucked Greta under one arm and reached for the card. "Just go now."

****

"That's so sad," Dorie said, looking out the window of the van as Mike drove away from the old farmhouse. "That lady, Sarah, and all those little dogs."

"Yes, it is sad. It's more than just sad though. I think there's more going on than the obvious." He looked serious. "The dogs we saw were worrisome, but she really cares for them, as best she can. The ones we didn't see...I have a bad feeling about that."

"Bad feeling? What do you mean?"

"Keeping many big dogs like that. Valuable dogs, she said. She sure wasn't going to let us see those big, valuable dogs. We only got in the door because of dog food."

"True. But it's not too strange to be protective of valuable dogs, is it?"

He gave her a sideways glance. "I don't know. It smells off to me, and I don't mean that dirty house. I wonder what he's doing with those dogs? A puppy mill? Or worse?"

"Worse? What's worse than breeding dogs willy-nilly just to sell as many pups as possible?" Dorie felt outraged at the idea.

"There are some things that are worse, Dorie, but fortunately we don't see much of them here."

"Hmm. Well, it sounds like those dogs are taken care of, or at least fed. What can we do about Sarah's messy bunch?"

"Not a lot, to be honest. She has space. Apparently they get fed, and even though she lives in conditions I'd never tolerate, it isn't against the law to be poor and dirty. There's no reason for Animal Control to get involved, and County Rescue has no mandate to apprehend animals."

"Yeah, but she really needs some help."

"She certainly does. Help won't come from an agency though, because we don't have the resources to help unless there is overt cruelty or neglect. That doesn't stop a private citizen like yourself from dropping by with dog food every now and then." His sidelong glance spoke volumes.

Dorie looked at her lap. "They really need to be bathed, and they probably have fleas, too."

Mike said nothing.

"If I get involved there, it won't be as a County Rescue volunteer, I guess, right?"

"That's right. There's nothing we can do under the circumstances. However, I might look the other way if you dropped by to raid our dog food donation pantry once in a while." Mike offered her a conspiratorial smile.

"I get it. I suppose I might get a chance to get out there with some equipment and give a pup a bath, sometime."

"You're a good person, Dorie. Sarah needs help, even if she doesn't realize it, and there's not really any formal help for people in her situation. But informal help, well, that's what works."

Dorie heaved a massive sigh. This was what got her in trouble with her father. "Yeah, I get that, Mike. I just...I don't know. I'm supposed to be trying to make a living here, you know."

Mike pulled up in front of her shop. "I do know, Dorie. It's hard to sell services when you have the soul of a helper."

"Can't I sell my help? That seems like it might work. Why can't I be a helper and pay my own rent, too?" she complained. "I just can't seem to get that part to work."

Mike chuckled his agreement. "That's the challenge. Working for a non-profit sounds like the answer, but what you may not know is how much time I spend scrambling for donations and grants and organizing volunteers."

"Yeah. Well, thanks for the ride, Mike, and the talk. Oh, by the way, did you think Andrea was a little, um, peculiar today?"

He shrugged. "Not my place to talk about my fellow man, or woman for that matter. It was interesting that she went out based on a tip and took you with her."

"Well, yeah, I volunteer with BARC, too, sometimes."

"What I said before. You're a good person. You might not be a wealthy person, but you have the right heart."

"Yeah, yeah, yeah. I bet you say that to all your volunteers," Dorie jibed. "Or your kids."

Mike grew serious. "I do want my kids to become good people. Juliette and I have been working hard to help them grow out of that adolescent self-centered phase and into adults who care. I think your father must be proud of you, Dorie. I would be if I were your dad."

Dorie's eyes stung. “Mike, thank you,” she choked out. “My dad mostly thinks I need a real job and to get a life, but thanks for your view. That means a lot.”

“I meant every word. Have a good afternoon, Dorie.”

“Bye.”

She jumped down from the van and watched it trundle down the street. Mike thought a lot of her. He respected volunteering for animals. *Wow. I bet he's a great father. Too bad he's not talking to Dad.*

Pushing through her shop door, she looked around. What did a new client see? That guy, that Chad, what did he see when he was waving his camera around? A bittersweet feeling welled up, knowing that she was going to be leaving soon.

She took in the sight of the well-worn wood floor and tall windows that let in lots of light. But they also let in the cold these recent weeks of fall. The low wooden shelves held fancy dog toys, treats, and grooming supplies. Posters on the walls included notices about lost dogs, dog obedience classes, agility and field trials. A vibrantly coloured infographic warned about the dangers of buying puppies from puppy mills. Bowls held dog treats for anyone to offer to their pet. She even had a coffeemaker. People must think this was a nice place. A good place for dogs and their people. Only nobody came in. At least not enough people to make the business work.

Now I'm not even going to have this place to work in. Maybe I can get Chad to give me a copy of the video. Nah, I'm not sure I even want it. This is hard.

She wandered back to the grooming area where she'd had a plumber put in her bathing sinks. Mournfully, she gazed at her grooming table. She imagined that old lady, Sarah, holding her thin wrap closed against the chill of the day, and the dreadful smell of dirty, unkempt little dogs. *Poor old lady and poor little old dogs. I don't want to end up like them.*

She gave herself a shake. This was a temporary in-between situation, that's all. She wasn't going to end up poor, dirty, and unwell with dogs surging around her feet. *Sarah needs help and it's the right thing for me to do. Mum would agree. Dad might not, but I know Mum would.*

Feeling clearer about herself, Dorie thought again about Sarah's "little mutts." Those dogs needed basic hygiene, she thought, not pampering. Just bath and brush, and flea treatment. *What a sad state. I'm sure Sarah can't afford dog grooming, and she probably can't even bathe them. She doesn't look physically capable, and I think she might be stuck out at the farm. I bet she feels terrible about not taking better care of her pets. I would if it were me. Maybe that was why she was so antagonistic. I can go out to the house like Mike said. That could really make a difference. Like my sisters make a difference, and Corinne.*

Andrea makes a difference, Dorie thought. *Going to the capital and talking to legislators about dog protection. It isn't my kind of thing though.*

Andrea. Nice of Mike not to gossip, but I'm too curious for that. Something freaked her out, sent her running away. What spooked her? Surely not Mike. Andrea and Mike were always ending up in the same place. Mike said they worked on the same issues, just from different angles. But what had happened? Dorie gave a mental shrug, almost hearing her father's voice. *Not my problem.*

But those filthy dogs. I wish I could afford to give services away, like Andrea and Mike gave away dog food.

Maybe I'm not as good a person as Mike thinks. I just can't afford to give services away. Dad would kill me if he thought I was bathing dogs for free.

Stepping behind the counter, she knelt to look for the cream-coloured paper she'd kicked out of sight earlier that day. Might as well face up to it, she thought. But the sheet of paper was missing. She couldn't find it under the counter or anywhere on the floor. That's weird. *But it means I don't have to think about that right now*. With a big sigh, she heaved herself to her feet and prepared to go home.

When Chad went to work on Monday, there was a message from Jeannette. The subject line read *Checking in*. With some curiosity, he clicked.

Hey Chad. Wondered if you're up to doing another story based here, around this dog stuff? I'm looking into some of the non-profits that are supposedly helping animals. Interested? I think it might be a nice longer piece. There's some unusual activity going on in the province. I'm not so sure about that lady from BARC.

Work. He felt a mild interest. Longer pieces meant more airtime, more time to work with the nuances of telling a story in images. And what did she mean about the lady from BARC? He could only remember Mike, the bearded guy, and Dorie's sweet smile as she tried to explain her desire to care for dogs. He briefly wondered if she'd ever brought that degree of interest to a man. A flicker of something flared in his belly, but quickly he reminded himself that he'd screwed that up already. In less than one date. Oh, well. If he did this story with Jeannette, he'd have another chance to talk to Dorie, make it up to her. Or not.

Pulling up a new browser, he set up an alert for any information about dogs, dog hoarding, dog cruelty, dog grooming, dog breeding in the county. *That should get me a lot of useless information, but perhaps a few story ideas that could get me back to Stella Mare.* He left the email open and stepped away to fill his coffee mug. Chatting with his boss left him with three new pieces of work with fast turnarounds. When he returned to his desk, he closed the email without replying. *Too much to do here. I'll think about that later. But on my own. Not with Jeannette.*

Dorie slammed the door on her way into the kitchen. Custard, drinking at his bowl, looked at her over his shoulder. Unimpressed, he turned back to his water.

Heavily dropping her bag onto the table, she called, “Anybody home?”

Her sister Evelyn came from the living room. “Could you make any more noise? Dad's taking a nap.”

She scowled. “Why is he taking a nap? It's almost suppertime. And what are you doing here, anyway?”

“Nice, Dorie. What about, hi, dear sister, thank you for taking care of our father while I do whatever it is you do?” Evelyn's sarcasm nearly dripped.

“Snark begets snark, Evie. I've had another really bad day. Don't be so nasty.”

“Why does your bad day mean everyone in the house has to suffer? Get over yourself, Dore. Grow up a little.”

“Oh, for Pete's sake. Get off your high horse. You have no idea what I'm going through.” She flopped herself into a kitchen chair.

Evelyn put a hand on the table and leaned toward Dorie. Sounding grim, she said, “That's true, Dore. I don't know. But you always make sure everyone knows when things aren't going your way. You need to think about other people once in a while.”

“You? I need to think about you? What’s wrong with you?”

Evelyn sighed hugely. She sat in the chair across from Dorie. “No, not me, Dorie. Dad.”

Dorie scoffed. “Dad’s fine. He misses Mom, that’s all.”

"It's been almost three years. We all miss her. There's more going on than that."

"Like what?"

Evelyn looked away. "Well, actually, I don't even know. He won't tell me. He did ask me to pick him up at the hospital today though. He had some test or something that wore him out. He made me stop asking questions."

"What? Why didn't he ask me to pick him up? I'm the one that lives here."

"My question exactly, but he said you're trying hard to build up your business and he didn't want to interfere with the Pampered Pooch schedule."

"Oh." Dorie looked at the floor. "Yeah, well, today I wasn't even at the shop all day. I didn't have any appointments, and I was out with Andrea investigating a dog hoarding tip."

"I don't like that woman. She's not right, somehow."

Dorie was incensed. "She's a good person, Evie. She helps dogs. She's trying to make the world a better place." *But even I don't get what happened today.* "Mike from County Rescue was there, too." *Mike even thinks I'm useful, unlike my entire family.*

Evelyn asked, "What did you find?"

"Oh, it was really sad, actually. An old woman named Sarah something and her eight little dogs, mostly filthy, probably underfed. We gave her dog food. And somewhere else in the house there were big dogs, she said, that belong to her son. But she wouldn't show us the big dogs. It was weird."

"Sounds weird. That ruined your day?"

"Not only that. But what about Dad? What's up? He sure keeps his secrets. I didn't know there was anything going on at all."

"I know. I didn't either. I wouldn't even now, except he needed a ride."

Dorie sat silently for a moment. "What should we do?"

Evelyn shrugged. "Tell the sisters, I guess. Or see if they know anything. And Dore, don't make a lot of work and worry for him right now. Like don't come in slamming doors because you had a bad day."

Shame filled her about her outburst. It had been a bad day for so many reasons, but they all paled against the possibility of Dad being sick.

"Since I'm not allowed to talk to Dad about my troubles, can I tell you?"

Evelyn nodded. "Yeah, sure. Go ahead. I'm listening."

"Last week, I got a notice that the building is being sold. The one where the shop is. I have thirty days to vacate the space."

"Oh, no! You've barely gotten started there."

"You're telling me? Yeah. When I got the notice, I called the landlord right away, to see if I could buy the building, but that's out. It is already sold and they never gave me a chance to offer for it." Propping an elbow on the table, she leaned on her hand with a gusty sigh.

"Stinkers."

"Yeah. The truth is I couldn't have bought it anyway. I don't have any money saved, and the business is running in the red. You used to be able to rent downtown space for cheap, but now it's very expensive, even an old building like mine."

Evie made a sympathetic noise. "What are you going to do?"

"I still don't know. Since last week, I've been looking for a space to buy so I can't get evicted again. But you can't buy anything without proof that you can get a mortgage, so I went to the bank again, you know, where I borrowed the money to get started. Today I got a letter from them telling me that I can't have any more money. I'm not qualified." She rose and paced the room. "I hate that word. I'm not qualified for anything, including a loan to keep my business running."

"You're a qualified dog groomer."

"Yep. Not a skill that's gonna make me rich. I'm genuinely at risk of defaulting on what they've already lent me. I'm going to be out of business. No income, so no loan payment."

"Just because you're out of your space doesn't mean you have to be out of business, does it? How is business?"

"Awful. Business is so slow. When I am busy in the shop, I'm so busy that I can't answer the phone, and that's when the phone rings. I don't know how people make these one-person shops work. It seems like there is nothing going on, or I need an extra set of hands and roller skates."

Evie chuckled. "Well, that's an image."

"Isn't it? Like today, I was out of the shop all day, but it didn't really matter. I have three appointments scheduled for the entire week. But there was a day last week when I was thinking I needed to hire some help. Oh, I should just admit it. This business idea is not working out. You guys were probably right." *And that darn Chad, too.*

Evelyn was quiet. Dorie looked at her suspiciously. "What? You're too quiet."

Evie shook her head. "It's a shame that you can't make a go of it."

Dorie scowled. "Am I hearing you right? You're not telling me how ridiculous my idea was, or how this was my own fault for not doing market research, or that I need to grow up and stop relying on Dad, or whatever the criticism of the week is."

Evelyn said, "Okay, okay. You can hold up on the tongue lashing, even though I'm sure that I deserve some of it. It's time we tried to pull together instead of apart."

"That sounds good. It would be different, anyway."

"I know it's been hard to be the youngest, especially to be so much younger. I think Mum kind of made a big thing about you being the baby, like forever, and that didn't help foster sweet relationships between all of us."

"You're blaming Mum? Really?"

"Not blaming. More like trying to understand our family. You were the special baby, who came along when they were all finished with babies. Mum made a big deal and wanted us sisters to be as excited as she was."

Dorie nodded. "Yeah, that makes sense. You were not nearly as excited."

"Yeah," Evie sighed. "Teenage girls can be a little weird about everything, and their parents having a baby especially."

"Well, that's not my fault."

"Yeah, I know. But, oh, my, were you ever the baby. I think you slept in their bed until you were four, and we all had to praise every little accomplishment you made, like getting a new tooth."

Dorie found herself beginning to grin. "I even remember Mum baking a cake when I graduated from kindergarten, and Rett grabbing a piece and storming off to her room. I guess that might have been a little irritating."

"More than a little. We three were all born so close together, I don't think Mum or Dad had a chance to play or celebrate or enjoy us, because they were so young and poor in those days. Things were easier when you came along, and I guess Mum got to enjoy her last baby. But that didn't do much to make us like you."

"We pulled together when Mum was sick," Dorie demurred. "We did well then."

"Yes. It didn't last though."

Dorie pondered. "I can see what you guys might think. I'm here and you're all out in the world, doing whatever. I'm still trying to figure myself out, and you have it all together."

Evie burst out laughing. "Oh, right. I'm glad you think I have it all together. Let's leave that for another time, though." She sobered and said, "Right now we do have to pull together. I'm worried about Dad. I don't think I can bear the idea of losing another parent any time soon."

Dorie's stomach clenched. "Losing? Is that what you're thinking?"

She turned her palms up. “I don't know. It just reminded me of Mum. All secret stuff and then she was gone. It couldn't happen to two of them, though.”

Stomach churning, Dorie said, “Evie, you don't know anything. We don't know a thing. Let's not get crazy, not yet.”

“Right. You keep working on that. In the meantime, what about your work?”

“Honestly, I don't know. I was going to ask Dad's advice. He's usually pretty good about that, once we get past the 'I told you so' part. Maybe I shouldn't worry him right now.”

“Good girl. I wonder if he's more likely to talk to you? You know, about his stuff.”

“Fat chance. He's just like you sisters, treating me like I barely have a brain.”

“I'm going to try my best to remove myself from that group. I can try to be a nicer sister, especially if you try to be a grown-up sister, and not depend on Daddy for everything.”

“I really don't, you know. I cook more than half the time. I take care of those lunks of dogs mostly. I work.”

“Yeah, when you have work. It could be the time to reconsider university, Dore. Time for a course correction.”

“While we think Dad is sick? That doesn't make sense. Mum being sick is what took me out of that route before.”

“Maybe it doesn't. It's just an idea. For sure, Pampered Pooch is closing. What are you going to do?”

That was the question, wasn't it? Dorie sighed tiredly. “I don't know. I really just don't know.”

After Evelyn left, Dorie went upstairs to check on her father. James lay on top of his bed with a crocheted blanket over his legs, but his eyes were open. Dorie tapped on the door and then walked in.

“Kind of tired?” she asked gently.

Her father sat up immediately and swung his legs off the bed. “Nope, I'm good. I hope you're calling me for supper.”

She scowled at him. "You're an optimist. I'm sure we can find something down there. But why did you call Evie to pick you up from the hospital instead of me? I'm supposed to be helping you."

He gazed at her fondly. "I'm the father and you're the youngest. You're here because you still need to be at home. Not because I need you."

"Well, I think we got different stories. I figured you needed me after Mum died, so I just stayed here."

He laughed softly. "Is that right? All this time I thought you stayed here because it was too scary to leave, or too much work to finish university, or that you wouldn't be able to have any fun if you had to work two jobs like your friends."

She stuck out her chin. "Is that really what you think of me, Dad? That I'm lazy and afraid to leave home?"

He shook his head. "I never said lazy. You work hard at what you want to work hard at. It's just that you haven't always worked hard at things you should have. Like mathematics. Or even school in general."

"Dad, why did you go to the hospital today?"

"Ha, changing the subject, are we?"

"Don't do that. Yes, changing the subject, but I really want to know. Are you okay?" She was sure her face reflected her worry.

He shook his head but didn't meet her eyes. "I am fine. I told your sister the same thing. If there is ever anything you girls need to know about me and my health, you'll be the first ones to know."

Dorie felt comforted to a degree, but Evie's worry stayed with her. Would Dad really tell them? They were all still feeling the loss of their mother, James perhaps even more than Dorie and her sisters, so would he try to protect them?

She decided to let it go for now. "Okay. I'm going to try to believe you. I'll drop the subject. Let's go downstairs and see what's in the fridge."

"You bet. Get out of here, you." James nodded her off and rose to his feet. Dorie caught a glimpse of him wobbling a bit and her stomach lurched. This felt bad in a too-familiar way.

Chapter 4

Less than a week later, Dorie had some good news. "Andrea has offered me a part-time job at BARC," she told James over their meal.

"That Andrea Chase, you mean?"

"Yes, the executive director of that social action organization, the place that advocates for dogs."

"Her. Where'd she come from, anyway?" James was frowning.

"Oh, Dad. Everyone doesn't have to grow up in Stella Mare to be good people. I don't know where she's from. I just know she offered me a job and I don't have a job."

James was still scowling. "Okay, so tell me about the job."

"It's about fifteen hours a week doing mostly social media stuff. Since I closed the shop, I might as well take it."

"Fifteen hours? What kind of social media stuff does that woman need?"

"Dad! You don't have to call her 'that woman.' Besides, it's the organization that needs help."

"Okay, then. What do they need with social media?"

"You, know, posting stuff about dogs and legislation and keeping up the newsletter and all of that. She wants someone to do it, I know how to do it, and why not?" Dorie turned up her palms. "It's not a career position, and I know it isn't a lot of hours. Maybe I can still do some grooming at the pet store in St. Stephen. I sent a message to my old boss there. Andrea said there could be a full-time job at BARC sometime."

"Full time doing what? That BARC always seemed like a one-woman show, and mostly for show." James still looked unimpressed, but he glanced at her with what she thought might be something like cautious approval. "I hope you'll prove me wrong."

"Well, Andrea said that the board wants more social media presence. I guess that's helpful for raising funds as well as awareness. We already know there's an epidemic of animal cruelty. Besides, she wants me to learn about grant writing, too."

"Grant writing. Probably not a bad thing to learn about. Your sister Evie has been living on grants, I think." James gave her a crooked grin. "Okay, daughter. I'll stop my interrogation. It sounds like you're set on this, and since otherwise you don't have anything, you might as well. At least until you find a real job."

"And Dad..."

"Yes?"

She tilted her head toward him. "I don't need permission. I just wanted to let you know."

James chuckled. "Of course. Sorry if that sounded like permission. You can become a circus clown if you like."

Dorie laughed. "Except I don't have the skills for that. I've still got work to do clearing the shop. I start this job ASAP, and I'll keep looking for anything else I can find, Dad. I know you can't be supporting me forever." She glanced to gauge his reaction, but he seemed preoccupied. Biting her lip, she headed for the kitchen to scrounge up dinner.

After a meal of sandwiches, Dorie took Custard and Mallow out for their evening stroll. The big dogs wandered slowly, and though Dorie meandered with them, her mind raced. The last week had been busy, trying to sell her grooming table and equipment, having a "going out of business" sale and moving out of her downtown shop. A bitter taste flooded her mouth as she recalled the locals who had flocked to her shop for the sales, many of whom had never come in for a service the whole six months she'd been open. *They only show up if they think they're getting something for nothing, or almost nothing. No wonder I can't make it work.*

Now she would try something new. BARC's president, Mr. Barrett, was nice and interested in her creating a splash for them. As she dawdled along at big dog speed, she recalled her meeting with Mr. Barrett in the boardroom at the BARC office.

Last Friday, Andrea showed Dorie into the sunny space. A tall man in a grey suit stood up to shake her hand. Mr. Barrett had that kind of grey hair that looked distinguished rather than old. On his wrist was a heavy gold watch, and around his neck, a tasteful necktie. Pretty fancy for Stella Mare, Dorie had thought, but then remembered Andrea's careful coiffure and immaculate BMW.

Her conversation with Mr. Barrett was a strange interview. He hadn't asked about her qualifications, interests, or plans. He just gave her a laundry list of things that he wanted done.

"We have virtually no social media at the moment," he had told her. "Anything you can do to increase public visibility of our mission would help. We need to cement our reputation with the public."

"Okay." Dorie wasn't sure what she was agreeing with, but it had seemed like the thing to say.

"We have donors," he said, "but we don't have any way to keep them in touch with us, so we need a plan there, a newsletter or something. Andrea doesn't have time to do this sort of administrative work, as her job is really out in Fredericton or in Ottawa, and the board wants to hire you to take that administrative burden off her."

Dorie's heart had sunk a little. "Administrative burden" was not an attractive phrase. But a job was a job. "Do you think it can be done in only fifteen hours a week?"

"Oh, yes, of course." Mr. Barrett had been very clear. "You young people are used to multitasking. The internet is your second home. I bet you can handle the social media without even looking. Then you'll have plenty of time to work on files and documentation."

"I'm not so sure about that. What if the work exceeds the hours?"

"Well, you can take that up with Andrea. She'll be supervising your daily and weekly work. The board wants a good person, someone who cares about our mission, in this role. That is you, isn't it, Doris?"

"Dorie. Yes, that's me, Mr. Barrett. Taking good care of dogs is what I do."

"Excellent. Check with Andrea about your start date, but the board needs your help immediately."

And so it was decided. Andrea said she would start on Monday.

Returning to the house after trudging through the fall evening, Dorie felt slightly optimistic. She'd told Dad and he hadn't gone ballistic about her needing to find a full-time job. She would figure things out. She just didn't know when. Or how. It was breathing room, at least for a while.

Dorie headed to work at BARC on Monday. She debated about what to wear, recalling Mr. Barrett's suit and Andrea's heels. *BARC seems like a fancy organization. I don't really fit into a fancy place.*

Since her closet was limited to jeans and not-quite jeans, she settled for clean jeans and a sweater. She was doing online work anyway. Though she did consider the possibility for an emergency call. Jeans definitely were sensible. The last time she'd worked with Andrea things had gotten messy. Sarah's place and all her dirty small dogs remained a vivid memory. Which brought back the strange way Andrea had beat a retreat. Dorie pushed that thought aside. Andrea was now her boss. Today, everything was new.

I wonder what it will be like to be a real employee at BARC? She brushed at the dog hair on the front of her sweater following Andrea, coiffed, suited, and heeled, into the boardroom once again.

"We don't have any extra office space, so you'll work in here and, of course, you can do a lot of your work at home or whatever. The board meets in here monthly, and sometimes I have donors in for meetings, but for the most part, you can camp out in here."

"Sure. This looks nice." She looked around at the tastefully appointed room. Along with the usual long table with substantial chairs, the walls were filled with framed photographs of Andrea with groups of people, mostly men in suits, standing in front of the legislature in Fredericton. In another Andrea stood with arms around a celebrity known for her interest in dogs. *There sure are a lot of pictures of Andrea. Oh, there she is with Mr. Barrett in front of some golf course. Wait, is that Mr. Barrett?*

"Is that Mr. Barrett in that picture?"

"Which one? Oh, that's Old Mr. Barrett. He hired me. Charles, who hired you, that's Young Mr. Barrett."

No kidding. The grey hair, the suit, the watch. Young Mr. Barrett was fifty at the very least. Only in Stella Mare. Dorie was relieved to realize she had not spoken that thought aloud.

Her gaze went last to a portrait of a tall woman with two Labrador retrievers at either side of her, one black, one yellow.

"Wow, that's an impressive painting. Who is that?"

"It's quite something, isn't it? That's Miranda Barrett, who founded BARC. Have you heard of her?" Dorie shook her head. Andrea went on. "As you can see, she was a dog lover, and she was also an attorney here in Stella Mare. She was a tireless advocate for dog safety. Her estate was used to start this organization."

Dorie turned to look at Andrea. "Her estate? So she's not around anymore?"

"No, Miranda's gone. BARC started nearly forty years ago. I've been the executive director for nearly twenty, but before that, Miranda's son ran the show, Old Mr. Barrett. Before that, it was Miranda herself. Now her grandson is president of the board."

A family affair. Like a monopoly?

"BARC is a family organization, I guess."

"It has been. I was the first non-family member. You're the second."

Dorie was quiet for a moment. "Well, I'm grateful. I need this job right now."

Andrea was brisk. "I'm grateful to the board for recognizing that I need some help. I expect you to be an asset. The board's goal for you is to create a positive public presence for BARC. We want people to think kindly of our group, to assume the best, and to feel good about donating. Today you can get started on whatever it is you do with social media. In there"—she pointed toward a closet— "are the files that need organizing. Plus I've enrolled you in an online grant writing and fundraising course. You have plenty of work to do."

Internally Dorie rolled her eyes. *Online training. Oh, joy.* She preferred hands-on work, like grooming dogs. "It sounds like more than fifteen hours a week."

Andrea gave her a sharp look. "We have funds for that many hours. If you work more, you won't get paid. It's your job to pay attention to your time."

"Sure. I can do that." *But how do I decide what is most important to do? Hmm. Don't ask too many questions today.* Again she heard her father's admonishing voice in her head. *You don't want to sound negative.*

Andrea led her to the file room she'd pointed out earlier, its small door almost hidden in the far wall of the boardroom. Ceremoniously she handed Dorie a large skeleton key. The key ring was a heavy dimensional sculpture of a Saint Bernard. "Go ahead. Try your new key."

After wiggling the key in the lock. Dorie opened the door onto a tiny space, almost a closet with a window. Andrea flipped the light switch. The room was full of dusty file cabinets.

"This is our organizational system, believe it or not. We haven't digitized any of the old records, even though we're currently doing most of our business online. If you ever find yourself with nothing to do, there's an entire lifetime project here of organizing, refiling, and digitizing. From 1986 until after 2015, the board maintained records in paper."

"This job just keeps on growing, doesn't it? I won't run short of work." Her heart sank. She didn't want to spend a lifetime digitizing old files.

Her face must have shown her dismay because Andrea laughed. "Don't worry, we're not expecting a miracle for our fifteen hours a week. These files have been here for years. I just wanted you to know that you'll never be at a loss for things to do."

Relieved, she smiled back, straightening her shoulders. "Okay, thanks for that." *This is a job. It is better than no job, and it could be a good job.* "What about involvement with the dogs?"

"I imagine you mean direct rescue work. There isn't any."

"But..." Dorie tried to control her disappointment.

Lifting her chin, Andrea went on. "I do try to keep up with what Mike is working on, because the stories of rescue and rehabilitation are what sell our concept. When I go to the Capitol to talk about animal cruelty, I use what I've learned from Mike and Maureen at Animal Control. You still volunteer with County Rescue, right?"

Dorie nodded.

"Good. You can use what you learn there. People are hungry for feel-good stories. Make compelling tales of cruelty and happy endings along with a plug for donations. That way your volunteering supports your job here. Okay?"

She nodded. Of course that was okay. Even Dad might agree that her volunteer work was valuable if it helped her paid employment.

"What's the first thing I should start on?" They stepped out of the dusty archives and Andrea looked on as Dorie carefully locked the door with her new key.

"The priority is the social media accounts. That will be your area entirely. I sent you a file that includes your new BARC email and access information. If you brought your laptop, you could get started on that right away."

"Great. Okay, then, I'll work here in the boardroom."

"Sure. First, though, can you go get us some coffee? The Sunshine Diner is right down the street. I want a skinny soy latte with extra whip. Get something for yourself, too. Just tell Cassandra to put it on BARC's tab. Sooner or later I'll have you paying the coffee bill every month."

"Sure," Dorie agreed, but her head was reeling. "Coffee. First."

So, now she was also the coffee girl? And digitizing old dusty files. Boring. *Why did I take this job? Because it is a job, and it is better than no job. Ah, right.*

Despite the job, her spirits lifted as she walked down the street toward the Sunshine. The crisp sea air felt good on her face, and she smiled at the gulls complaining down by the water. She could even imagine the taste of delicious coffee. This wasn't so bad. Fifteen hours was only three hours a day, then she could do whatever she wanted. Well, as long as what she wanted included finding more work or what James called "a real job." In the meantime, this might not be so bad, and it would get her family off her back. Free coffee was a bonus.

Almost cheerfully she pulled on the heavy door of the Sunshine Diner. The place was nearly empty this time of the morning, after the fishers were out on the water and the retail workday had begun. Dorie headed to the counter as Cassandra, Sunshine's waitress, came from the back.

"Dorie Madison! I haven't seen you in forever. How the heck are you?" Cassandra's wide smile warmed Dorie.

"I've been around. You don't have a dog, do you, Cassandra? You'd have seen me if you had a dog."

Cassandra shook her head. "My mother has dogs, but you're right, not me, not how I'm living now. What about you and dogs?"

"The Pampered Pooch. That was my shop."

"Was it? What happened there? I noticed the other day that the sign is down."

"Yeah, the landlord sold the building and evicted the tenants. I had to close up shop. So now I'm working for BARC."

Cassandra grinned again. "Skinny soy latte with double whip, you mean?"

Dorie flushed. "Yes, actually. I'm now the coffee girl. At least the coffee-getter. Sounds like you know Andrea's order by heart."

"Every day about this time. Sorry about the shop thing, but at least you'll be working with dogs."

Dorie shrugged. No point in going into details. She changed the subject. "I haven't been in here for ages. I'm surprised to see you still here. I thought you went to art school or something."

"Yeah. Well, life has other plans, right? I'm working at the Seaside Gallery learning how to handle artworks. Did you know there's a science to packaging them and hanging them, and an art to displaying them?"

"I guess like a lot of things, you don't know the details until you get right into them."

"Yes, and it's always more complicated and sometimes more interesting than you expect. I thought I wanted to be an artist, but now I'm thinking differently. But the Sunshine, here, this is what pays the rent. At least right now."

Dorie got it. "I guess it's the same for me. I thought I wanted to own a dog spa, but it just didn't fly here. So now I have this job and I have to figure out my life"—she made air quotes— "as my father would say."

Cassandra's smile deepened. "It is really nice to see you, Dorie. We haven't seen each other much since school. You were what, a year ahead of me?"

"Yes, I think so. Seems like forever ago."

Cassandra agreed. "Yeah, we're old folks in our twenties. And I guess you'll be a regular in the Sunshine now."

Dorie snickered. "Yes, I guess so. Not my first career choice, but at least there's good coffee."

"The very best. What'll you have?"

Cassandra made the two coffees and waved her off. Walking back up the street to the BARC office, Dorie did her best to embrace her new routine.

Chapter 5

Chad stood in the break room. Dave was talking about his great weekend with the family as Chad and Peter listened.

"Yeah, the best part about coaching soccer is you get to be there every single time with your kid. Her ball-handling skills are developing so fast, and the kids are learning about teamwork. It's pretty great. Weekends get wild though, with kid birthday parties, all three of them heading in different directions, and on Saturday Jennie went out with her friends, so the kids and I made pizza. They like cooking with their old dad."

"You know, there's specially ground flour to make pizza dough like the Italians do," Chad said. "You get this finely ground flour, start the dough the day before, and it develops the best flavour."

Dave looked puzzled. "Frozen pizzas, Chad. I dress 'em up with more cheese."

"You can make a better dough yourself though. I can send you the directions. What do you use for sauce?"

Dave frowned. "Never mind. I've got some work to do." He headed out and down the hallway.

"Is it me?" Chad asked Peter.

Peter shrugged. "Dunno. I'm here for the coffee." He went to the coffeepot on the counter and poured some into a #1 Dad mug. "I was on baby duty all weekend so my wife could try to sleep. Did you know that six-week-old babies don't sleep at night? Or more than a couple of hours at any time? I'm bagged."

"You could try swaddling. I've read that swaddling helps babies stay calm."

"Knock it off, Chad." Peter elbowed him. "You know nothing about babies and we both know that."

"Yeah."

"Or pizza making, for that matter."

"I guess. I don't know why I do that. Even my grandmother told me off for being a know-it-all."

"Maybe you're a slow learner." Peter waggled his eyebrows.

Chagrined, Chad sighed. "Yep, I guess so. I bet it sucks to have no sleep. Is having a baby worth it?"

Chad mentally patted himself on the back when Peter chuckled. "You bet it is. At least my baby. But I'm glad the coffee never runs out here."

Asking a question instead of telling went well. Hmm. "Yeah. Okay, Pete. See you later."

Heading back to his desk, Chad wondered what it was like for Dave to have those kids, and now for Peter to be living with a tiny baby. *I don't usually even notice, do I? Mostly I'm relieved that I don't have to deal with that. I like working late at night on my projects, and sleeping late, and not having to consult with anyone about how I spend my time. Those guys seem to like their lives though.* Nan was right. He was a little bit like his father. Not in a good way.

He felt a bit uneasy. Fatherhood. His talk with Nan about his dad was still vivid in his memory. *I wonder what kind of dad Dave is? Do his kids like him?* It wasn't that long ago that Dave and Pete were like him, creating careers, working and playing hard, going out with different women. Now these regular guys, now they're fathers. Somebody's dad.

What kind of father would I be? If I ever got a chance to be one? That was too weird to think about, so Chad turned his attention back to work. Somehow, though, he kept seeing Dorie in his mind. Not the image of her angry and telling him goodbye, but her messy bun when he brought Frou into the shop, her smile when he picked her up for dinner, and her earnest face on the video he'd collected around the dog hoarding story. He felt a strange emptiness in his middle.

At his laptop, he pushed the feeling away and opened his email. Absently scrolling through work notices, he clicked on a search engine report of web items about cruelty to dogs. Oh, look, more dog issues near Stella Mare.

Chad thought back to his brief, disastrous date with Dorie. *Maybe she's forgotten. Surely I can get in touch about, well, other stuff?*

A few minutes later, he started a text.

Hey. Remember me?

Delete. Of course she would remember the critical geek.

Good morning, Dorie. That might be okay. More professional. He kept tapping.

Good morning, Dorie. I have been thinking (about you) about the plight of dogs in our province.

Ugh.

Hey, Dorie. I see there's more trouble for dogs down your way. Are you working on this issue? My colleague is interested in following up and I wondered if we might talk?

No, no, no. No "colleague."

Hey Dorie, I see that there have been more incidents of trouble for dogs in NB. I might like to follow that story. Would you talk to me? I know I was kind of a jerk the last time we talked. I would like a chance to redeem myself. Chad.

Before he could second-guess himself again, he pressed send. Immediately his stomach clenched. He shoved his glasses up his nose and squinted at his phone. *Why do I feel so unusual? This whole day has been strange. Or it's me.*

He pushed himself to look back toward his work, but he found himself again on his phone, scrolling through social media, searching for Dorie.

There wasn't much on her personal page, except a few cute pictures of her with some gigantic hairy dogs. He searched instead for that organization, BARC. Bingo! A news release a few posts down, posted by that Andrea but with a picture of Dorie. There she is! For a moment, he stopped reading just to look at her face. Oh, she was prettier than he remembered. What a smile! He felt a big hole in his heart. *I want that smile turned on me. I might have screwed that up completely, but I still want it.* That feeling. That woman.

For another moment, he lost himself in imagining her, her smile, her laugh, the way she popped up from behind the counter at her silly shop (not silly, he told himself, that's what got you in trouble already).

With effort, he turned his attention back to the text. Oh, she was working for BARC now. Wow, a great rationale for connecting around the dog stuff. "Yes!" He pumped his fist into the air.

"Hey, Chad! What's all the excitement?" Dave stuck his head around the doorframe.

He looked up, confused. "Did I say something?"

Dave laughed. "Just some noise. What's so exciting?"

He shook his head. "Just a story idea."

He got a skeptical look back. "Pretty exciting story then. I thought you just trailed Jeannette around."

"Thanks, friend." Chad scowled. "I get to have ideas, too, you know."

Dave laughed and clapped him on the shoulder. "I don't think any story warrants that level of excitement from my serious buddy Chad. I bet there's a woman involved. Am I right?"

He felt himself flush. Dave caught on, clapping him on the shoulder again. "Can't wait to meet her, buddy."

Mute, Chad just shook his head. Dave was laughing when he went out the door, but Chad was less amused. Dave was right though. It was really about Dorie, but the dog thing still might make a good story.

In the middle of the afternoon, Chad was editing film when his phone pinged. He caught his breath when he saw it was Dorie.

Hey, Chad.

He grabbed up his phone and typed quickly, before he could think about it. *Yeah, I'm here. How are you doing?*

Good enough. I'm working at BARC now.

He smiled. *Yeah, I saw that. How's that going?*

The screen didn't change for a long moment. Chad could almost imagine her shrugging. *It's kind of okay. It's only been a week or so.*

He didn't know what to say to that. *Can I call you?*

No, not now. I'm at work. Later.

Tonight? What time? He wondered if she thought he was being too pushy.

Tonight is good. About seven.

Dorie leashed up Custard and Mallow right after dinner and headed into the dark, phone in her pocket. *I wonder what Chad*

really wants? Well, she could wait to find out. She was busy enough without having a guy in Saint Jacques to think about.

Oh, but you do think about him, her inner voice taunted her. *His dark hair and those deep brown eyes, and the shoulders.*

Stop! Just stop, Dorie told herself. *Mr. Good Advice. He was a jerk to me.*

She walked a little farther. *Okay, he was a jerk who wants to apologize.*

Her inner dialogue was so intense she almost missed the phone when it rang. Breathless, she clicked and said, "Hello?"

"Hi. Dorie?"

"Yeah, it's me. Hi, Chad." Oh, it was nice to hear his voice.

"It's really nice to hear your voice," he said.

She couldn't help herself; she laughed. "Okay, honestly that's exactly what I was thinking. Only about you."

"Well. That's good, I guess."

"Yeah. Funny."

"Yes, so first things first. I was a dumb jerk to you last time I saw you, and I'm sorry and I was trying to be helpful. At least I thought that was what I was doing. I'm going to try to keep my helpful comments to myself from now on. I have been doing that. Practising."

"How's that working?" Dorie was genuinely curious.

"Well, when I'm not telling other people how I think they should do things, I don't have all that much to say," he admitted. "I'm trying not to spend all my time wondering what I should say next."

Dorie was quiet.

"Dorie? You saying nothing isn't helping me stop worrying about what to say."

She laughed. "You're right. That wasn't intentional, sorry. I got a little lost in my thinking. I'm the youngest in my family, so I've had more than my share of people telling me what to do and how to do it. I recently talked to my sister about that. I might be oversensitive."

"You have a sister?"

"Oh, yes, I do. Many sisters. Too many. I'm the fourth daughter. I have three big sisters who all think they know better than me what I should be doing. You know my mom's gone, but my dad is also pretty invested in telling me everything I do that's wrong."

"It must have been annoying when I did it too."

Dorie laughed. "Nicely put. Yes, annoying and way too familiar. The worst part is you were right. You and all the rest of my family. You might be happy to know the Pampered Pooch is no more." She tried not to sound bitter. "It was a concept that just could not fly in Stella Mare."

"No, really? You closed the shop? That's too bad." Chad sounded genuinely sad. A pleasant warmth grew in her belly.

"A lot of things happened all at once. The biggest was that I lost my lease," she explained. "But I was lucky because Andrea offered me this job with BARC about the same time. It isn't enough hours. but I'm going to figure something out."

"Now you work for BARC. Are you involved in this latest dog hoarding story I saw?"

"Not involved. Supposedly BARC doesn't get involved, but Andrea sometimes gets fired up and we end up out in the field. Our reason for being there isn't very clear. But the story might be bigger than hoarding. Mike at County Rescue thinks that there is more going on, but nobody is saying too much. At the moment it's mostly rumour."

"What's the rumour?"

"Well, we've been involved in shutting down some puppy mill businesses, and that got ugly."

"What's a puppy mill? Sounds like a factory."

"Pretty much. It's a setup where somebody breeds dogs without much concern for the health of the bloodline or breeds them too often or raises them under factory-like circumstances."

"How is that different from a breeder?"

Dorie warmed to her topic; she so seldom got a chance to talk about what she knew. "Completely different. Purebred dogs all come from a limited gene pool, as you can imagine. They are bred specifically to have those characteristics that make the breed. Labrador retrievers are friendly, loyal, and like to fetch things. Border collies are focused, determined, great at rounding up strays, and tend to bond with one person."

"Yeah, and dogs like Frou-Frou are curly haired and tenacious. And irritating."

Dorie giggled. "Well, except for the irritating part, you've got it exactly. The same narrowing of the gene pool that makes dogs have breed characteristics can cause characteristic problems too. Like Labs can be prone to hip troubles. So good breeders watch the bloodlines for all those problems and try hard to ensure that they are raising dogs who don't have them and won't pass them on. But puppy mill breeders only care about getting pups that approximate the breed so they can sell them. It's not good for the individual dogs, and not good overall for dog breeders and dog lovers."

"Are there puppy mills in New Brunswick?"

"Not as bad now. County Rescue has done a lot to raise people's awareness about where purebred dogs come from, and to cut off puppy mills at the sales end as well as shut them down when we find them. BARC pushes the legislative levers. Andrea is working on ways to limit the number of dogs on a property."

"What if somebody wants to have a lot of dogs though, and takes care of them? Like sled dogs or something?"

"Of course people can do that. We just want to stop situations in which dogs are being harmed. Sled dogs are well treated, usually, at least by the people I know who have them. We do have some dog hoarding going on, though, and that's different from puppy mills." She stopped to think about Sarah and all her little dogs.

"Different how?"

"That story where I met you, that was dog hoarding. This guy just kept getting dogs and he didn't have the means to take care of them. He kept adding more and more to his house. It was awful inside. I got to see some of the pictures that the police took, after the fact. The poor man wasn't really in his right mind, and the dogs had taken over the house. It was so horrible." Her nose twitched at the thought. "Honestly, I'm glad I didn't get to go inside there. We helped to place some of the dogs in foster homes, but some of them were so far gone our vet recommended euthanasia."

"You sound sad."

"Well, of course. It wasn't the dogs' fault they were in that mess." Teariness pulled at her voice. *Get a grip, girl.*

Chad's voice, when it came again, was a lot softer. "That sounds terrible. I can see why you want to stop things like that from happening."

"Yeah. Dogs are friends for people. There are so many hard situations. Like when old people can't care for their dogs. That's super sad. My aunt Corinne is a social worker, and she sees that problem all the time. It's not due to intentional cruelty, just life."

"Life."

"Yeah. Did you ever have a dog, Chad?" Dorie stopped walking and thrust her hand into Mallow's thick, silky neck. He turned his head to look at her, then nuzzled her knee.

"No, I never did. My uncle had retrievers, always, but they were working dogs. When I was a kid, I wanted a dog to sleep on my bed, but my mother didn't believe in animals in the house."

"That's terrible!" Dorie was shocked. "I can't imagine no animals in the house. We have always had dogs, usually two at a time, big ones, and there were always cats around. My first pup was a golden retriever when I was five. Okay, my mum and I took care of him together because I was only five, but still. He was the best dog ever. Chester. I loved that mutt."

"What happened to Chester?" Chad's voice sounded like there was a smile on his face.

"Chester was the best. But he was hit by a car and killed instantly when I was thirteen. He ran out in the road after a squirrel across the street. I was trying to hold the leash and had to let it go."

"Oh, no! You saw the whole thing. That's rough."

"Yeah. Yeah, it was awful. I had nightmares for weeks. I kind of got over it, and my dad brought home a new dog, not a pup, but Maxwell, a mixed breed from the pound. He wasn't Chester, but it helped. We already had Chester's older sister, Nell, and then a few years later Mallow and Custard joined the menagerie."

"Sounds like a lot of animals."

"Yeah, I guess so. I think it was mostly my mum who was the big animal person. Dad likes our dogs, but I don't think he'd be out getting new family members if these guys were to disappear."

"Have I met these guys to which you refer?"

Dorie laughed again. "I should introduce you. Custard and Mallow, the biggest lunks you'd ever meet. And sweet. Not very excitable. Honestly, not excessively smart. Not like your grandmother's Frou-Frou."

"It's possible I haven't really had a chance to get to know any dogs very well. Frou-Frou only likes my Gran. He had an attitude toward me right from the start. I shouldn't assume all dogs would be like that."

"You'll have to come meet my guys. Mine and Dad's, that is."

"Is that an invitation?"

Was it? *Oh, why not.* The man had apologized. "Sure. When are you coming back to see your grandmother?"

"I don't know about that. But I could come to work on a story, say, about BARC and dogs. Especially if you were willing to spend some time with me."

Flirting? Is he flirting? He's really bad at it. "You mean to work on the story about BARC?" she asked sweetly.

Sounding flustered, Chad answered, "Oh, oh, yes. Of course. On the story."

She waited.

"Come on, Dorie. I would like to see you. I'd make a trip to Stella Mare just to see you if you'll have me. I might get a story out of it, and I can visit my grandmother. But the main reason I want to come is to see you."

"That was very direct."

"Yep. I've been told that my social skills are pretty poor."

That is correct, they are. Okay, I can be direct too. "Okay. I would like to see you again. We can be friends. If you come for a visit, I'll make some time for you. But don't be travelling here just to see me. I barely know you, and the first time we tried to get together it was not so great."

"Okay, right." Chad sounded excited. "I'll be in touch, okay?"

Dorie hung up with a sigh. *Did he hear me say friends? I hope so.*

Chapter 6

Friday afternoon, Dorie was in the office wrapping up the following week's social media posts when she got a series of texts from Chad.

I've been reading up. Puppy mills, dogfighting, animal hoarding, plain old neglect and abuse, we've had it all here in the province.

I'm piling up footage to use in a feature. You could be my consultant.

And how about dinner tonight?

And did I say I am sorry I was a jerk before?

He even sent a brief video of himself whistling in his truck, captioned with something about being happy to go to Stella Mare.

Dorie shook her head, smiling. *He's not really like other guys. Chad's himself. That's all there is to it.*

She looked over her planned posts. Images of happy animals and people, superimposed over sad, starved puppies. Heart wrenching, she thought with some satisfaction. Get their attention and tug on the heartstrings. That'll help them open up the wallet. The winter holidays were coming, and BARC always ran a fundraising campaign at the end of the year.

When she was nearly finished, her phone pinged with a breaking news alert. Simultaneously, Andrea stuck her head in the door. "Dorie! There's a big one. Come on."

Grabbing the phone and her jacket, Dorie tried to read while jogging to the parking lot. "What's up?" she asked breathlessly.

Andrea pulled on her seat belt. "On the police scanner. Multiple dogs on site out in Bakersville. It sounded pretty nasty." She looked at Dorie. "They weren't all alive."

"Oh." Dorie felt shocked. Dead dogs. Not something she wanted to think about too much. But there were some out there that needed their help.

She checked her phone again. "I wonder if this is related. The news flash is about police activity. They've locked down the village of Bakersville and asked people to stay inside and not post anything about police movements." Dorie looked up at Andrea's determined face. "Are you sure we should be going out there? It sounds serious."

"Of course it's serious. Any time an animal is in danger, it is serious. And that's our job, Dorie, to help."

"Okay. If you say so," she murmured, chastened. Tapping surreptitiously, she sent a quick text to Mike at County Rescue. *Heading to Bakersville with Andrea but not sure why.*

Her father almost certainly would disagree with Andrea about her responsibility for dogs. She could almost hear his voice: let the police do their job. The dogs will wait for you. She remembered Andrea telling her on her first day of work not to expect to do any direct work with dogs. *There are some peculiar mixed messages going on here. But this is way better than admin, and I'm on the clock, so I'm just going to go with it.*

Forty minutes later, approaching Bakersville, Dorie heard a siren. Were they calling in more police? No, it was an ambulance coming toward them, out of Bakersville, probably heading to Saint Jacques, to the hospital. This was feeling more and more like a crisis Dorie didn't belong in, but she was stuck in the car with Andrea, who looked to be in intense mode. Her jaw was set firmly and she had a vise-tight grip on the wheel. Gazing away out the car window, Dorie tried to relax.

Dark began to fill the fields as the BMW skimmed across the country roads. A pale moon rose, silvering the hayfield stubble and making the forest look like a paper cut-out against the darkening sky. Dorie caught the scent of woodsmoke, and the evening itself looked peaceful in contrast to her pounding heart and churning stomach.

Bakersville was only two blocks long, so she saw the police immediately. An old garage at the far end was wreathed in bright yellow police tape and illuminated with portable floodlights against the deepening gloom. Andrea parked in front of the little post office, ahead of where an officer routed traffic away from the scene. She swooped out of the car, and Dorie followed in her wake.

Still wondering what she was going to do to help, Dorie trotted along behind Andrea. *Guess I can watch and see how this is done.*

Andrea marched up to the police tape where an officer was standing. “I'm Andrea Chase from BARC. We had a tip that there were dogs involved here.”

The man looked at Andrea without curiosity. “Animal Control is on the way, ma'am. No concern of yours.”

“I disagree,” she said clearly. “BARC is here to help. I want to see those dogs. You can release them to me.”

Dorie was startled. What would they do with dogs in Andrea’s BMW?

The officer sighed. “Animal Control is on the way, Ms. Chase. You can talk to Maureen when she arrives.” He turned and walked away along the police line. Andrea made a sound of annoyance and looked toward Dorie.

“We could be here a while,” she said sharply.

"What did you mean about taking dogs? We can't take any dogs."

She raised her eyebrows. "Acting like you belong sometimes gets you more information," she said firmly. "I want to know what's going on here."

"Do you think Mike Maybee knows about this situation?" Dorie neglected to mention that she'd sent him a text.

Andrea scowled. "Mike is involved in everything."

"Well, he's the director of the rescue organization. I didn't know that Maureen at Animal Control worked with us. I thought she only worked with Mike at the County Rescue."

"It depends."

"Depends on what? I didn't know BARC did any rescue work, or investigation. I mean, we went out to Sarah's, but you left."

Andrea made an exasperated sound. "Dorie, right now, I just want to know what's going on. I'd like to get a good look at the people who perpetrate this kind of cruelty." Her face was tight.

"What kind of cruelty? Do you know what's going on here?"

Instead of offering any answer, Andrea marched away along the police tape. Bemused, Dorie followed her. No dogs or people milled around the old gas station. She saw just the police tape and officers with the floodlights. There had been the ambulance earlier, but now, there was no visible action.

Andrea looked grim. "Bad stuff for dogs. Whatever it is, it's bad."

The fact that Animal Control was coming was the only confirmation that there were even animals on site. Dorie pulled out her phone and took some pictures of the scene. There might be something useful for her media campaign here.

A wild racket of barking, shouting, a scream, and a series of loud bangs erupted in front of her and Andrea. The front door and the garage door of the building burst open at the same instant. Dogs emerged, barking and growling. They charged toward Andrea and Dorie, outside the police line, and at the officer they'd been talking to. Behind them ran a man and woman, closely followed by other uniformed RCMP. An engine roared to life and a big vehicle tore off across the field behind the gas station. Two ATVs tore across the field, and a police cruiser took off behind them.

Dorie counted six dogs, even though it seemed like three times as many when they were all barking and snarling. Once clear of the building and away from the people, the dogs quieted. Four took off into the woods beside the gas station, one collapsed on the ground, and another stood over the fallen one, snapping and whining.

"Oh, no! She's hurt," Dorie said. She lifted the police tape and slipped underneath, heading for the fallen dog.

"Dorie! Come back here!" Andrea's voice was full of alarm. "You don't know what will happen."

Dorie approached slowly. The watchful dog issued a warning growl.

"No worries, I'm a friend," she said, tentatively offering the dog her hand to sniff. She hoped the dog didn't think she was offering a hand to chew. These dogs could all be starving, though these two looked well fed. With her other hand, she fished in her jacket pocket for her omnipresent dog treats. Oh, yes, thank goodness. When she extended the treat toward the guardian dog, it immediately dropped all pretense of meanness and flopped to the ground to chew. "You little trickster," she murmured. The dog was a sturdy terrier mix, brindle-coloured, female...and young.

She turned her attention to the injured animal but maintained a healthy distance.

"What can you see?" Andrea asked.

Dorie shook her head. "Doesn't look good. She's bleeding, a lot, from the shoulder, I think." The dog gave a deep sigh and her body relaxed on the ground. "Oh, no, Andrea, I think she just..."

Before Dorie could complete her thought, the uniformed officer bore down on her.

"Get out of here. You're not safe here, miss. Get back behind the line." The guardian dog leaped up and growled. The officer backed off slightly but was still insistent. "Miss, right now."

Dorie looked up at him. "This dog is badly hurt. We need to get some help."

"Miss, people might be getting hurt. Get out of here. Right now."

Another burst of sound and activity came from behind the garage, and the officer ran off, hand on his holster. Dorie turned to see Andrea pulling a leash and more treats out of her bag and slipping under the police tape.

"Do you think we can move her?"

Dorie looked again at the inert dog. "No. No point. It's too late for this one, Andrea. But this one"—she gestured to the other dog finishing the treat—"this one is good to go. I think."

Andrea approached, treat in one hand, leash in the other. "Good dog," she said approvingly. Without fuss, the brindle allowed Andrea to slide the lead around her neck as she crunched another dog snack. The two women quickly walked back under the tape, the dog trotting easily along with them.

Handing the leash to Dorie when they got to the car, Andrea grabbed her camera. "Put her in there and let's go. Those other dogs headed into the woods."

"But isn't that Animal Control's job?"

Andrea scoffed. "All of this is Animal Control's job. But do you see Animal Control? You see a dead dog over there, right, and nobody prevented that." She turned toward the gas station.

"Andrea. Come back."

"You're not coming? Well, suit yourself." She marched back down the street.

Dorie felt unaccountably tired. *I just watched a dog die.* She watched Andrea getting farther away with every furious step. *I got yelled at by a cop, and now, you're off acting like you're going to make the world safe for dogs when it's not your job. At least I don't think it is. I'm not actually sure how I got into this. But this is as far as I go. There's a dog right here and this one I can help.*

She looked down at the tightly muscled brindle dog. The dog gazed at Dorie, her yellow eyes mournful. Dorie could swear she looked sad. Maybe she just needed another treat. Unfortunately Dorie was out. "You've had a rough night, girl. You can settle in the car for a nap." Rummaging around, she searched for a blanket to cover the backseat; Andrea's BMW didn't really look like it had been used much to rescue dogs. Not finding a blanket, she pulled off her own jacket to make a bed for the dog.

Dorie's phone buzzed in her back pocket. *Oh, my goodness, Chad! What time is it?* It was dark enough that she had to pull out the phone to get the time; her old-fashioned wind-up watch was useless at night. Yes, it was Chad texting.

Hi.

Hi. I'm out on a dog rescue mission. Sorry to be running late.

Where are you? Can I come help?

Well, that might be a good idea. I'm here with my boss, and I don't have my car, so I might be stuck here for a while. Can I just send you the coordinates?

Sure. I'm sure I can find you. Is there a story to this rescue?

Probably. Some bad guys, lots of police, a dog casualty, and there are some other ones missing. Sounds like a story but I don't know the plot.

I should be there within an hour.

Dorie turned from her phone toward the now-quiet building. Where was Andrea?

A big black car squealed to a stop next to Dorie at Andrea's car. She squinted, trying to see through the tinted glass. A door slammed, the car took off, and there was Andrea, looking bedraggled and annoyed.

"Who was that?"

Andrea pushed past her and opened the car door. "Never mind."

"Was that Mr. Barrett? It looked like..."

"Just get in the car. We're leaving."

"But..."

Andrea looked into the backseat. "Oh, we've got that dog in here. Is she okay?"

"Of course she's here. You told me to put her in the car."

"Right, of course. I guess we have to keep her." Andrea was slightly dishevelled, and her usual confidence appeared rattled.

Dorie looked at the brindle curled up on the backseat. "She seems okay. A little scared but not hurt. What about you? What's going on?"

Andrea shrugged one shoulder as she looked behind her and squealed out of the parking place, cranking the steering wheel, and turned back toward Stella Mare. Once on the main road, she settled and looked toward Dorie. "It'll be best if we both just forget what was going on here."

Incredulous, Dorie blurted, "What? That's crazy. A dog died. This dog was, I don't know, abandoned. We can't just forget what we saw."

"Trust me. Just let that go."

"Ten minutes ago you were stomping down the road with a camera. What happened?"

She raised her voice. "Nothing happened. We just don't belong there. Didn't you say that before? Let it go. We're done there."

Annoyed, Dorie looked out her side window. This made no sense whatsoever. Forget troubled dogs? This BARC thing was just peculiar. That's all there was too it.

She tried again. "Andrea, how can you just let that go? Was that what that man, Mr. Barrett, said?"

"What? No, of course not." Andrea's profile was tight and angry. Or was it scared? "Just let it go, Dorie. I don't want to see you writing anything about any of this. Got it?"

"Yeah, I hear you. I don't understand."

Andrea shook her head. "You don't need to. Just let it alone."

"Okay. I hear you." Dorie tapped out a message to Chad.

"Who are you writing to? I just told you to keep this quiet."

She was furious but kept her voice even. "I said I would. It's just my friend that I was supposed to meet. No worries."

"Okay, then. I'll drop you at your house. But I mean it, Dorie." Andrea's look was searing.

"I heard you."

Dorie understood Andrea wanted her to leave the story alone, but how did she explain the new foster dog to her father? She hoped James would be napping again.

Tugging the brindle along, she went into the house. The dog was clearly not accustomed to walking on a leash, but Dorie eventually got her into the house. The brindle's nails clicked on the tile while Dorie grabbed treats from the basket hanging by the kitchen door.

Custard, normally asleep, let out a mighty woof, and the brindle startled and growled. The two big dogs padded into the kitchen. Dorie felt the brindle tense at her side.

"Hi, guys. Nice of you to take notice," she commented. "As you can see, we have somebody new here. Be nice." Mallow meandered over to Dorie to get a head pat and to sniff the newcomer. She threw herself on the kitchen floor and bared her hairy belly. The brindle softened and leaned in for a sniff, then sat. Custard sat placidly waiting for his turn to be sniffed by the new girl.

"Good dogs," Dorie praised. She knew the big dogs wouldn't be a problem. They were accustomed to fosters showing up. The brindle, though, had been an unknown quantity. Scared, young, and perhaps used for fighting. Or at least breeding fighting dog stock. Scared dogs were more likely to be aggressive. Still watching the dogs carefully, Dorie got out a third bowl and filled all of them with kibble. Feeding the brindle first, she then set bowls out for the big dogs, well separated. The brindle scarfed down her food, then pushed Mallow out of the way to eat from her bowl. Mallow looked toward Dorie, clearly affronted.

"Yeah, I know." She sighed and grabbed a handful of kibble, using it to lure the brindle back to her own bowl where Dorie added more food. "See, girl, we feed everyone here." The big dogs lurched out of the kitchen and back toward their beds, while the brindle tongued out all three empty bowls and looked expectantly at Dorie.

Dorie frowned back. "Any more and you'll be throwing it up. Here, let's go outside in the yard. You probably need it." She had picked up the trailing leash to walk her new charge outside just as Chad knocked on the kitchen door. Unaccountably, Dorie felt her heart lift.

"Hi." He pushed up his glasses and pocketed his video camera.

"No, please get that camera out again. This girl has a story to tell, even though I don't know what it is yet."

"Okay. You've got my interest."

"Let's take her for a walk around the yard and I'll try to fill you in."

An hour later, Dorie and Chad settled into a booth at Jessie's Pizza. It was eight p.m. but felt closer to midnight. Sliding along the seat, she relaxed for the first time in hours. The restaurant was warm and the smell of sizzling pizza, frying onions, and french fries was driving her wild.

She gave Chad a brilliant smile. "I'm pretty sure the last thing I had to eat was coffee this morning."

"Coffee's great but it doesn't sustain you all day. Why didn't you eat?"

"Just busy. I don't know when I've been so hungry. Have you ever noticed how delicious everything smells when you're starving?"

He grinned back at her. "I'm glad you're hungry. Let's get you fed, first thing. Then we can try to sort out what's going on out in Bakersville."

They negotiated their order and Chad gave it to the hovering server. Cold beer and hot mozzarella sticks arrived immediately, and Dorie dove in. Finally coming up for air, she sighed deeply. "Oh, I feel so much better," she announced.

"There's pizza yet to come," Chad encouraged. "So, tell me more about your day."

"Yeah. Well, I still don't know everything that's going on, but Mike, you know Mike? The County Rescue guy? Mike thinks there's a dog-fighting ring, you know, people setting up fights and betting on them."

"Yes, I read an article that speculated on the rise in dog fights, even though it's against the law."

"Yeah, I know, it's been banned forever. But some people live to break the rules, especially if they think they can make money from it. So it might be that those dogs, the dead dog and the one we rescued, and the other ones that ran off into the woods, they might be fighting dogs."

"Isn't that brindle pup a female?"

"Yes, and the one that died on scene, both female. Females aren't used for fights, but they do need them to breed more fighting dogs. It could be a big ring. People who fight dogs and people who raise them for this so-called sport."

"So-called?"

"Yeah. It's a sport, like horse racing is a sport. People bet on the winners, lots of money changes hands. There's a big market for big, muscular, aggressive dogs trained to kill. Because it's illegal, that sort of thing is attractive to criminal sorts."

"Yeah. Not to the kind of criminal that, say, knocks off convenience stores, but the smart organized kind of criminal. The ones who know places to launder money."

"I never really understood that. What does it even mean?"

"You've heard the phrase, to follow the money, right?"

Dorie nodded.

"That's because money leaves a trail. When you have a job, the government knows your salary, keeps track for taxes. When you had your business, you had to report your income, right?"

"Right. And pay taxes."

"Yes. But if you're making piles of money illegally, you don't want anyone to be able to follow that trail. Big wads of cash make people take notice. You can't buy a house with all cash, for example, without being able to say where it came from. So criminal organizations need legitimate businesses to push their illegal dollars through."

Dorie looked around the pizza restaurant. "If I owned a restaurant, but I made a pile of money by dog fighting, I could just make deposits into my restaurant bank account and pretend that it all came from pizza sales."

Chad nodded. "Then the money would have a legitimate source. You'd pay tax on the income for the pizza restaurant, but if you were making tons of money, you'd spread it out over a bunch of little businesses, so the tax bite was less."

Dorie smiled at him. "How'd you get to be so smart?"

He scoffed. "Thinking I'm smart is what gets me in trouble. I've just worked in the news business for about ten years. You do see a lot. It would be hard to avoid picking up a few things."

Dorie pondered. "If there is a dog-fighting ring, there may be a few people making money and needing to wash it, right?"

"Launder. Yes."

"Why would anybody bet on a dog fight? It's awful. Dogs fight to the death and if they don't die, they're maimed. The training is brutal, and sweet, kind dogs are taught to be aggressive killers. Then people, regular people, get ideas that some dogs are born killers which is just, I don't know, just so unfair. What's the sport in that?"

Chad shook his head. "People bet on dogs for the same reason they bet on anything else. They hope to make a killing, and I don't mean dogs. I mean big money."

"Yeah."

I wonder what Andrea has to do with any of this. Dorie opened her mouth to mention Andrea to Chad but stopped. He worked for the news. Andrea was her boss and had told her to drop it. While she hadn't exactly dropped the topic, she decided to leave Andrea out of their conversation.

The server slid a massive pizza onto the table. Steam rose and conversation lagged while Chad expertly slid a large piece onto Dorie's plate and took one for himself.

"Mmm. This is just as good as I remember."

"Remember? When was the last time you had Jessie's pizza?"

Chad got a faraway look. "It was a while ago. Probably high school. I left right after that and only came back to visit Nan."

"No friends? No high-school sweethearts?"

"I had friends. But once we weren't in school, there wasn't much in common. I know some people here in town, but I wouldn't say they were friends, if you mean the kind that keep in touch."

"You were in my sister's year in school, right? Evie? Evelyn?"

"Yeah, I knew Evie. Knew who she was anyway. One of the Madison sisters."

Dorie looked down at the table. "Yeah, one of the sisters. That was always my label. People seemed to expect things from me based on my sisters. At least the ones who had been around when my sisters were coming up through school."

"Like what? You girls weren't big troublemakers, were you?" Chad was smiling.

"No such luck. That might have been some fun. No, my sisters were a lot older than me, and they were all 'high achievers.'" Here Dorie made air quotes with her fingers. "And I have never in my life been a high achiever. This girl just wants to have fun, you know?"

Chad grinned at her. "You know how to have fun...chasing down people who are mean to dogs, making the world safe for animals. You have your own kind of fun, I think."

"Yep. That's me. I need a superhero cape," she added thoughtfully.

He propped his chin on his elbow. "And what's your superhero name? Dog Saver?"

"Oh, that's lame."

"Yeah, I agree. What do you have?"

"Not much. Uh, Princess of Pampering, canine version?"

"Oh, that's really bad. What happened to the pampering of the pooches, anyway?"

Her smile evaporated. "Lost it. The business, I mean. I was evicted, couldn't borrow money to get another place because I already borrowed money, and besides, everyone was right. Except me. You were right, my sisters were right, my father was right. Pampered pups don't fly in Stella Mare." Her voice bitter, she added, "Dog fighting, yeah, we have that. Dog pampering isn't our style."

Chad put his hand over hers on the table. "I'm really sorry, Dorie."

She waited a beat and pulled her hand away. “I am getting better at admitting my mistakes. I just don't seem to learn much from them.”

“Does anyone? I know I keep making the same mistakes over and over.”

She looked at him quizzically. “You? Like what?”

Chad shook his head and looked at the table. “Sometimes I talk too much.”

She smiled. “Well, tonight you've had to listen to me. Why did you want to come to Stella Mare, anyway?”

He didn’t answer right away, but finally said, “News. Dogs. I have alerts set up, and there were two items in the police blotter down in Charlotte County about dog cruelty. I thought there was a story.”

She sat up straight. “Well, there probably is a story. This mess that happened today, that's a story. We just don't know the whole story.” Sinking back down, she thought about Andrea's grim face in the car. “Do you know Mike Maybee? He could probably tell you more.”

“The rescue guy? Yeah, I sort of met him the day I sort of met you, at that hoarding story in September.”

Dorie was busy scribbling. “Here's his number. I don't think I can follow this up with you, but he's good.”

Chad looked puzzled. “What do you mean, you can't follow it up?”

“It's just best if I keep my nose out of it,” she admitted. “Even though my nose really wants to know what's going on.”

He squinted at her. “This doesn't sound like the woman I know. You're going to step away from a possible dog-fighting story?”

“Yeah. Yes, that's what I'm doing. We should talk about something else.” She picked at the last bit of cheese on her plate.

“What just happened? Did I say something wrong? Again?” He looked upset.

She shook her head. "No, not at all. It's just, well, I just started this part-time thing with BARC."

"Isn't BARC about advocacy for dogs?"

She shrugged. "Yeah. But this, well, this is out of my area. I've been told." She raised her eyebrows meaningfully.

"You've been told."

She nodded. "I really don't want to say any more about it."

"Okay, then. I 'll respect that. Is it okay if I follow it up as a story though?"

"You do whatever it is you do. I'm only responsible for me, right?"

Chad chuckled. "Right. I guess you wouldn't mind if this story got a little daylight, especially if it kept some dogs safe."

Dorie pantomimed zipping her lips and smiled at Chad.

"Okay. Message received," he said. "Let's talk about something else. You're at BARC? What's your job there?"

She drew a breath. This felt like solid ground. "Mostly boring admin stuff, but I do get to keep the socials running and that might be fun, except it appears I have to be careful what I draw attention to. Cute puppy pics are okay. But what about you, Chad? Do you love your job? Photojournalist sounds pretty exotic."

"Yes, I live an exotic life in Saint Jacques," he said with a straight face. "Filming car accidents, city council meetings, and new ships in the harbour. Sometimes we even have political infighting."

She couldn't help but grin. "Imagine that. I was sure anything would be more exciting than Stella Mare."

"You sound like me at eighteen. Haven't you lived away?"

"Well, I spent three years in Fredericton at university. Does that count?"

"Sure. What did you study?"

"Ha. Partying, mostly. I didn't manage to get my degree, but I was studying marketing. That makes me partly qualified for my part-time job."

"Hey, hey," he chided, "don't put yourself down like that. Things are going to work out."

Vaguely comforted, she allowed herself to smile. "But you. You left here at eighteen?"

"Mum died when I was little, and my father moved out west to work when I was eleven. He was killed out there in the oil sands. I was here with Nan."

"Oh, man. I'm sorry about your parents."

"It sounds more sad than it is, because I had Nan. She was the whole world. My father was a techie guy, could fix anything he could get his hands on, but he was hard to talk to. Nan's been pretty good. But when I was eighteen, I couldn't wait to leave. I thought any place was better than here."

"Where did you go?"

"Ontario for school. After that, I lived a few different places. Halifax. St. Johns for a year. Saint Jacques is okay. It's close to here, which is good, in case Nan needs me. The job is a job."

"Saint Jacques is just okay though? I would have thought it would be great." She imagined busy streets, rushing pedestrians, news teams zipping off to cover exciting stories. How could that be only okay?

"It's okay. I like it okay. I come home to an empty apartment though."

Ahh, this. "You need a dog. I've got a brindle terrier I can let you have cheap."

He laughed out loud. "I do not need a dog. I can't imagine my life with a dog in it. I never know for sure when I'm going to get home from work. A dog wouldn't put up with it."

Neither would a girlfriend. *Better keep that to myself.* "When you're not working, what do you like to do?"

"I like to look at things. Places. People."

"Look at people?"

"Not in a creepy way. Mostly through a camera. But when I look at someone, I wonder how they got to be the way they are. What caused the wrinkles in the face, or the limp, or the big smile. What is the story of their life that made them be who they are right now? Everyone has a story."

"I guess so. I never thought about that."

"I think about it a lot, and I wonder how to tell the story in pictures. You know that saying that a picture is worth a thousand words?"

"Sounds like something my father would say."

"Well, it's one of those old sayings. But think about it. Have you ever seen a picture that told you, like, everything? You got it all in one look, no explanations needed?"

Dorie was unsure. "Maybe. I don't really know."

"Well, that's what I'm interested in. I want to know how to put together pictures, images, that tell a story, so that you don't need a lot of words. I've made a few short films, and I take photographs, too, well, digital images, and that's pretty much what I do."

"Wow." Dorie was impressed. "You have a passion for your work."

He laughed. "Not necessarily my paid work. But yes, I love to look for the pictures that tell the stories."

"Well, thanks for telling me that," she said, wonderingly. There was more to this guy than she'd realized. "Will you show me some of your work?"

Again he laughed. His laugh made her feel warmly included, like they were sharing a joke. "Isn't it the guy who is supposed to ask the girl up to see his etchings?"

Dorie was nonplussed. "I didn't mean, I wasn't..."

"I'm just teasing. I'll show you some stuff sometime. But right now, let's figure out about this pizza. Had enough?" Chad looked at the remains on the table.

"I'm full. But I can take it home unless you want it. Dad and I always fight over who cooks, so this way I can get cooking credit for warming up pizza."

He grinned at her and then gestured to the server for a box. "Glad to help you out. Cooking isn't your thing, huh?"

"Correct. Dad reminds me that I'm terrible wife material, but I tell him he's a sexist old man and that men can cook as well as women. We both like to eat but neither of us likes to cook."

"I like to cook," he admitted. "I hope that doesn't make me good wife material in your father's eyes."

Dorie felt her grin widen. "He's really not sexist like that. I just like to give him a hard time. Have you met him?"

"No, I don't think so."

"Let's go then. Come on over to the house and you can meet James. You already met the brindle. But you haven't met the big dogs yet."

"The big dogs. Right."

Chapter 7

Despite Chad's interest, within two days the unclear story of shots fired in Bakersville was over. The news moved on to the next thing. He was nagged by a sense that there was more to the story, though. He searched the archives for old stories on dog fighting and organized crime. He wondered whether he really cared about the topic, or if his interest lay more in the energetic young woman he'd seen most recently over pizza. It really didn't matter though, because Dorie was clear that they were only going to be friends, and not close ones. He might as well focus on the dog stuff, since the woman stuff wasn't getting anywhere.

Most days he got nowhere on the dog stuff, too. Dorie told him Animal Control had located three of the four dogs that had taken off through the woods in Bakersville. There was no news on the humans. The brindle was still at Dorie's house and her future was undetermined, since nobody seemed to know who owned her. Besides that, questions remained about her background and whether she'd be a safe pet. Dogs needed certain types of socialization, Chad learned, to be good around other dogs, people, and especially children. Animals retrieved during the commission of a crime could be apprehended from their owners, he'd learned, but it wasn't clear yet that the Bakersville site had been a crime scene, or at least nobody was charged for anything. Yet. And the owners of those dogs? Still unknown.

Dogs. I might need a dog; Dorie could be right. It's lonely here. Arriving home in the dark, he turned on a single lamp, warmed up his dinner from the refrigerator, and sat with his laptop. *This is not how I expected my life to be.* For a moment, he imagined Dave's house: young children sitting at the table, a pretty spouse smiling at Dave, everyone happy and glad to be together. Chad's apartment felt cold.

He picked up his phone. Dorie's face flashed on his screen. He'd have to remember to take her off his home screen before she realized he was looking at her every day. How long until his next trip to Stella Mare?

How's your girl you rescued from Bakersville? He attached a picture of the brindle he'd taken at Dorie's house before their pizza date. Dinner, not date. The text message sat there on his phone. *Should I? How many times a day can I text her before she gets annoyed with me? Oh, whatever.* He clicked send, then put his phone facedown and turned back to his laptop.

Eating his warmed-up dinner, he opened the file where he was keeping information about animal safety and dog fighting. An idea poked at him, from the back of his brain, and he wanted to give it some space to expand. What if...

His phone pinged at his side. Dorie? He flipped it over. Nope, Nan.

Dear Chad,

He snickered a little. Nan still treated texts like they were formal letters.

I need a little help from you. My doctor says I need to have a procedure. It is no big deal, nothing to worry about, but I need someone to take care of Frou-Frou. Can you come down for a few days? You could even see that nice Dorie. Love, your Nan.

A procedure, huh? She was always trying to keep him from worrying about her or about anything. He called her.

"Hi," he said when she picked up.

"Oh, Chad. I didn't want to bother you with a call," Nan explained, "so I just sent that message."

"What kind of procedure, Nan?" *I'm not letting her get away with being vague this time.*

"Just something the doctor thinks I need. Nothing to concern yourself with."

"I am concerned. You're not in charge of how I feel. When is this un-concerning procedure taking place?" He felt his eyebrows raise.

"Oh, yes. When. I don't know yet, but I wanted to be sure you can take Frou-Frou. He's a good boy, you know, but he needs someone who understands him."

Chad laughed. "Nan, you know perfectly well that Frou and I are never going to be friends. But I'll take care of the little snot for your sake. I might even be nice to him."

"Oh, Chad, I know you'll be nice to him. They're supposed to give me the details on Monday. I'll send you the date then, okay? Is it really okay with your boss?"

"Sure. I'll make it okay." He hoped he sounded more confident than he felt. He was already getting some heat for being away last weekend, even though it had been approved. "The Maritime News Network puts family first, according to our HR manual."

Nan laughed. "Well, here's a chance for them to prove it. I'll call you Monday. You go get some sleep now, okay?"

Chad could hear Frou-Frou barking. "What's up with the dog? Intruders?"

"No, I think he just misses you."

"Hardly likely. You make sure your doors are locked, okay?"

"Chad. This is Stella Mare. I don't know if this back door lock even works. Besides, nobody's going to come in here without my say-so."

“Right. When I come, I'm getting that lock fixed. I'll talk to you soon and, even though it pains me to say it, tell Frou-Frou good night from me.”

Nan would be smiling at that. That was enough, to keep her smiling. “You're a good boy, Chad. Even if you forget that Stella Mare isn't the big city like you're used to. Good night.”

Chapter 8

Chad had developed a morning habit of picking up a coffee and sitting in the parking lot at the coffee shop scrolling social media. *I have to see what's going on*, he told himself, but also noted his tendency to hit both the BARC site and Dorie's personal page before anything else. *I'm just staying up to date.* A week after his visit to Stella Mare, the BARC site was hopping.

Dorie had posted some grim pictures. Chad wondered where they had come from and why Dorie was suddenly talking about something she'd been told to hush up. It had been clear she suspected dog fighting in Bakersville though there was no proof.

"There are people in our communities who are profiting from the suffering of animals. Who is setting up dog fights? Who is betting on those dogs? This is a blood sport that was outlawed long ago but has shown up right here. Do you know anyone who is participating in dog fighting? Name them here, and let's stamp them out of our community. Our companion animals deserve better than this. Help BARC help dogs by donating below."

Wow. What had happened to staying out of this? I was sure she couldn't stay quiet about that. To the point of getting herself in trouble. He shook his head. *Oh, Dorie. This is going to blow up.*

He was wrong though. Looking at the comments, he could see that it had already blown up:

"It's them Macintoshes. They never were no good."

"Mafia! The mafia from Montreal. Nobody from here would be doing that."

"Watch out who you accuse, BARC. You might be BARCing up the wrong tree." Chad snickered at that one. But the next one gave him pause.

"Hey, DORIS. You better watch your back. We know where you live." As Chad looked, his screen refreshed, taking him back to his home screen. He scrolled, frantically, looking for Dorie's post, but it was gone. The post disappeared in front of his eyes. He felt like Dorie herself had just flickered out, like she'd never even been in his life.

Is she okay? He was shocked at the fear that washed through him. *Hey, get over yourself. Of course she's okay. It's just social media.* He took a steadying breath. *There are some dangerous people out there.*

He scrolled to her personal page, almost to reassure himself that she really was okay. He couldn't help but smile at her picture, with that giant black dog's chin propped on her shoulder. Custard? Mallow? He didn't know, but it didn't matter. She loved those darn dogs. Perhaps he could like them too.

Here was something new, posted by Vergie, a woman he didn't know, but then, he didn't know that many people in Dorie's life.

"You guys looked like you were having fun. Here's to Thursday happy hour!" The picture was Dorie, indisputably Dorie, (*my Dorie*), dancing close to some guy. Extremely close. Forehead to forehead. Some guy with long dark hair, straight as an arrow, had his arms wrapped around Dorie (*my Dorie*), his hands on her backside sliding into her back pockets. And their faces so close together... Chad felt a wave of rage. How dare this guy put his hands on her like that? He looked again. She looked... she looked like she liked it! What the hell!

Chad felt suddenly sick to his stomach. Party girl, she had told him. Well, it seemed like she was still a party girl. He had been wrong about her. He thought she was focused on making a safe world for dogs, but there she was with some guy at a St. Stephen club. *Last night. While I was alone here in Saint Jacques, thinking about her.*

Ugh. What a pathetic mess I've turned out to be. Just put the phone down, man. Hating himself, he kept on scrolling.

What else was on this page? Another post from this friend, Vergie. Dorie stood with a bunch of women, their arms around each other posing for the camera. Group selfie, Dorie in the middle with one arm around a friend and her other hand holding a cocktail glass. "The best girls' night ever" was the caption.

Chad was reeling. First there were people threatening the woman he, well, the woman he was interested in, and then she's out being a party girl and he thought she wasn't really that, and who was that guy! That tall, skinny, long-haired confident dancing sort of guy with his hands all over her? Furious, worried about her and afraid he'd never see her again, Chad felt just a little bit sick. *Now I have to go to work. Well, this has already been a crappy morning.* He put the truck in gear and drove off too fast.

Dorie woke up with a headache and a sense of impending doom. James banged pots in the kitchen below. *Uh-oh*. What time was it? Picking up her phone, she peered at the time. Oh, no. Almost nine a.m. Late for work. Dad hated it when she slept late on a weekday. She hated it, for that matter. She squinted at the phone and saw a pile of notifications.

"Ugh..." She tossed it on the bed and threw herself back onto the pillows. Ouch, that was hard on her head. What had they been doing last night, anyway? She could barely remember getting home, but she did recall Vergie picking her up along with a couple of other girls and heading to St. Stephen where there was at least one bar that had live music on Thursday night. *I just wish I had thought a little more before I started doing shots with that guy*.

Guy...that was his name, wasn't it? He was pretty cute, with all that long hair, but still. He was no Chad, Dorie thought briefly. Weird how much she thought about Chad. He'd probably have been super uncomfortable in that bar last night. *Well, at least I had fun. I think I had fun. It was a lousy day yesterday, so going out seemed like a good idea. But was it worth this? I feel awful, and honestly, I hope I didn't make a huge fool of myself. I used to like being the party girl. Now I wonder if that was how I coped with awkwardness.*

She stopped for aspirin in the bathroom before braving her father in the kitchen.

James looked at her over his shoulder, eyebrow lifted. "Well, there you are."

"Yeah. Coffee ready?" She sat heavily at the table. The brindle came to rest at Dorie's feet. "Hi, girl. Sorry I didn't get up to walk you." Dorie scratched behind her ears and the dog gave a little moan. *At least she's not mad at me.*

"You need a glass of water first," James said with a critical glance. He put a big tumbler in front of her. "Coffee's coming." He sat at the table across from her.

She drank the water thirstily. Yes, he was right. Water was what she needed. How did he know?

"Dorie, it's Friday morning, you know that, right?" James looked serious.

She nodded. "Ooh, that hurt." Hand on forehead, she looked up and said, "Yes, I know."

"Don't you have to work today? You're getting a little old for these kinds of shenanigans."

"Dad. Please. You don't have to lecture me." *In fact, I was just thinking that myself.*

"I'm not trying to be nasty, daughter. But I don't know how to get through to you. Raising you was my job. Growing up is yours." James put a mug of steaming coffee in front of her, slopping a bit on the table.

"Thanks, Dad. It's not really my fault that Vergie decided we had to go into town for drinks, or that the bank won't give me a loan, or that the miserable miser who owns my building decided to evict me. Or the woman I work with runs hot and cold. You know, it really isn't my fault that all these things happen to me. I don't know how everyone else seems to have their lives together, but stuff just happens to me. I try and try, but nothing ever goes right." She dropped her face into her palms, sniffling. In a minute, she felt James's big hand awkwardly patting her on the back.

"Now, Dore, I know things haven't been easy for you with Mum gone," her father said gently. "It's not fair that you had to come back home after school to help me, either, and I do appreciate that you did that. But I worry about when you're going to make a real life for yourself."

She peered up at him through her fingers. "A real life? What do you mean by that?"

Her father turned toward the stove where a frying pan sizzled. "Oh, you know, purpose. A family. Meaning. Happiness."

"I don't need a man to have a life, Dad."

"It's a good thing, too, since you don't seem to have one," he said, sounding irritable now. "What happened with that nice young man you brought over last week? Where'd he go?"

"Chad? Back to Saint Jacques, to his exciting life there. He has no interest in me or Stella Mare."

"He seemed pretty interested. I'd say it's you that has no interest in him, or our town. You're the one who can't seem to settle into where you are, doing what you are doing. Always on the lookout for something more fun."

Dorie was stung. "Dad. I just went out for one night. For the first time in months. I thought you had my back."

"I do, baby girl. I really do. But having your back isn't the same as propping you up. Besides, I'd like to see you settle down, right here in Stella Mare. What about that nice boy from Saint Jacques. Isn't he Alice's grandson?"

"Dad...my head hurts too much for this conversation. Can we just leave it for now?"

A plate of toast landed in front of her. The pink jam made her stomach turn. "You should know that your sisters are coming this weekend."

"All of them?"

"Well, no, just Rett and Evie."

"That's enough. Dad, what have I done to deserve this?" He just raised that eyebrow. "What, were you tattling on me to the big mean sisters?"

"I didn't have to, Dorie. Have you seen Facebook this morning?" He waved his phone at her. "You should pick your friends better."

"What? You go on Facebook in the morning now?" She grabbed at his phone, which immediately went blank. "Can you show me?"

He pocketed his phone. "Eat your breakfast. Whatever is on there will be there when you've woken all the way up." He refilled his coffee cup and left the room.

Dorie's sigh was gusty. It wasn't enough that she had to live her miserable life, but everyone else had to have an opinion about it. Scraping the jam off her toast, she took a meditative bite, looking at the back of her phone as it rested on the table.

As long as I don't look, I don't have to think too much about it, right?

It was a good idea, but it didn't work. She couldn't remember much about last night. *It's been a long time since I drank that much. I wonder if Chad saw whatever it is. And oh, Rett and Evie! Perhaps I can go out of town. Forever.*

Custard meandered over to her and leaned his big head on her knee. She bent down to his doggy skull and rested her cheek. So silky and soft. She scratched behind a big ear. "Hey, buddy. Why does stuff always happen to me? What's wrong with me that my life is so, ugh, messed up?" He groaned with pleasure and leaned into her hand. *Why can't my life be as simple as a dog's life?*

Okay, no point in further delaying the bad news. She flipped her phone over and kept one hand free to keep on scratching Custard.

She'd been right, there were a lot of notifications.

Really a lot.

Like a scary amount. She clicked through to her page.

No. No, no. A video, of her doing shots and...what kind of dancing was that? No, no, no. She could see comments from Evie. Not encouraging comments.

And what was this? Who was this guy with the hair? Oh, Guy, right. That guy. *Oh, my head is really hurting now.*

Did I really do all that stuff? Well, there's Vergie too, and Cait. At least it wasn't just me. Who has seen this stuff?

Dad, obviously, even though probably Evie sent it to him. Evie. *Turncoat,* Dorie thought savagely. *You probably sent it off to all the sisters.*

Wait. Who else could be seeing this? Privacy was set to...p ublic. Oh, no. Chad. Dorie deleted the posts immediately and changed her privacy settings.

She really liked Chad. In fact, they'd been texting daily for the last couple of weeks. He was the first person she thought of when she heard something interesting ("Oh, what would Chad say about that?") even though they weren't in a "relationship." She liked him, plain and simple. *But he's in Saint Jacques, a big city with stylish women, working in journalism, a profession where elegant people are side by side all day long, and here am I, mucking about with dogs, wearing clean jeans on my best days, and not able to compete in any kind of way. But oh, I hope he didn't see these pictures.*

She clicked on his page and found herself looking at the bare minimum. He's blocked me, she thought, incredulous. *What did I ever do to him? Oh, for crying out loud. This is one miserable day.* Her phone rang. Andrea. That was odd.

"Hey, Andrea."

"Dorie, we have a problem."

"Okay. Yeah, umm..." What am I supposed to say to that, Dorie thought irritably. *Is this my problem?*

"I told you to let it go, Dorie. Why aren't you following directions?"

"What? What are you talking about?"

"I took your post down. You were told explicitly to stay quiet, and you posted on social media. This is a problem."

"My post? You took down my post?" All Dorie could think about were the posts from the club last night. What had she posted and what the heck was Andrea doing in her personal accounts?

"Dorie, are you listening? You don't sound like you're hearing me."

She shook her head, hard, and barely managed to avoid a groan. Custard lumbered away to check his bowl. *You big lunk, where are you going when I need you? Even my dog has given up on me.*

"I'm here, Andrea. What's the problem?" Dorie tried to make her words crisp and clear.

"I want you here in this office immediately. Mr. Barrett alerted me this morning to what you've done. The board is very concerned."

Dorie's head was spinning from more than her hangover. *This is about work, not about my personal life. What is she worried about?* "Do you mean the post about animal cruelty? That's what BARC is fighting, right?"

Andrea's voice got louder. "Dorie, come in. Right now. Mr. Barrett will see you at ten sharp."

"Right, right," Dorie agreed. "Ten sharp."

She clicked off and slumped back on the old wooden chair. The fall sunlight slanted through the dusty windows, making patterns of light and shadow on the oak table, her mother's old lace runner, and the trailing ivy sprig rooting in a jar of water. *How have I messed things up so much? It's a good thing Mum isn't here to see what a mash I've made of my life.* Wiping her eyes with her fingers, she headed upstairs to get dressed for work.

Dorie was barely on time for the ten a.m. command performance at BARC headquarters. That was partly due to the small crowd of men assembled on the sidewalk and up the old granite steps of the building. When Dorie started up the steps, the biggest one leaned in front of her.

"Going somewhere? Going to your cushy little office?"

"Excuse me," Dorie said politely, not making eye contact.

"No excuses, little girlie. Who you calling a criminal? You need to watch yourself."

Another man chimed in. "Yeah, we know you. Know your father, too. Be careful what you say and where you say it."

In the middle of an upwelling of noise now, Dorie's aching head could make little sense of it. It was perfectly clear, though, these men meant some level of harm and she needed to get out of there quickly. Somehow she had to get through them because her boss and her boss's boss were waiting for her inside. "Excuse me, please," she said, breathlessly. "Let me through."

One of the men growled. "Why should we? You stab us in the back, and you expect us to just take it? Keep out of what don't concern you, Doris, and it will be okay. None of your business."

"I'm not stabbing anybody." She looked at the speaker and made her voice strong. "Don't engage in animal cruelty and I won't point a finger at you."

During another upwelling of sound, Dorie pushed through the small crowd to the door. Andrea pushed the heavy door open from the inside and said, "You all, go on now. Get out of here. You're harassing my employee."

"Harassing! We'll do more than that. You BARC better get out of town. Nobody messes with our business, lady."

"I'm very sorry," Andrea said, not sounding sorry at all. "You need to go now."

"You're gonna be hearing from my lawyer," one of the men tossed back as he was heading down the stairs.

Dorie slid inside the door and leaned against the wall, breathing heavily. What was going on? Andrea closed the door and locked it from the inside, then turned to look at Dorie. "See what I mean about a problem?" Her face was set in grim lines as she led the way down the dark hallway to the glass door labelled BARC.

"Should we call the police? They were a little scary."

"Absolutely not. We need to get this quieted down, not ramped up." Andrea marched ahead.

"But...he was nasty. Mean."

"We're going to take care of all that right now." Andrea opened the door to her office.

Young Mr. Barrett sat in the chair in front of Andrea's desk. He stood as they entered, but pointedly did not shake Dorie's hand.

"I didn't expect to see you under these circumstances," he said, unsmiling. "Please sit down."

Dorie looked around for a chair while Andrea went behind the desk. She pulled a folding chair away from the wall and opened it up to perch on the edge.

She figured this wasn't the time to say anything, so she sat and looked first at Mr. Barrett and then at Andrea. Both faces were stern. Angry.

Looking at Mr. Barrett, Andrea said, "Those people out front were harassing Dorie. There were threats."

He shrugged. "You poke the bear, he gets mad. Dorie, we need to talk about your work here at BARC. There were people who took issue with your post yesterday about dog fighting."

"It was just the truth. I didn't say anything that wasn't true."

Mr. Barrett sighed. "You stated as fact some things that are suppositions."

"No, no, I didn't. I was very careful about that." Dorie turned to Andrea. "Right, Andrea? I only said that there may be a dog-fighting ring that's having events around here, and that dog fighting is both illegal and cruel to animals. And that BARC is opposed to all forms of animal cruelty. What's wrong with that?"

"There's no proof of dog fighting," Mr. Barrett said heavily. "No convictions."

Andrea's grim look persisted. "What you said was inflammatory, Dorie. You got over a thousand comments on that post before I pulled it this morning."

"You pulled it? That's engagement! A thousand comments! That's huge. We could only hope for that."

Mr. Barrett grimaced. "A post that threatens people's livelihood. Raises suspicion of citizens. Engagement that connects BARC to threats of violence. Did you see those comments, Dorie? Andrea took screen shots before she deleted. It was ugly."

"Dog fighting is ugly. Animal cruelty is awful. People whose livelihood depends on animal cruelty should be shut down. Isn't that the point?"

"Dorie, you were skating the edge of libel, and who knows the kind of people who might be involved in that stuff," Andrea explained. "BARC, we, can't be associated with that kind of nastiness. This organization gets by on grants and donations. Nobody's going to donate to a cause that foments violence."

Oh, yeah? With effort, Dorie kept the words in her head, but her face must have spoken because Mr. Barrett picked up the theme. "Andrea's right. We count on law-abiding, caring people to fund us. They don't want to have anything to do with these threatening kinds of things."

"So we just don't cover anything that's controversial?" Dorie argued. "Just nice pictures of puppies and not really show people what happens when animals are abused like this?"

"Dorie, please," Andrea said. "You're not being attacked here. But BARC is. And we have to make sure that doesn't persist."

Mr. Barrett pushed his glasses up his nose and looked at the tablet in his hands. "You said that there are links to organized crime, Dorie, and there is no evidence of this."

Not yet. "I'm surprised you don't want me to dig into this further, actually. What if we uncovered a whole ring? What if BARC could actually end a cruel practice locally, instead of just lobbying about regulations?"

Mr. Barrett sat even straighter in his chair. "Apparently you don't see our work as valuable as direct intervention. You might want to rethink that if you plan to continue to work for BARC. We are not about getting people all riled up and angry. We are about keeping connection to our lawmakers, so they remember to protect animals in legislation."

If I plan to continue to work for BARC? Why, were they thinking of firing me over some people's comments on my post? This makes absolutely no sense whatsoever.

Dorie sat back in her chair. *I need this blessed job, or I would just walk out the door right now. He's talking to me like I'm a kid who's been bad or something.*

"Perhaps I need to refresh myself on what we're trying to accomplish with social media." She aimed for a conciliatory tone.

"Yes, let's look again at the goals we set for you," Andrea chimed in. "I think we need a process, too. Apparently, you weren't monitoring that post, or you would have seen what happened when people started calling out names and libelling groups."

Dorie shook her head. "No, I wasn't. I finished working, the post was scheduled to launch, and I figured it would get the usual kind of response and that would be that. I had no idea that this one post would cause such a fuss."

"It's not just the loudmouths who commented. There are other people who got upset, and that's the problem." Mr. Barrett sounded firm.

Other people? What other people? Was he protecting someone? With effort, Dorie tuned in to listen further.

"You need to issue an apology. I've got the board attorney, Naomi Snow, working on language for that. I want to make sure we forestall any libel suits, or even angry donors."

"Me? I need to apologize?"

"We need to be clear that you acted on your own, that BARC does not condone this sort of thing."

Dorie was still confused but trying to hide it. *I cannot go home and tell Dad I lost this job. I'll do whatever it takes.* Lost for words, she stared at Mr. Barrett.

"This is a very serious matter," Andrea reminded her. "I'd hate to let you go, because I still think you can be an asset to us. You know a lot more about social media management than I do, and I am willing to give you another chance, if Mr. Barrett and the board agree. But you're going to have to do things the way we tell you to." Andrea looked at Mr. Barrett, who took a long moment to gaze back at Dorie.

Despite her confusion, Dorie willed her face to be clear and open. "Well, I will do whatever is necessary to restore the confidence of our donors and the board." *Oh, wow, listen to me. Don't I sound grown-up? Not even hungover anymore. What a faker.*

Mr. Barrett looked mildly relieved. Andrea actually smiled and said, "Well, Dorie, that's more like it. It sounds like we can all agree on how your work should continue with BARC."

Dorie allowed her chest to relax a tiny bit. *Hopefully I haven't lost this job, too. At least not yet.*

Andrea added, "We'll have to work on that retraction or apology or whatever it is that Naomi Snow is working on. That must go out ASAP, not only for BARC, but for your protection. There were some threats."

Dorie frowned. "Not like real threats, right? Just like social media trolls?"

Mr. Barrett shook his head. "I don't know anything about trolls. The comments on your post were made locally. Some included threats to your home, your father, and your dogs. I think getting this apology out soon is in your best interest."

"My home and my dogs? I do need to call the police. I don't want anybody bothering my father," Dorie said with vigor. "I didn't think there would be real threats. Those morons out front were a little intimidating, though."

"There are blowhards everywhere, of course," Mr. Barrett said. He sounded more relaxed now. "No police. We are not calling the police. BARC can never be associated with threats or threatening behaviour. Even when we protest, we don't cross that line. We lobby the legislature, or rally to support animals, but we don't hold with that rough stuff."

Dorie's marketing brain was working. "We could use the threats. Show people that threatening is the opposite of how BARC works. Call out the people who made threats."

Before she finished her sentence, Andrea was already shaking her head. "No, no, no. No more calling out, Dorie. That's what caused our problem."

"This could be a golden opportunity. Any publicity is good publicity, right?" She pondered aloud, "What if we got some coverage of what happened and why it isn't our way?"

"No." Andrea and Mr. Barrett spoke as one.

Andrea added, "Stick with puppy pictures for a while, please. Nothing inflammatory."

Mr. Barrett looked grim once more. "Naomi will get in touch later this morning, Andrea, and then, Dorie, you will get the apology underway." He rose to leave. "I want this managed quickly, and never want a problem like this again." He looked hard at her.

What is he, my high school principal? Makes me feel about fourteen and in trouble.

Andrea walked him out to the hall, giving Dorie a moment to check her phone. Did she delete everything she could from last night? What was left on the BARC page? Hmm. Not a lot. Her personal page had a lot of notifications, too, but Andrea returned before she could look.

Coming through the door, Andrea said, "The threats were nasty, Dorie. I don't even really want to show you the screenshots."

"Why are people so freaked out about what I said? Dog fighting is a bad thing. It's been illegal in Canada forever, so why is it a big deal?"

"Think about it, Dorie. People were naming other people in the comments. People were calling each other criminals. Threats are, well, threatening."

"You think there really is a dog-fighting ring that people are profiting from? I was just guessing."

Andrea raised her eyebrows but said nothing.

"You do! You think those threats are the evidence that it's organized crime. Wow!"

"Hardly evidence."

Dorie was excited. "This is huge, Andrea! It's a real thing! Do you have those screenshots? We can figure out who the big culprits are."

Andrea held up her hand. "Stop right there. This is not our business. I made a mistake even going out to Bakersville last month. We barged in and it wasn't okay. I got in some trouble for it, too, which you don't need to know about," she added, looking away.

Dorie bit back her questions. "Oh, okay, okay. Not our business. But will the police do a good job with this? Can they make 'organized crime'"—she used air quotes—"stop dog fighting in New Brunswick?"

Andrea shrugged. "They'll do whatever they do. In the meantime, we need to separate BARC from all this nastiness. We're not vigilantes for canine justice, Dorie, no matter how romantic that might sound. Now I've got to get some work done. I imagine you do, too."

"Oh, yeah, sure. Let me know what the lawyer says I have to do." Dorie walked purposefully into the boardroom with her laptop. What a day, and it wasn't even noon yet. What else would happen?

By eleven thirty, a document arrived from the lawyer, with directions that should absolve Dorie and, by extension, BARC, of any sins in the arena of public opinion. She sat with Andrea to critique her planned social media posts. It was not the thing she wanted to do, but she needed to do it to keep her job.

"Andrea, how are we going to stop this bad stuff, if we don't call it like we see it?"

Andrea gazed at her. "We've discussed this to death, Dorie. BARC does not call out individuals. BARC uses legislative action to put these people out of business."

"But the legislation is already there. Dog fighting is illegal. Has been forever, but that doesn't seem to stop it. Why can't we mobilize social media to put pressure on? That's what happens everywhere else."

"Individuals put pressure on that way, Dorie. Not BARC. We depend on government and other organizations for funding. We can't behave like cowboys, yelling about whatever bothers us, and still keep a reputation for being a worthy and safe organization, a place that everyday animal lovers feel good about donating to."

Dorie was pretty sure she was giving Andrea "attitude," that thing that irritated her father and sisters. With an effort, she pulled back. "Okay. I'm the new person here, and you've been with this group for a long time. And I don't know what I don't know. But I think pretending we don't see the animal cruelty in our community makes it feel safe for those people to continue doing what they do."

Andrea glared at her. "You've made your point. Now I'm making mine. Mr. Barrett and Naomi told you what you need to say to represent BARC. I have told you what you cannot say. You already violated that directive once. Do you want to stay in this job? If so, you'll have to keep your personal opinions separate. Can you do that?"

Dorie pondered for a moment then she exhaled. "Yes. Of course I can do that. But Andrea, do you understand what I mean?"

She looked annoyed. "It does not matter one bit if I understand you. It doesn't matter if I agree with you. I want to be perfectly clear. No more of this, Dorie. If you're working here, you support BARC. You don't undermine it."

Dorie felt contrite. No, she didn't want to be undermining BARC. "Yes, I get it. I'm sorry, Andrea. I'll keep those opinions to myself."

Andrea seemed to soften then. "I know you care about the dogs. I do too. The way I show it is through keeping BARC running."

"Right. Got it."

"I know this just sits wrong with you, Dorie. How about a change of scene? We had some dog food donations this week. Do you know anyone who could use them? You can deliver. Off the clock, of course."

"Oh, yes, thanks, Andrea. Good idea." Dorie thought about Sarah and the incredibly loud barking from the main house. "Remember Sarah and those little dogs? I wonder what her son does with those big dogs?"

"Dorie," Andrea said, a warning in her voice.

Dorie went on. "I bet he's got fighting dogs out there. Her son, you know, remember what she said?"

"Dorie Madison. Stop it right there."

She grinned. "Just pulling your leg. I said I'd stop and I'm done. Promise."

Andrea sighed. "Sometimes you're just like a kid. Anyway, I'm sure Sarah can use the small-dog kibble from the donation that arrived on Wednesday. Mike's going to take the rest to the rescue. It's in the back hallway of the building. Let me know if you need any help."

"Nope, I'm good. I can get it. Thanks."

Andrea left and Dorie finished her workday in better spirits. Even if she couldn't say what she wanted to say on BARC's pages, she could still do the thing that she liked to do: help people do a better job taking care of their dogs. She finished her work then piled bags of kibble into her car. Going to Sarah's might be, well, entertaining. At the least it would lighten up her day.

Chad got almost nothing done at work that Friday. He kept scrolling on his phone to Dorie's page, though by nine thirty there was nothing left to see. The online news wasn't local, but he did call a friend in Fredericton who promised to let him know about any breaking stories about dog fighting or animal cruelty or anything in the southeastern part of New Brunswick. In between, he tried to call Alice, but she didn't answer, and he didn't even try to leave a message.

Between worries about his grandmother and the overwhelming wash of feelings about Dorie, he felt exhausted but restless. Extreme effort to focus got him through the essential tasks of the day, but by then he'd had more than enough.

He stuck his head into his boss's cube. "I'm cutting out for today," he told Rob.

"Feeling okay, Chad?" Rob asked kindly. "You never take time off."

"Yeah, I'm okay. I have some things to sort out. I need some time."

Rob shrugged. "Sure. You know how we operate here. I'll call you if something happens, but really, it's been a pretty slow day."

"Yeah. Thanks."

Leaving the studio, he walked toward the harbour. It was cold and clear. That would help his head get clear too. His mind was full of Dorie, her laugh, her smile, her love for those dogs. But those images were overlaid by others, the ones from the pictures from the club. Was this the same girl? He couldn't shake the picture of that guy with his hands in her back pockets, wrapped around her curves. *Arrgh! Why does this bug me so much?*

He walked fast, hands in pockets until they warmed up, and his breath came faster. *I need a run. That's the thing. Get me over this fixation once and for all.* This girl clearly wasn't who he thought she was, and so he needed to turn his attention elsewhere, like back to fitness. The last time he'd taken on running in a big way was after his father died. Chad remembered pounding down the road, kilometre after kilometre, leaving grief, anger, and loneliness in his wake, and feeling the good tired of physical exertion, washed clean of painful emotions. All that was left was his strength and his fatigue. Yes, running could help. Right in this moment though, he was wearing work clothes and a heavy jacket. He'd have to change.

His phone pinged with a text from his friend in Fredericton. Hmm, a note to watch the news at six on the competing network. *Okay, I can do that. But right now I'm going running.* He headed back to his truck.

"Dad! Hey, Dad!" Dorie called as she entered the house, dim in the late afternoon light. "Oh, sorry, Dad." James sat up, rubbing his eyes. "Hey, have the dogs been out?" Apparently he had been napping on the living room couch.

"What time is it? I must have fallen asleep."

"You think?" she teased fondly. "I've got a dog food run to do for BARC and I thought I'd take the beasts if they need an outing."

Custard raised his head thoughtfully. Mallow continued to snore on his huge bed in the sun porch.

"I'm sure they'd be happy to go. You probably need my van though, if you're taking a pile of dogs. Keys are on the hook. How you feeling, anyway?"

Dorie grabbed leashes and keys. "I'm good, Dad. Water, coffee, and getting over myself at work. I still have a job, in case you were wondering."

"You left in a rush this morning, late and all. I didn't know that your job was in question. Do you want company on your dog food run?"

"No, not really. Unless you suddenly feel a need to volunteer." She peered curiously at her father. He stretched and stood up.

"Nah. But I get what you're doing. You're making yourself busy, so I have to think about dinner."

She laughed at that. "Wasn't my plan, Dad, but now that you mention it, I seem very nefarious."

"Well, I think Evie said something about coming and bringing a casserole, so try not to be too late, okay?"

"She's getting an early start on the sister weekend, huh? Is she going to lecture me?" Dorie asked. "Because I don't need her casserole that bad."

James laughed at her. "Get going so you can get back. I have no idea what your sister is going to do. Never have had. Go on with you."

"Okay then. Should be home by six," she tossed over her shoulder. "Come on, mighty dogs. Let's go for a ride." The big hulks laboriously rose, but the brindle was already wired for action. She bounced as Dorie slid on her leash. Treats in pocket, Dorie shepherded her pack to the car.

Chad kept picking up his phone, even though he had blocked every possible way he could look for Dorie or she could look for him. *What is wrong with me?*

Running hadn't been enough to work out this restless feeling. After his sprint around the harbour, he headed back to the newsroom to catch the competitor's six p.m. broadcast. His own network broadcast a national feed at six, so there was no activity in the studio.

He wandered into the uncharacteristically quiet space. His Fredericton connection had said to watch the six p.m. news, but with no more information than that, he had to catch the entire broadcast. Chad settled in to watch.

It wasn't a big story, apparently, because it was the last little bit before the end of the show, more like a joke than news. "Tempest in a teapot," the anchor said, who went on to note that there had been a kerfuffle on social media about a dog-fighting ring. Dorie's boss, Andrea, was interviewed.

"BARC is always on the side of the underdog," she said with a big smile, "and as you know, we work hard to make sure that dogs' lives are cruelty-free. At the same time, we know the hardworking people of New Brunswick cherish their dogs, and we would never want to suggest otherwise. BARC apologizes for implying otherwise." She smiled widely at the camera. *Oh, she is good. But what do you really think?* He was skeptical of her skillful image management. *She's hiding something.*

The film quickly switched to somebody's cell phone video, taken outside the BARC office. Oh, look, there was Dorie, trying to get inside, and those goons were yelling at her. Chad jumped to his feet, temperature rising. *Those guys!* She needed some protection from these jerks. He saw her look behind her as Andrea opened the door for her to slip in. Her eyes were dark and haunted.

Poor thing. Then he remembered the other pictures he'd seen that morning. *Right. Maybe those dark eyes aren't haunted, but hungover. I don't need to worry about her. Or feel sorry for her.*

He tried to feel annoyed at her for partying, but mostly he felt bad for her. And for himself. *I really like her, I guess. Even with the silly partying. I thought she had outgrown that stuff.* The image of her dancing with that guy reappeared in his mind. *I'm just not her type, I guess. Just gotta let go of that idea.*

Despite his efforts, though, Dorie was what he thought of when he closed his eyes. Now he had this video, where she looked like she needed help, to stick in his mind. *Now I'll be worried about her*, he thought with irritation. *This will not do.*

Friday night's casserole dinner was a hit. Evie was a good cook. Dorie had to give her that. Corinne showed up, too, which made quite a crowd around the big table. Dorie had hoped everyone would bring their dogs. The pups usually enjoyed the family gatherings more than the people did. *At least more than I do when they're all gunning for me*.

The casserole was a seafood lasagne. Dorie warmed up garlic bread and tossed Evie's salad before sitting down to eat. A bottle of crisp white wine went around the table, too, and the big dogs snoring in the sun porch provided a counterpoint to the conversation.

Evie pushed her plate away. "Oh, that was good, if I do say so myself." Dorie squinted. It was coming.

"How'd your day go, Dorie?" Corinne asked. "It looked pretty rough on the news."

"What? I was on the news?" Dorie was genuinely surprised.

Corinne nodded. "Didn't Andrea let you know? Somebody made a video of those guys harassing you on the way to work this morning."

"Really? Why wasn't that on social media? That would have made it a little easier to deal with the president of the board."

"What? You had to meet with the board?" James sounded scandalized.

"Come on, Dad, you knew that. They were annoyed with my coverage of dog fighting. That's why I had to race downtown this morning. To get chewed out by everyone. And issue a big apology written for me by BARC's lawyer. It could have been worse, I guess. I didn't get yelled at by the whole board, just the president, that Young Mr. Barrett."

"Oh, Young Mr. Barrett," James said thoughtfully. "That's another one who doesn't miss any opportunity." He returned to his plate.

Dorie straightened her shoulders. "You guys, go ahead. Do your worst. I've been yelled at by citizens, chewed out by my boss and her boss, had the lawyer lecture at work. What else can you do to me?"

Corinne patted Dorie's shoulder. "Sounds like a rough day," she said sympathetically.

Evie snorted. "Would have been rough anyway as hungover as you probably were, right, Dore?"

Dorie glared at her. "Must you?"

Evie went on. "Yeah, Corinne, you must not have checked your phone. Thursday's party night apparently. Not just for college kids, but for those who still think they're college kids."

"Nasty, Evie. What good does this do you? I thought you were going to try to be a better sister." Dorie's tone was bitter. "I'm surprised the rest of the pack hasn't come to chew me out."

"Oh, no worries about that," Evie said blithely. "Rett's coming for dessert."

Corinne brightened. "Rett? Is she bringing the kids?"

"I doubt it. She wants to give me a piece of her mind. You know, this day was hard enough," Dorie said flatly. "I am determined, though, to see the brighter side. I still have a job, even though I got yelled at. This afternoon I got to help an old lady get food for her dogs. So do your worst, family. You can't beat me down."

James leaned back in his chair. "You girls are always fighting about something. Dorie's got a point, Evie. She kept her job. She took what was coming and didn't quit."

Wow, was Dad defending her? "Thanks, Dad."

"Now I don't hold with drinking on a Thursday night though." James shook his head. "Going to work hungover isn't how we raised you girls to behave. Your mother, well..." He choked a bit.

Great. Now I get to feel guilty because of my poor dead mother. Nope, Dad is not defending me. He's just got his own axe to grind.

"Yeah, I get it, Dad. I just got a little carried away. Vergie said let's go to town and so we really went to town. It was a mistake."

Following a noise at the back door, Dorie's sister Rett came in, cake box in hand. "Hi, everyone!" she called in her musical voice. "Did you save me any?" A small boy and a medium-size yellow Labrador retriever followed her.

Evie inspected the lasagne pan. "Yes, I guess so. How many kids with you?"

Rett came to the table to look. "I only brought Mason with me tonight. He wanted to commune with Mallow. But of course Charlie came, too."

"Oh, yes, Mason and Mallow. Soul mates," commented Corinne. "Boys need dogs, but those two are a special pair."

Dorie smiled at Mason, a miniature version of his dad Harry, as he slipped in behind his mother. "Hey, Mason," she said. "Let's go see the dogs. We got a new one. She's in her crate. Make sure Charlie is nice to her, okay?"

Mason nodded to Dorie. "Hi, Dorie. Yes, he'll be nice. Hi, Grandpa," Mason murmured as he gave James a quick hug, then started to leave the room, Charlie the Lab and Dorie trailing him. The brindle was crated, but Dorie was curious about how she'd react to another dog.

James called after him. "Seafood lasagne, Mase? Will you have some?"

Turning in the doorway, Mason shook his head. "No, thank you." He walked out to the sun porch. Dorie followed him and Charlie.

Mason walked carefully around the brindle's crate, leaning down to say, "Hi, new dog." The brindle rested her chin on paws, nose pointed toward the dining room. Charlie wandered in long enough to sniff at the two big dogs, then he backed out of the room and headed toward the people.

"Hi, Mallow," Mason said quietly. The big lug looked up and groaned a welcome, and the child sat down next to him and wrapped his arms around the shaggy neck. Head pillowed on the big dog, Mason gave Dorie a blissful smile. "Mallow's my best friend," her nephew said.

Custard stretched out on her side, and the brindle sighed and closed her eyes. The dusky sun porch was a peaceful, pleasant place. *Wish I could curl up here, too*. "You guys have fun," she said to Mason and headed back to the table.

She arrived at her seat to see Evie hand Rett a plate of seafood lasagne.

"Just what I needed," Rett enthused as she tucked in.

"Are you working too hard, Rett? Forgetting to eat?" James asked.

"Me? Nah. Today was just a busy day. But this hits the spot just right."

"How are things at the Sunrise Home?" James wanted to know.

"Oh, you know, busy. Understaffed. Trying to keep people active and engaged." Rett worked in a long-term care home in Saint Jacques. "I'm happy that it's Friday, I can tell you that."

"Is Mason going to eat?" Evie held a plate over the lasagne pan.

"Probably not. Harry fed him and the girls before I got home from work. He'll have cake later, I'm sure."

Dorie looked around the table at her family. Corinne and Rett were chatting about their work, Evie was trying to give James a second helping, and the gentle sounds of snoring dog came from the sun porch. *If only it would stay this peaceful. No attention on me.*

Swiping her plate clean with garlic bread, Rett sat back in her chair with a sigh. Charlie, lying on the floor behind her chair, rolled onto his side and uttered a matching sigh.

"Good food, Evie."

"Thank you. That cake looks great, too. Chocolate with peanut butter frosting?"

"My signature." Rett grinned. Then, sobering, she leaned across the table. "So, Dorie."

Here it comes.

"No. Just no, Rett," Dorie said. "I've heard it all. I don't want any more advice. Instead, you could let me tell you about my day."

Rett sat back. "Okay. Go ahead."

"I got up with a massive headache because I was stupid drunk last night. Emphasis on stupid. I got called on the carpet for misrepresenting BARC and nearly lost my job. People screamed threats at me actually. To cap it off, I had to agree to use a lawyer's carefully crafted statement to keep people from being offended by the truth and purge the social media sites I've spent the last weeks building. But I didn't lose my job. Just my self-respect. Good enough for you, Rett?"

Her sister was silent.

"Well?" Dorie looked around the table, slightly belligerent.

Rett was a tough case. "So did you learn anything?"

"Geez, Rett! Why is it always me that's done wrong? I've learned that it's harder to get sympathy from your family than from strangers on the internet."

"Wait. Did you say threats? Who threatened you?" Evie looked worried.

"That was what was on the news. Dorie being harassed downtown," Corinne added.

Dorie continued. "I don't even know who they were. A bunch of rough-looking guys waiting downtown at the office, said they knew where I lived, and Dad and the dogs, too. Andrea said there were online threats, too, but I didn't see them."

James raised his eyebrows. "Are you sure you heard that right? What were they all haired up about?"

Dorie shrugged. "I don't know for sure, but if you mention dog fighting around here, people suddenly get very sensitive. It's like I suggested shutting down the fish plant or something. Like everyone's livelihood was involved."

"Probably not everyone, but some people who don't mind using threats," James noted.

Silence fell around the table. Then Corinne said, "Well, there is good news. Dorie still has her job. Even though she did have to eat a pile of crow."

"Eat crow? That's a funny expression, but yes, I guess I did. I had to remove posts about local animal cruelty, even dog fighting, plus issue an apology. I feel like I caved, but yes, I still have employment. The day wasn't a total loss. I did get to help an old lady feed her dogs. At least I'm not a total waste of space."

James shook his head. "Dorie, Dorie. Always the drama. You're not a waste of space and nobody ever said that. You just do some unexpected things for someone who's a full-on grown-up."

"Yes, going out last night was pretty adolescent. I don't think I'll make that mistake again. So can we please talk about something else?" she begged. "I've done everything everyone has asked. I still have a job. I'm doing what I'm told to do. What else do you want?"

Rett looked thoughtfully at Dorie. "You do know that we love you, right, Dore? That you're our baby sister and we really want good things for you?"

Dorie felt doubtful. "Funny ways to show it."

Undeterred, her sister went on. "I remember when you came home from the hospital, you know. You were so little, and I was so excited to have a baby, a real baby sister. Not like Evie, there."

"Thanks a lot, Rett. What was wrong with me?" Evie objected.

"Oh, you know. I was practically a baby when you were born. But when Dorie came along, well, I was already almost twelve and a baby was about the most wonderful thing Mum could ever have done for us. For me anyway."

Corinne made a little sound of assent. "Yes, I remember too. I was so much younger than your mother, Dorie, and when she had you, I was only about the age you are now. It was magical to have another baby around. I was living here with your parents then, which you probably don't remember."

"But I remember," Evie said. "I remember being so mad at you, Corinne, because you tried to help Mum out with us girls and I didn't want you, I wanted my Mum. Only she had this new baby." Evie gave Dorie an evil grin.

"Oh, you guys. I was just the baby. I didn't have anything to do with all those dynamics."

James was lost in a reverie. "It was wild around here for a while. Your mother was so happy when she found out we were going to have you, Dorie. We already had three little girls, but one more seemed like the icing on the cake."

"And I've been disappointing you ever since," she said quietly. "I know Mum hoped I'd have a career and a family like Helen and Rett. Or do something artistic, like Evie does. It just didn't work out for me the way she hoped."

Evie sighed loudly. "Listen, Dore, can you just take a minute to listen to yourself? You're the one who says you're a disappointment. Maybe we don't think drinking on a weeknight is smart, and you ended up in financial trouble with your business because you don't take anybody's advice, but that's just you. You don't have to assume that we're all disappointed all the time."

Her father leaned back in his chair. "I remember being so happy that we were having another little girl. Everyone in the world seemed to think I should be disappointed, no son, but I knew girls. I already had three. I knew about daughters. Another one was a pretty nice thing. Your mother was thrilled, and I was too."

Dorie's throat grew thick, and her eyes prickled. "Oh, Dad," she choked out. "I thought this evening was about giving me grief, but everybody's been really nice. I don't understand. Do you all know something I don't? Do I have a terminal illness or something?"

"Who does?" They all looked up at Mason standing in the doorway to the living room.

"Nobody, buddy. Come on over here," James indicated his lap.

Mason walked over and leaned against his grandfather. "I'm not a baby, Grandpa," he said.

"I know," James said "No babies here tonight. You left those little sisters at home, too, didn't you? Want to help me take the dogs out?"

Mason nodded, and James pushed himself to his feet. Grabbing a handful of leashes, he called to the dogs, and a veritable flood of canine enthusiasm poured into the kitchen.

"Watch out for Charlie," Rett called out, "he'll take off on you."

Evie got up. "I'll come too, you guys. That's a lot of dogs."

Mason protested. "No, me and Grandpa can do this. We got it."

Corinne rose. "I'll go. You don't mind your old aunt, do you, Mason?" The boy shook his head and Evie sat back down with a laugh.

"Okay, okay," she said. "We'll let the older and younger generations do the work. We'll just sit here and, well, drink wine."

With a mad scramble of jackets and leashes, dogs and people headed out. The brisk evening air blew in, causing Dorie to shiver. When the door banged shut, the three sisters sat in silence for a moment.

"Dorie, how is Dad really?" Rett asked seriously.

"What do you mean? He's himself. He's fine, just like always."

Evie shook her head. "I don't think so, Dore. Like I told you, he's secretive about his health. He had me take him to that appointment, but he wouldn't tell me a thing about it."

"But he's fine. He's got normal energy, and I think he gets out everyday, and he's connected. I don't know what could be wrong."

Dorie felt herself shrink a little under the gaze of her two sisters. "Really, you guys, I think he's fine."

Rett shook her head. "He's not likely to tell you anything that worries him, Dore. Evie either. I think he still sees you two as his girls, young, and in need of him to take care of you."

Evie straightened her back. "No way, Rett. Dorie, but not me. He doesn't take care of me. I take care of myself."

Rett nodded. "Yeah, I know that, but what I mean is he won't ask you to take care of him. Like even now, Dorie lives here but he's right in there, doing the dog things. I bet he cooks half the time, too, right?" She looked at Dorie.

"Listen, Rett, neither of us claims being a good cook. We just muddle through and appreciate when Evie brings us dinner. Or Corinne."

"Okay, that's not a great measure. But he told Evie not to tell anyone about his appointment, and he won't talk about it to any of us."

Dorie snorted. "Like we wouldn't talk about it among ourselves."

"He could be talking to Helen, for all we know. Are any of you in touch with her?" Evie looked around the table. Both sisters shook their heads. "Yeah, me neither. But we should be. She hasn't been home since forever."

Rett raised her eyebrows. "That's true. Since the summer after Mum died. Ottawa's not that far away."

Dorie felt moved to defend her oldest sister. "Yes, but she's got the Jake and the law practice, and you know they're all involved in Jake's hockey."

"Well, whatever. But we need to keep in touch about Dad. I'm worried about him," Rett declared.

Evie shrugged. "Sure. I get over here once a week or so. How often do you come to Stella Mare, Rett? It's not like you're here all the time. When you say you're worried, I think you mean Dorie and I are supposed to be worrying."

"Pfft! No need to be nasty, Evie. I'm just thinking that Dad isn't getting any younger, Dorie isn't really helping all that much, and we need to pay attention."

Dorie was incensed. "What do you mean, not helping all that much? I'm here every single day."

Rett scoffed. "You live here and work a part-time job. You can't even make dinner for Dad most nights. You let him support you and you're barely able to help him?"

"I knew this night was too good to be true. For Pete's sake, Rett, what do you want from me? I've had a terrible day, and now you want to tell me I'm useless to Dad. Well, thanks a lot, dear sister. You should try living here for a while. I noticed you didn't stay in Stella Mare."

She gathered her dishes and stomped to the sink. Turning the taps on full so the splashing water drowned out her sister's words and her own angry thoughts, she looked over her shoulder. Evie was reaching toward Rett's shoulder. Dorie snapped off the faucet in time to hear Evie say, "Leave her alone, Rett. She's okay. It's best that she's here."

"What? Now you're talking about me in the third person? I'm right here." Dorie was incensed.

Evie looked at her imploringly. "Dore, I was saying that it's best for you to be right here with Dad. You can be the eyes and ears of all the sisters. You can be the one to let us know if he stays okay, or if there is something else going on."

Dorie, mollified, returned to the table.

"I haven't seen anything," she pointed out. Rett didn't meet her eyes.

"See?" Rett asked pointedly of Evie. "She wouldn't notice."

"It's possible there's nothing to notice, Rett," Evie said, relatively gently. "We all could be oversensitive after losing Mum the way we did."

Rett's face softened. "That's true. I am worried about losing Dad, but not because I know anything. Mostly because I don't know anything. How can a sixty-nine-year-old man be in good enough shape that he's not dying? When his wife died so young?"

"Fifty-eight wasn't all that young, Rett."

"The older I get, the younger it sounds," Rett said. "I work with ladies in their seventies and eighties doing all sorts of things, and I wish that could have been Mum's life."

The three sisters were quiet for a moment. "Rett, I promise I'll try to take care of Dad, not just live in the house," Dorie said. "I can't bear to think about anything happening to him. It's just not possible."

Evie patted her hand. "I'll help, Dore. I can try to come in more often. We should connect with Helen, too. Just see how things are with her. We only have each other."

Rett smiled. "We only have each other, but we do have each other." She turned to face Dorie. "I really am sorry for taking a bite out of you. You're not the annoying little sister and sometimes I forget that."

Dorie laughed. "Oh, but I am the annoying little sister. I'm just a lot of other things too."

Evie stood. "Let's get this cleaned up before the dog crew gets back. I heard Rett brought dessert."

"I'm happy to clean up if I get to eat Rett's chocolate cake," Dorie said with a grin. "Hey, you guys. You annoy the pants off me and I love you both."

"Yep. Me, too," said Rett.

Evie put an arm around each of them. "Having sisters is a blessing and a curse, and you can never tell which it is going to be. I love you guys too. Now let's get busy!"

When James, Corinne, Mason, and the multitude of dogs returned, the kitchen was immaculate, and the sisters were in the living room with music blaring and wine flowing.

"Looks like a nice evening," James said approvingly.

Dorie looked around. Yes, a nice evening. Except for the not-so-nice parts. Getting up, she planted a kiss on her father's cheek, prompting a flush and surprised exclamation.

"You're a good dad," she said. "Want a glass of wine?"

"Nah, I better not," James demurred. Evie threw Dorie an arch look.

"Since when, Dad?" Rett demanded.

"What is this, the third degree? I just don't want any more wine, thank you. Keeps me awake."

Corinne held up a glass. "If anybody's pouring, I'll have some."

"Sure, Auntie Corinne," Rett said, brandishing the bottle. "Does it sound normal to you, Dad saying no to a glass of wine?"

Corinne scoffed. "Cut the guy a break, girls. He just knows when to say no."

"Oh, ho!" Evie shouted. "Look who's talking!" There was a burst of laughter and conversation, while Mason settled onto the couch beside James, who tucked the boy under his arm matter-of-factly. Dorie smiled gently at the pair. *I wonder if I'll ever have a boy like Mason? I hope it happens before something happens to Dad.*

"Who's up for cards? Do I ever have a game for you," James invited.

There was general noise and shuffling of chairs and searching for the cards, complaints about cheating ("Cheaters! I raised a household of cheaters. Mason, that's your mother right there, cheating at cards. You better tell your father..." "Oh, Dad, you're the worst. Watch him, Mason, look at how he distracts us and then flips the cards around. Don't learn from Grandpa...") until the cake was gone, the wine had been supplanted by water, and Mason was asleep on the sofa.

"Who's sleeping where?" Dorie asked.

"Rett and Mason are coming to my place, since Jase is away for the weekend." Evie said. "I assume you're going home, right, Corinne? You're welcome to sleep on my pullout couch if you'd rather."

"Or here," Dorie added. "On the couch."

Corinne snickered. "I think I can make the three kilometres to my house, girls. Thanks for the invitation. It's been fun. Hey, James, come out for coffee with me next week, okay? I'll give you a call."

"Sure, Corinne. Always."

"We're going pumpkin-picking tomorrow and hit some farmer's markets," Rett said. "Evie says she knows some good ones. Anybody else want to come along? Mason and I'll be heading home early afternoon."

Corinne shook her head but had an idea. "I don't need any pumpkins, Rett, but let's meet for lunch before you leave. That work okay for you, Evie?"

"Sure. Just don't ask me to cook."

"Hey, am I invited? I also don't like to cook," Dorie added.

"Of course. Everyone's invited," Corinne assured. "Noon tomorrow at the Chowder House?"

"Great. That sounds perfect." Dorie felt warm and contented. "Too bad Helen lives so far away. It would have been fun to have everyone here."

James sighed heavily. Nobody else said anything. After a moment, Corinne got her coat, Rett gathered up her son and her things, and Evie collected pots, pans, and dogs. The house was very quiet once everyone was gone.

James sat quietly on the sofa. Dorie turned off lights in the kitchen and, returning to the living room, she sat in a pool of light from a table lamp.

"Everything okay, Dad?" She tried to keep a light tone.

James gave a slow smile. "Yes, fine. It is just so nice to have you girls here and getting along."

"Mostly getting along. Rett let me have it while you were out, but we worked things out." A moment passed. "You know, Dad, they're worried about you."

Silence.

"Dad?"

"No reason to worry about me, Dorie. I'm going to be around here for a long, long time. I promised your mother I'd help you get grown up, and I'm not going anywhere until that job is done." He smiled at her in the dim light.

"I'm trying hard, Dad."

"I know you are. You're making progress too. I saw you getting along with those sisters of yours, and a couple of years ago the fighting would have been off the charts. So yes, I can see things are changing for the good."

"Yeah. Thank you." Dorie stood up. "This has been a really long day. I'm going to bed. Good night, Dad."

"Good night, Dorie."

Chapter 9

Chad had hurriedly packed a weekend's worth of clothes into a duffel, then he grabbed a bigger bag and piled in more jeans and shirts. *Who knows how long I'll be gone?* Gathering his computer, cameras, and lights, he piled everything in the truck. *What else?* His chest tightened as he looked around his small apartment. *How long will I be gone?* He opened the refrigerator then closed it again. *No time to clear that out. Just time to get going.*

"Yes, an extended leave of absence." He spoke toward his phone hooked into the dash's audio. "I'm heading out of town now." He turned onto the bridge out of Saint Jacques. "I'll let you know as soon as I can."

"Okay, Chad. There's a form to fill out, but I'll have Human Resources email it to you. You'll have to let us know how long you'll be out, but there's no rush to get that done. You just take care of things where you are. And, Chad," his boss added, "take care of yourself, too."

"Yes, thanks. Thank you. I appreciate that." He clicked off and let out his breath. Okay, work was settled. The apartment, well, it was what it was. He had no idea how long he'd be away. *Oh, Nan, be okay, please be okay.*

Frou. What about Frou-Frou? Dorie? He pushed the image of her at the club out of his mind. He needed her help. *Can't hurt to ask.*

He sent her a voice text. "Hey, it's Chad. My grandmother is sick. Can you take care of Frou today? Her key is under the mat at the back door. I'll call you later."

He had no idea whether Dorie would or could take care of Frou-Frou, but he had to do something about the dog. Nan had been taken away by ambulance and the dog was probably upset. Nan would want him to handle it.

The early morning phone call rang in his head. *"Mr. Simmons? This is the Regional Hospital in St. Stephen. You're listed as emergency contact for Alice Simmons. She arrived this morning by ambulance."*

"Can I talk to her?"

"No, Mrs. Simmons is unresponsive. I am notifying you as her emergency contact."

"I'm coming. I'm coming from Saint Jacques, but I'll be there as soon as I can."

He stepped on the accelerator. This was going to be the longest trip he'd ever made even if it took the shortest amount of time. *Oh, Nan. Please be okay.*

After half an hour on the road, he started to think maybe he was being rash. Couldn't he have gotten in touch with any of Nan's friends in Stella Mare? Drat it! He should have done a better job of keeping track of her life. She had friends all over town, but did he know any of them? Of course not. All involved in his own life, far away, and boring as it was. *Self-involved millennial, isn't that what they say? Be okay, Nan. I really need you to be okay.*

Full of good feelings from her family weekend, Dorie planned a new start at work, so, on Monday, she went in before the sun was up. BARC's social media accounts had a clean slate; pretty puppy pictures prevailed. Per the lawyer, she had apologized for allowing unfettered commenting on her post. Naomi's skill at writing impressed her. No one was accused, but it still allowed for the fact that awful things were happening to dogs. She filed that away. A good skill to have, perhaps.

She tackled the dusty file cabinets with her new-found energy for her job. *Why not? I'll get something done that I won't have to undo.* She was still crushed about losing all the social media capital with the bad post.

In the archive closet, she clicked on the light. The oldest cabinet was labeled 1986 – 1992. She sneezed when she dislodged the dust. It looked like nobody had been in here since then. The dusty file drawer sparked her imagination. What did ancient files look like? Would the paper even be intact? How long did it take for stuff to decompose in a filing cabinet? Hmm, perhaps there would be a body in here, or some mysterious treasure. She was just starting to get herself interested when her phone pinged with a text.

Seven a.m.? Who was texting at seven a.m.? *Who is even awake at this hour?*

Chad. *Hmm. I guess he unblocked me.*

Scanning the text, her heart clenched. *Oh, Chad. Poor Alice. Oh, no. Poor little Frou-Frou.* Quickly, she sent back a single word.

Okay.

Grabbing her coat, she rushed out of the office. Should she get her car? Yes, Chad's grandmother was out in the country a little way and there was frost on the ground. She tugged her gloves on while trotting up the sidewalk. Turning left, she passed the Sunshine, promising herself to come back later for coffee.

Alice's house looked still in the predawn light, surrounded by skeletal trees silhouetted against the brightening sky. Dorie heard barking as she approached the house. Focused on finding the dog, she barely noted the old red barn, tidy porch, and carefully raked lawn.

When she called out to Frou and stepped up onto the back porch, the barking intensified. She found the key under the mat just as Chad had said. What had happened to Alice? She unlocked the kitchen door and Frou-Frou charged at her, leaping up to lick her face.

"Scary stuff, hey, buddy?" She scratched behind both his ears as he sat in front of her. "Here, let's go out and then we'll find your food. You can come with me today." The house was cold and quiet, except for the dog's nails on the floor. After doing a turn around the backyard, Dorie returned to the kitchen to locate his bowl and kibble. Deciding he needed to be fed, Dorie filled his bowl, but he just sat beside the full bowl and stared at her.

"No good, huh? Guess you miss your family. Well, you come on. We're going for a ride in the car. I know there's dog biscuits in the car." Frou willingly followed on the leash, leaving his bowl of food untouched. She gathered his bowl and the bag of dog food.

She took a picture of Frou-Frou climbing into the backseat of her car and sent it to Chad. *There. At least he won't have to worry about the dog.* For a moment she wondered why she cared, but then she thought about the long days when her mother had been hospitalized. Other people, like Alice, had been so helpful then. This way Dorie could repay that kindness. *Oh, Alice, please be okay. Frou-Frou needs you. And probably Chad does too, but I don't know about any of that. I am glad I can help out with the dog.*

Back at Dorie's office it was still early. Frou-Frou settled under the boardroom table and Dorie returned to the archive closet.

Now how were these files organized? Oh, yes, a drawer per year, and within the year? *Oh, what a mess*. Income, expenses, minutes of board meetings (looks like a board of two people). Wait. What's this? A file of handwritten notes and cards?

Ugh. She pulled out a thick file and took it into the boardroom. *I can sit and read*. Frou-Frou settled against her ankles. She became absorbed immediately, trying to piece together the story of how BARC came to be, making notes for future posts.

The office door opening roused her. Andrea stuck her head in the boardroom door. “Dorie? You're in early today.”

“Yes. I wanted to get started on this project.” She indicated the paper files in front of her. “By the way, we have a guest.”

Frou-Frou had wandered over to sniff and investigate Andrea. She leaned over to pet his head. “Who is this? I thought you had big dogs?”

“He’s not mine. This is Frou-Frou. His mum had to go to the hospital this morning and her grandson, a friend of mine, asked me to watch him. Is it okay for him to be here?”

“Of course. He seems well behaved. And a poodle, too, so no dog hair.” Andrea looked down again. “Welcome, Frou-Frou.” She frowned. “Is that actually his name?”

“Yeah, I know. It's bad. Apparently, my friend told his grandmother the dog was too ‘froufy’ when he was a pup, and that's what his grandmother made of it. Maybe he has another name, but I haven't heard it.”

Andrea grimaced. “Takes all kinds. I'm looking forward to my coffee.”

“Yes, I'll go. These files are a lot more interesting than I expected. I'm just going to leave this here, okay?”

“No, you better lock it back up. I don't expect anyone in here, but the board has always been very particular about those files. It's BARC's only history.”

“Okay, then, I'll have your coffee in a bit.”

"Dorie, thanks for taking our recommendations seriously. I'm glad you're going to be able to stay on. We were close to disaster last week."

She nodded tightly, still unsure it had been the right thing to do. It felt bad when she thought about it too much. But it did keep her job, which kept her family placated.

Chapter 10

Near three p.m. Chad called Dorie. By that time, she and Frou-Frou were out walking in the woods, and she'd brought Mallow and Custard along. The brindle was bristling in her crate in the back of James's van.

"Hey, Chad," Dorie said cheerily.

"Hey." His voice was flat and low, tired. "You got Frou?"

"Yep," Dorie agreed. "I've got your boy Frou and a bunch more. How's it going?"

"Can you keep him a while longer? A few days? I'm probably going to be tied up."

She sat on a stump watching the dogs mill around. "Sure, Chad, whatever you need. How is Alice?"

Chad sighed and her heart squeezed in sympathy. "She's not so good. She's still unconscious. They think she had a stroke or something."

"Oh, no. That sounds terrible."

"Yeah. Nobody knows how bad, not yet. I just can't believe it."

She groaned. "I'm so sorry, Chad."

"I don't feel like I can leave the hospital, not really. I'm her only family." His voice cracked.

"Well, don't you worry about the dog. Frou is fine with me and the gang. He can have a sleepover. Or three."

"Thanks, Dorie. I really appreciate it. Nan will too, if—no, when she wakes up and I tell her." His voice cracked again. *Is he crying?*

"I'll take good care of Alice's dog, Chad."

"Thanks." After a pause, he said, "I have to go now."

"Okay. Chad, take care, okay? Good-bye."

Dorie clicked off. Still thoughtful, she got up to walk with her horde. Poor Alice. And poor Chad. His only family member in hospital unconscious. For a moment she remembered what that had been like: cafeteria coffee, sandwiches from a vending machine, smell of antiseptic everything. *Ugh. But Chad's alone. At least when Mum was sick there were lots of us. Nobody was alone.*

Calling to the dogs, she guided them all deeper into the woods. Mallow and Custard seemed willing to walk farther than usual with Frou on hand. *No wonder Alice loves Frou-Frou. He's a good influence. Canine charisma.*

Frou looked at her. "What?" Dorie demanded. "Can you read minds, too?" Frou-Frou stepped firmly to the rear, clearly pulling Dorie backward. "For Pete's sake, dog. Do you want to go home?" He whined a little, the first time Dorie had heard him make such a sound. "Okay, you got it. Come on, Mallow, Custard. The lord and master says we're going back. Let's go!"

She headed back to the parking lot. Before they arrived, she could hear the brindle complaining at top volume from the back of James's van. "Coming, we're coming," Dorie muttered. "Impatient, that one."

But no. The brindle's agitation was about the men leaning on the van. One had a crowbar and was prying at the tailgate.

"Hey! Hey you! Get away from there!"

Frou and the galoots barked, and Dorie dropped her leashes. The dogs ran for the van. Before Dorie could even get a good look, the men leaped onto big motorcycles and roared out of the lot.

Running toward the van, Dorie saw words finger-swiped into the dust. One of the words was a nasty expletive. The others said, "Watch yourself, dog lady."

"Oh, for Pete's sake! Not very original. Pea-brained vandals. What next?" She squinted. "What? Dog lady? I suppose that's me. Or Andrea? But this is my dad's van. Who would know?"

The brindle barked helpfully in her crate. "Oh, you. You might be the giveaway. Hmm..."

Still thoughtful, she bundled the dogs into the van. She poked around for a rag and wiped the nasty message off the paint. She saw no damage on the tailgate either. *I guess I was just lucky to get back when we did.* For a moment she remembered Frou-Frou pulling her back toward the parking lot. *No. Just a coincidence.*

The brindle stopped barking and whined a little in her crate. No one had come forward to claim the brindle yet and she couldn't help feel more attached. *You're a pretty good watchdog.*

"Yes, your turn is coming," Dorie told her. She settled the massive pooches onto their seats, called Frou and clipped a leash on the brindle before letting her out of the crate. The muscular terrier was more than eager to get going.

Yeah, you're valuable to somebody. But why don't they say so? Refreshing the supply of dog treats in her pocket, Dorie and Frou took the brindle for her walk.

"Well, Frou, I'm happy you're well trained," she commented to the poodle. "This lady here doesn't know too much about walking with people, but at least she's willing to go along where you go." The three paced around the field next to the parking lot, Frou watching Dorie carefully and the brindle bounding along, keeping Dorie's arms—both hands on the leash—at full length.

She tried to use treats to hold the brindle's attention and keep her at heel, but the dog was too wired to notice.

"Those guys got you upset, didn't they?" She stopped and Frou-Frou stopped obediently beside her. The brindle continued to pull on the leash, but when she looked back to see Frou and Dorie, she also sat. "Good girl."

Dorie scratched the soft ears. She slipped Frou a treat and offered one to the brindle. "Okay, if you're sitting and calm, you can take it. That's good to know. I guess some scary stuff has happened to you." The three of them started again to promenade around the field.

"Whew, this is a workout." Dorie panted. "Nobody could pay me enough for this. It's a good thing I volunteer." After their second tour, she steered her charge back toward the van and coaxed the brindle back into her crate by tossing treats inside and the dog followed. Once done, Dorie perched in the back of the van next to her crate.

"Whose pup are you?" she asked, once again admiring the blocky head and yellow eyes. "You're a pretty girl and strong. Somebody is probably missing you, if only because you're valuable." The brindle lay in her crate, head on paws, gazing at Dorie. Frou was on the ground, looking up. Dorie absently patted her knee, and the poodle leaped into the van and curled around in Dorie's lap. Leaning forward, Frou poked his nose into the crate, and the brindle lifted her head to touch noses with him.

"Friends. I guess we can all be friends, of a sort. And Brin, you're with us as long as we get to have you." She poked another treat through the crate grating and slid Frou off her lap. Time to get going.

Once in the front seat, Dorie looked over her shoulder at the snoring dogs and then wrestled with Frou's dog seat belt. "Well, Frou, you think you're in charge and the galoots don't seem to mind," she said. "Even the brindle is willing to let you be the leader, and she's a dominant dog. I think we make a deal. You lead them, and I lead you. We have an understanding, right?"

Frou had curled on the seat but opened one eye. Dorie gave his head a rubdown before she started the van, oddly comforted and feeling protected by her canine crew. She pushed out of mind those motorcycle guys and their crowbar and headed home.

Chapter 11

On Wednesday afternoon, Chad paced the lobby of the hospital. *I don't know how much longer I can stay awake, but I don't want her to wake up alone.* He thought he should call someone Nan would know, but he didn't know anyone. Except Dorie. Even though his vision was foggy, he conjured up Dorie's warm smile and green eyes. He called her despite a tremble in his fingers. *I can check up on the dog.*

"Hi, Chad. I am so glad to hear from you."

Ahh. Chad felt himself take a breath. That felt better. "Hey, Dorie. I just wanted..." Chad stumbled. "Is Frou behaving himself?"

"He's the best, Chad. He's smarter than those two lunks of mine put together. He's well trained, I swear he understands English, and he even makes it possible to walk the brindle on a leash. He's Super Dog."

Chad laughed shortly. "Sounds like he's got you convinced. You sound like my Nan about him." His eyes smarted as he spoke.

"How is she?" Dorie asked, suddenly sounding serious. "Dad was asking, too."

"Not too good," he said sombrely. "She still hasn't regained consciousness."

"Oh, no." Dorie sounded sympathetic. "Have you been there all this time?"

"Yeah. I just can't, I can't let her wake up alone, you know?" He cleared his thick throat.

"You must be wiped out. Can I come stay for a bit? You could go home, get a nap or something."

Chad felt his heart squeeze. "That's really nice, but you don't even know her."

Dorie let out little giggle. "Yes, but she was pushing you in my direction a little while ago."

That made him smile a little. "That's the truth. But instead, could you help me sleuth out her friends? I feel kind of foolish that I don't even know who she hangs around with, but I just don't."

"Of course. I'm happy to help. Dad will be too."

"I remember a couple of ladies she plays cards with, but I don't know anybody's last name or anything. Can you go back to the house and get her address book? She keeps it in a kitchen drawer. The one nearest the wall phone." Chad shifted uncomfortably. "I really feel stupid that I don't even know who her friends are."

Dorie giggled again. "Of course she has an address book. My father does too. But, listen, I think we can do this an easier way. I bet she goes to church."

"Of course! That's brilliant. Yes, she goes to St. James, or at least she did when I was a kid."

"So okay, I'll do this. I'll stop by with Frou and talk to the secretary or the minister or whomever. Information travels fast in Stella Mare, but it does have to get started."

"Thank you. I know she'll want her friends to know, or at least I think she will." Chad suddenly second-guessed his idea.

"Well, whether she wants them to know or not, you can't be the only one looking out for her. I'll pass the word and get the information train going. Is there anything I can bring you or do for you?"

His exhausted brain constructed an image of sinking into Dorie's arms. Quickly he reeled in his thoughts. "Uh, no, I guess not." *I sure could use a shower and a nap, and decent food.* "I don't want to leave her. What if she wakes up all alone?"

Silence. *Oh, geez, what kind of a wuss does she think I am now?*

Finally, she said gently, "I get that, Chad. It wasn't all that long ago I was there with my mum. Only there were a bunch of us to keep watch. I'm going to get you some help. Alice has a lot of friends here in Stella Mare. Don't worry. We'll get some reinforcements."

He felt better immediately. Alice did have friends, and if she got mad at him for sharing her personal business, that would be okay. "Thanks a lot. I appreciate it. I know you're busy."

"Not that busy," she said with a laugh. "No death threats so far this week. I'll let you know what happens, okay?"

"Okay. Thanks."

He clicked off and his shoulders slumped. Dorie was a good friend, even if things had started out kind of rough. His traitor mind kept imagining the softness of her face, the curve of her waist under his hand. *Stop it!* With a huge effort, he turned his focus back to friendship. Friends. A friend who liked that annoying fluffy dog. Nan would certainly approve.

Dorie could have phoned the church, but she figured having Frou-Frou in hand would give her credibility. First, though, she checked in with James, finding him in the living room reading.

"Hey, Dad, Chad says Alice still isn't so good, and he hasn't slept since Sunday."

"Oh, I'm sorry to hear that." James shifted. "So that's why Frou is still here."

"Yeah, but Chad needs someone to spell him at the hospital, and besides, Alice has friends, maybe from church. Chad said she goes to St. James, so I thought I'd let them know."

James snorted. "Now that's a smart idea. Once Ida Mae Maybee gets hold of that information, everyone in town will know."

"That's what I was thinking. Okay, Frou and I are heading downtown to church. Watch out, Ida Mae."

"Bring home some dinner, will you?"

Dorie scoffed. "Leftovers getting tiresome, Dad? I'll see what I can do."

James was right. Ida Mae was horrified to hear that Alice was in hospital and was prepared to act immediately to get Chad some help. She took Chad's number and had the phone in her hand before Dorie and Frou were out the door.

"Mission accomplished." Dorie headed back out to the street with Frou. She wondered if Chad would come to see her when he got back to Stella Mare. For a moment, she was lost imagining him walking up to her, reaching for her... Frou made a little noise beside her, and she started. "Right, then. Okay, Frou, the cavalry has been called in. The ladies of Stella Mare have things under control. I bet they'll even be feeding Chad before long. In the meantime, though, I have to feed Dad and myself."

Frou waited outside the store while Dorie wandered the aisles looking for inspiration. A jar of pesto and a bag of premixed salad went in her basket. *It's not gourmet but it will do. Dad will think he's in heaven to have something other than sandwiches.*

Staring blankly at the pasta selections, she heard voices from the next aisle. "...those busybody do-gooders need to keep their noses to home," a rough male voice said. *Uh-oh.*

"Shh. No need to get unpleasant, Joe. I talked to Andrea. She knows what side her bread is buttered on. She and Charles will keep things under control. They shut the young one down."

Dorie's ears hurt with the effort to listen harder. Really? Were they really talking about BARC? Charles Barrett? And the young one? Was that her?

She slid the tortellini into her basket then casually walked to the end of the aisle. Looking up the next one, she saw only a denim-clad back with a ball cap on the head. She didn't recognize the person, and she was more relieved than not to find the men had disappeared. Still, those words stuck with her. "*They shut the young one down.*"

Is that what happened? Had she been shut down by Andrea and Young Mr. Barrett? What were they hiding? Who were they trying to protect?

Lost in thought, she paid for her food, collected Frou, and walked toward home. On the way, she called Chad. Maybe he'd like dinner, too.

"Hey, the ladies of St. James are on the case," she reported when his tired voice answered. "I think you'll be seeing some of them soon."

"Yes, thanks, Dorie," Chad said. "Ida Mae called me and gave me the rundown. I think she was really looking for news about Nan, but there isn't much."

"Are you coming home tonight?" Dorie asked.

"Home? You mean to Nan's house?"

Dorie felt a little uncomfortable. Of course Alice's home wasn't Chad's home. "Uh, yeah, I guess so. I was going to say you can come over to our house if you like. I'm actually going to make food."

She could hear Chad's smile. "I cannot even tell you how good that sounds. But I can't. She's still asleep or whatever, and I just don't feel right leaving her. But thank you."

"Hmm. Okay. You're always welcome at my house. Dad would be happy to see you again, and of course Frou is here, too." *And so am I, even though I don't want to tell you how much I'd like to be with you.*

"Right. Thank you for all you're doing, Dorie. I really appreciate it." The fatigue in his voice cut her right to the heart.

"Yeah. Well, good night."

Dorie had trouble that evening. She managed to cook dinner just fine, but when she sat down to eat, she couldn't stop thinking about Chad at the hospital. She knew that place well and didn't think it had improved since her mother's illness.

"You could just go keep that boy company, Dore. "

Dorie looked up, startled from her thoughts, and squirmed. "Yeah, but we're not, like..."

"You don't have to be anything," James pointed out. "You know what it's like to be waiting there, not sure what's going to happen. He's all alone."

She frowned at him. "You can come too, you know. If you're so sure he needs company."

"Well, I dunno about that. I think he'd rather see you. I'll hang out here with his dog."

"Alice's dog," Dorie corrected automatically. Perhaps Dad was right. She could just be a friend. "Okay, Dad. You're right. Is there any of Rett's cake left? I could take him some of that."

"Not likely. That was last week. Go through a drive-through or something in St. Stephen. You can take my van if you like. And a few dogs?"

"No dogs, Dad. Dogs are with you. I'll call you if I'm going to be late."

St. Stephen was about thirty minutes from Stella Mare, the winding road rising from the bay. Dorie was used to the drive, but it still didn't do to be too casual at night: large wildlife sometimes meandered across the road after dark. It was late when she got to the hospital and she had no idea where to go. She sent Chad a text.

Hi. I came to see you but where are you? I'm downstairs in the main lobby.

A few minutes later Chad arrived, warm with surprise but he looked almost flattened by fatigue. He had that hospital pallor family members tend to acquire when supporting someone who is ill. He approached her with a tired smile and reached toward her. She reached back with one arm, but then they both pulled away at the same moment and laughed.

"Awkward, eh?" Dorie grinned. *We'll do better next time.* Her heart hurt a little at the exhaustion in Chad's face.

That seemed to rally him a little. "Awkward is my best thing," he deadpanned.

Dorie snorted. *Maybe things aren't as dire as I feared. He's kept his sense of humour.*

"Dad thought I should keep you company." *Lame, Dorie. Blaming Dad.*

"Well, I appreciate it. It's so good to see a familiar face. Your face. You." There was a pause. "Ida Mae's reinforcements haven't arrived yet."

"Probably in the morning. Church ladies are active in the morning, in my recollection."

"Let's find some coffee," he suggested. "They aren't going to let you in to see Nan, and the nurses have my cell number in case anything changes."

"No need for coffee. I brought you some takeout, coffee included." She hefted the drive-through bag. "You couldn't come to supper and Dad thought you might need something other than vending machine food."

Chad's real smile caught her off guard. "The nurses up on the floor have taken pity on me and are making sure that I get a meal when Nan is supposed to be eating. Hospital food but still food. However, I can smell french fries, and no hospital food is going to compete with hot, fresh french fries. Let's go find a seat."

As he dove into the bag, Dorie thought about what he'd said. "You've got some nurses looking out for you?" Oddly, she wanted to be the one looking out for him.

"Yeah," he said around a mouthful of fries. "Mm, these are good. Sue McGinty, I went to school with her... She remembered me. She's up there. And Darren Peters. Do you know either of them?"

Dorie shook her head. No, these people would be contemporaries of her sister Evie or even Rett. The conversation made her feel young and inadequate. "At least you're not all alone up there. You've connected with the nurses."

He looked uncertain. "Well, if by connected you mean slight recognition. They have a lot of work to do and I'm just hanging out there worrying. It was nice of Darren to feed me though. Not as nice as these fries." He smiled at Dorie and her heart gave a little jump. *What was that? Not the time, girl. His grandmother is sick and he's worried.* But she couldn't seem to stop herself from gazing at the bulge of his shoulders in his worn T-shirt.

"Do you work out?" She popped a hand across her mouth. *Uh-oh*. "Sorry. No filter." She grimaced.

Fortunately, he laughed. "Not lately. But I do haul a lot of heavy equipment into some strange places. Why do you ask?"

"You look like you do."

He flushed. "I'm going to take that as a compliment. What about you? Do you work out?"

She squinted at him. Was he flirting? With his grandmother unconscious here in the hospital? She decided that it was a straight question. "Yes, actually. I go to the gym in town. It helps with the dog wrestling that I used to do. You know, getting uncooperative pooches all pampered up."

"You're not doing that anymore?"

"Probably not." The silence after that felt comfortable. Chad slid down so his head could rest on the back of his chair.

"You look so tired. Can you get some sleep?" Dorie asked.

"Yeah, I can catch a nap in the family waiting room. I've done that a few times. I just wish she'd wake up, and then we could have some idea of what's next. The docs aren't willing to say anything about her prognosis." He sounded desperately sad.

"Hmm." Dorie reached to lay her hand on Chad's, as it rested on his thigh. He turned his hand over and grasped hers. His grasp was warm and dry, and very firm. It felt good. Dorie gazed at their linked hands and drew a breath. Feeling a little shy, she looked up toward Chad's face, but his eyes were closed, and his breathing was slow.

"Are you asleep?" She pulled her hand away and stood. "Wake up. You need to go take a real nap or something."

He jumped in the chair. "Asleep, right, you're right. Sorry, I'm not good company." He knuckled his eyes.

"Right, you're terrible company. But I forgive you under the circumstances. You really have to take care of yourself. Please. Go back upstairs and sleep if you can. We can talk tomorrow." She watched him nod.

"Yep." With an effort, he pushed himself upright. He stood, too, slightly wobbly and dazed.

"Oh, man, it's a good thing you're not going to drive that twisty road to Stella Mare tonight. You're a mess. Go on, get upstairs." She gave him a crooked smile, paused, and then stuck out her hand.

He reached for her hand then pulled her in close. His arms went round her and he buried his face in her neck. She breathed him in, feeling his chest under her cheek, but before she could even register what she was feeling, he stepped away, holding her at arms' length.

"Sorry."

"No need to apologize. That was nice."

"Yeah. Nice." He paused, then added, "I really appreciate that you came all this way and the food, and your help with the dog and all. I can't tell you how much it means."

She gave him a quick, tight smile and nodded. "Good night, Chad. Now go upstairs and sleep."

"Good night. Drive safe on that road." She nodded, pulled on her jacket, and headed toward the exit. She didn't look back.

When she woke at six, Dorie found a text from Chad. *Nan's awake. They'll be able to do some assessment today. Thanks again for last night.*

Still in bed, she tapped a reply. *That's great news! Keep me posted.*

She found herself whistling as she fed the pack, ate her own breakfast, and called Frou-Frou to go to work with her. Once again, she went early to the office and found her way into the oldest files. By seven fifteen, she was immersed in BARC's history.

The work wasn't thrilling. How can something that sounded so interesting be so dull in reality? The files from the 1980s were full of boring invoices, spreadsheets, and newspaper clippings. One file held an old print magazine that featured BARC as one of the newest tools to help fight animal cruelty. Each year of records included the minutes of the Boards of Trustees. Dorie decided to pull them out to read in sequence. That would help her to get a clear picture of the development of BARC over time.

Frou was happy to sleep under her chair, and when ten a.m. arrived, he accompanied her to the Sunshine Diner.

Though she stepped out to tell Andrea she was making the coffee run, she didn't find her. Odd. Dorie gave a mental shrug. A boss didn't need to answer to her part-time social media lackey. The coffee walk was a fun part of her morning routine, so Dorie didn't let Andrea's absence deprive her of that or the enjoyable walk through the village.

Cassandra called out to her when she pulled the big wooden door open.

"Dorie! Welcome!"

"Hi, Cass. It's just me today. Got any of that fancy pumpkin spice?"

"You bet. Big latte, right? And how about a biscuit for your pooch?" Frou looked mournfully through the sidelight window.

"Not my pooch, but sure. He's visiting. Belongs to Alice Simmons."

"Oh, yes, I heard she was in hospital."

Dorie nodded. "Is she okay?"

Shaking her head, Dorie said, "I don't know any details. Her grandson said she woke up this morning, but I think it's still pretty dicey."

"You know her grandson?"

"Yeah, Chad. Older than me. Your mum would know him, probably."

Cassandra laughed comfortably. "Yes, she knows everyone who ever went to high school in this town. I don't remember a Chad Simmons though. Is he nice?"

Dorie squinted at her. "Is that a code word for cute?"

Cassandra laughed. "Could be, I guess."

"Okay, then, yes. Kind of shy and cute, and also he can be a total pain in the neck. But right now, he needs help, so I'm the dog sitter and community liaison."

"Dog sitter because Alice is in hospital?"

"Yeah. You know my aunt Corinne? The social worker?"

Cassandra shook her head.

"Corinne works with seniors, and when they can't take care of their animals, it's a big problem. Like a by-product of getting old, there's no good way to care for your pets."

Cassandra frowned. "I guess I never thought about it. If my mum got sick, I'd probably have to figure something out for her dogs. Not that she's old. Are you helping out old people with their dogs?"

Dorie shook her head. "No. Nobody is really. I'm just Chad's friend so I have this one for now, but I met an old lady with a bunch of dogs and I think she's going to need help soon. It's all so unfair. If you're old and sick and you need more care, you have to go somewhere your dog can't go. Even if your dog is your best friend."

Cassandra nodded. "There's no special care homes for old dogs, are there?"

"Right. Old people don't necessarily have old dogs, but old dogs are a problem in themselves. They need more care, often cost more due to medical expenses, and they're basically un-adoptable."

"So that poodle, does he need a home?" Cassandra nodded toward the big plate-glass windows where Frou-Frou sat, his curly hair highlighted.

"I hope not. I hope Alice is going to come back home to her pup," she said, startled. "But I'm starting to realize how easily it could become a problem for just about anyone."

"Well, he's a cutie. I hope he gets home to his mum."

"Me, too. Thanks for the coffee and dog biscuit, Cass. See you tomorrow."

Taking her steaming cup in hand, Dorie headed back uptown to the office, Frou-Frou politely trotting at her side. What if Alice couldn't take care of her dog? What about Sarah, out in the country? What about all those old people and their dogs, some old, some not very old? She shook her head. She could almost hear her father. *You can't save them all, Dorie.* Maybe he was right. *But I can take good care of this one and keep checking on Sarah.* But her mind went to work on possible solutions while she got back to work.

Once at the office, her fragrant coffee helped her to focus on years of minutes from BARC board meetings. Not brilliant reading, but less boring than the financial files. The original minutes were typewritten and carbon copied, and the files included a photograph of the Board of Directors for that year. Dorie perused the pictures with interest. They could be useful in her media campaigns. Early pictures featured Mrs. Barrett, front and center, invariably grim.

I wouldn't want to get in her way. She looks like a force.

Dorie leaned back in her chair, gazing at the portrait of Mrs. Barrett on the boardroom wall. In her carriage and direct gaze, she saw a woman who knew her mind and brooked no interference in her affairs. Her regal bearing was mirrored in the dogs at her side. *Ruled the roost and left her considerable fortune to*

BARC, not Charles. Maybe she liked dogs better than her own son.

I bet he wasn't too happy about that, Dorie thought, yawning and stretching. She returned to piecing history together. *No wonder this has been a family-run organization. That was the only way to get to the money.*

Family-run organization for years. Until Andrea. Dorie dug out a newspaper clipping from 1999, complete with photo.

"Andrea Chase, formerly of Halifax, NS, becomes the first executive director of BARC, Inc., on January 1, 2001. Andrea brings her experience in working with legislative leaders on issues of animal welfare, her proven fundraising ability, and her desire to continue the important work of keeping canine safety at the forefront of the legislative agenda. We welcome her to BARC and to Stella Mare."

Dorie gasped at how young Andrea appeared, with a young-looking Old Mr. Barrett's arm draped around her suited shoulders. His face was oddly close to Andrea's. *Kind of familiar for a formal photo, but people were different then, I guess. So that's when Andrea got her job.* Squinting, Dorie thought she saw discomfort on Andrea's face. *Guess she had to learn to project that professional image.*

I wonder if running BARC was a career goal for Andrea? I can't imagine wanting to fundraise and talk to legislators and go to golf tournaments and galas all the time. She looked again at the photo of very young Andrea. *Maybe she just wanted to help dogs.*

Dorie stood up to stretch and Frou stood up with her. "Sorry, bud. I'm not done here yet." He gave a shake and curled up again.

Standing over the table gave Dorie a different perspective on the notes and photos laid out chronologically from 1986 to 2015, when the paper files ended. Dorie sipped meditatively, pondering the story of BARC as she walked along the long boardroom table.

In the early nineties, animal cruelty legislation was passed with BARC's influence. Annual reports reflected and celebrated success. But after 1995, not much seemed to happen, except Mr. Barrett hired Andrea. There were a lot of publicity photos of her, but not a lot of success reports. Then Young Mr. Barrett took over. Since then, well, not much.

Dorie stretched and glanced at a clock. Hours of reading and BARC was still a mystery. *BARC hasn't done anything material to change legislation for the past fifteen years. Who does BARC benefit?* They didn't rescue dogs, they didn't help dog owners out, and they didn't even do very much in the capital, at least not that Dorie could see. *Why does this organization exist? What the heck IS Andrea's job, anyway?*

Dorie sighed gustily. Frou-Frou, at her feet, sighed too. She reached down to give his ears a scratch. *What am I doing here?* She'd rather be working for Mike. Or helping out Sarah. Even hanging out with Chad. She set her chin and gathered her materials together to return to the drawer. Enough. Enough mystery, enough paper, enough tiresome files. That was enough for this day.

Chad hit Stella Mare about two p.m., parked in Alice's driveway, and found his way inside. Twenty minutes in a hot shower helped his tense shoulders to relax. Pulling on clean clothes, he made a cup of tea and took it to the living room. He settled onto the Chesterfield. *This might be a mistake*, was his last thought until he woke to late afternoon light slanting sharply through the window.

Sitting up, he scrubbed at his face. *I could sleep another week. But I'll get some more tonight. I hope.*

He poured out his cold tea in the kitchen sink. Picking up his phone to text, he shifted gears and called Dorie. *I have to check on the dog, that's all.*

"Hi, Chad."

Her voice brought him fully awake. "Hi." Something happened in that moment. His chest got tight and no words came out.

"Hey. How are you? How is everything?" He could almost see her smile, and then his chest softened, and he smiled, too.

"It's nice to hear from you," he murmured.

She giggled, a silvery sound. "I'm sure it is. But Chad, you called me."

"Oh, right. Yeah. Well, can I plead tiredness?"

"Anything you like. How are things going?"

"Nan was awake and had some company, so I came here, to her house. Caught a nap." He turned to look outside. "It was a long nap. Anyway, Nan is better and I'm here. At her house."

"She's awake and better? Oh, that's really good to hear."

"It's all pretty good news, I guess. She's going to have to go to the rehab hospital, but they think she's going to be able to go home after a week or two. They expect she will be okay." Mostly okay, he thought. *I'm not so sure about how she'll really be.*

"Wow, Chad, that is the best news. Really."

"It's a lot better than I thought it was going to be. It was scary when she didn't wake up right away."

"I can imagine."

"Turns out that being asleep like that is better for the brain. Helps it to start to heal, keeping the world kind of shut out."

"Hmm. I had no idea. That makes sense, I guess."

"I had no idea either. But anyway, they think she'll continue to do well, and that's really good."

"Good. So."

"So."

“Are you heading back to the city? Your work must need you.”

“Nope. I took a leave of absence for a bit. I really didn't know what she would need, and I’m her only family. I'm going to be here in Stella Mare.”

“Oh, that's wonderful,” Dorie exclaimed.

He puzzled over that. Wonderful? “Since I'm going to stay, I'll take care of Frou, but can you keep him until we get Nan settled in the rehab place? I'm going to be in St. Stephen a lot until then. It would be boring for a dog.”

“Yeah, of course. Frou's actually good company. My dogs like him, and that rescue I've got at the house is actually learning manners from him.”

“Frou. That fluffy bow-wearing thing of my Nan's?”

“Oh, Chad. He's such a good dog.” Dorie scoffed. “He's a good helper. I'm going out to see this old lady I met, take her some dog food. Frou's coming too.”

“You're going somewhere?” Ouch, did he sound wistful? *Stop it.*

“Just out to see this lady I met. Do you want to come? It's probably not very exciting.”

Not exciting was fine. He just wanted to see Dorie, now that he was clean and at least somewhat attentive. “I'd like to come along. I've got a couple of hours. Will that work?”

“Sure. I'll pick you up in about twenty minutes.”

Why did I ask him to come? Oh, well, he can carry the dog food. I am not excited to get to see him again. No, I am not. Oh, well. I invited him. If we get into a tiff, it'll be my own fault.

“Come on, Frou. We've got work to do.” She locked BARC and headed to the car, Frou trotting at her side.

Stopping at the rescue, she collected the bags of kibble and turned the car toward Sarah's place. Alice's farmhouse was more or less on the way, Dorie realized. Chad might as well come along. Pulling into the driveway, she honked the horn.

Chad must have been looking out for her because he came out before the horn stopped. He slid into the passenger seat and smiled warmly at her. "Thanks for letting me come along," he said. "I slept enough that I almost feel human."

She grinned at him. "I bet that felt good."

"Yeah, it did. Um..." he suddenly looked uncomfortable. "Uh, Dorie, I called you to help with the dog, because I, uh..."

She stared at him. "Because you needed help?"

He looked out the van window. "Dorie, are you seeing that guy?" He turned toward her, flushed and tense.

"Guy? What guy?" She was suddenly regretting her invitation again.

His face got even redder. "I saw a post with you dancing with some guy, right before, you know, all the trouble, and I wondered..."

"Wondered what?" Dorie held onto her equanimity.

He shook his head. "I called you for help with the dog, but I also wondered if you were dating someone else. I know we said friends, only friends, and I get that, but I also didn't know about this guy and I know it probably isn't any of my business but I want to know." He shoved his glasses up his nose and peered at her. His brown eyes were full of concern.

"You're right, it isn't your business," she said grimly, but then softened. He was sleep-deprived, worried, and as awkward as he could be, but he meant well. "No, I'm not dating anyone. Not that guy, for sure. It's too bad that my so-called friends had to document that night. Not my finest moment."

He looked relieved. "Thanks. I know I was prying. Sorry."

She gave a sidelong glance. "Forgiven. But you haven't spoken to your brother yet."

"Brother? Oh, right." He turned to the backseat. "Hey, dog." Frou-Frou pointedly ignored him. "Oh, come on, buddy," Chad chided. "I didn't take you away from your mum. We can still be friends, right?"

Frou curled up on the backseat and went to sleep.

"Oh, well," Chad said to Dorie. "I tried, right? You were the witness."

Dorie relaxed into good humour. "Frou-Frou has liked everyone he's met, except for you. I don't know what it is about you two. Sibling rivalry?"

"Maybe," Chad agreed. "I never had a sibling, so I wouldn't know."

"Oh, I know all about sibling rivalry." Dorie pointed the car toward Sarah's old house. "Four of us girls, remember? Always somebody in crisis, always some big drama. Never enough parent to go around for four girls. The sisters all blame me for everything bad, but honestly, I'm the little sister. I couldn't have caused all the family troubles."

"Well, I don't think I compete with Frou for my Nan's attention, but he might think so."

"Nah, he probably just knows you have no respect for him. I think he's a great dog."

Frou sat up and put his nose over Dorie's shoulder. "Yes, you heard me, didn't you?" She nuzzled him.

Chad shook his head. "He's never that nice to me."

Dorie raised her eyebrows. "Are you ever that nice to him?"

Chad shrugged. "Maybe not. He's the dog. That's what I know."

Dorie pulled down the long driveway past the front of the ramshackle house. "Here we are. Sarah is old and she's very suspicious. We can't go to the front of the house, and if there's another car here, I just drive right on by. Today it's all clear."

"What do you mean? All clear from what?"

She looked around as she got out of the car. "Help me carry this dog food and I'll tell you all about it later."

They each took a big bag and Dorie headed toward the ell door, where Sarah had allowed her in before. After knocking lightly, Dorie looked at Chad, judging that his pleasant, open face, nice brown eyes behind his glasses, and warm smile shouldn't scare Sarah too much. Frou-Frou sat politely beside Dorie, waiting for the door to open. The racket of barking from inside the house escalated as footsteps approached.

"Hi, Sarah," Dorie said rapidly, as the door opened a crack. "Remember me? I brought you some more food for your babies. This is Frou-Frou. And this guy here, he's Frou-Frou's owner."

"Cute dog." The old woman gave Frou a glance and then glared at Chad, but she opened the door slightly for Dorie to slip in. Dorie held it open for Chad and his bag of dog food, and Frou politely entered last. Sarah's little dogs spilled all around their feet, yapping and toenails clicking. Sarah led the way into the ancient kitchen, still overrun with small, unkempt dogs. The smell was nearly overpowering and the sound from the front of the house was deafening. Chad set the dog food down and held his hand to his nose.

"The big dogs are noisy today, Sarah."

"Oh, them. They always make a ruckus." Sarah squinted at them. "There you are, dearie," she said. "And who's this? Your boyfriend?" She looked hard at Chad with what Dorie recognized as a smile.

Dorie repeated herself, realizing Sarah either hadn't heard or hadn't registered what she'd said at the door. "This is Chad, Sarah. He's Frou-Frou's owner and my friend. He's helping me make deliveries this afternoon. How are your babies?"

"Oh, not so good, Dorie. Little Blackie, he's not eating, and I can't get him to get up. Come and see him." Dorie went into the other room, leaving Chad and Frou in the kitchen with a swarm of little dogs. Blackie listlessly lay on a dirty blanket near what

Dorie presumed was Sarah's bed. The little dog was covered with sores.

"Do you have a vet, Sarah? Somebody who could look after him?"

"Oh, no, no. I don't want nobody looking at my babies, Dorie. Besides, my son, he don't want anybody out here. You remember. Like your boyfriend, there, you better take him and go."

"Are you sure? I could ask Doc Hartley to come out, Sarah. He's really kind, loves the dogs."

"Oh, no, no. No. You have to go now, Dorie. Richie will be back soon. Go on, get your boyfriend and go." The old woman nearly pushed Dorie out into the kitchen. The racket from the front part of the house escalated so that Dorie almost didn't hear the roar of a motor.

"Quick!" she said to Chad. "We've got to get out of here." When they spilled out the door, Chad looked back toward Sarah.

"Is that a camera? Come on!" Dorie and Frou bounced ahead as they scrambled through the evening light toward Dorie's car. A heavy-set leather-clad man was heading toward them from the front of the house.

"Hey! Hey you! What you doing here?" the man roared. Chad stopped again to look, but Dorie grabbed his jacket and said, "Come on, Chad, get going."

In the car, she backed out of the driveway before the big man got close, but Dorie was speeding anyway. Frou barked from the backseat for nearly a minute before he settled down. Finally Dorie slowed to the speed limit when she reached the county road.

"Well, another adventure." She grinned at Chad.

"What was that all about?" His eyes were wide.

"I really don't know. I think Sarah is afraid of her son, but she lives there to take care of his dogs which we've never seen. They're the noisiest ones. Sarah's bunch are pathetic, because she has no money for food or grooming, and she's not able to care for them. The one in the back, Blackie, is very sick and she won't even let me call my vet. I've been bringing food out to her a couple of times a week, but I still don't know what's going on there."

"The son has dogs that you're not allowed to see? And that old woman takes care of his dogs too? Weird."

"Weird is right. The whole setup stinks, not the least because there's an old lady who might be sick herself, in that disgusting house with all those dogs that she can't care for. What if something happened to her like to your Nan?"

"Well, her son would step up. He'd have to, wouldn't he?"

"I don't know. All I know is what Sarah has said, and honestly, I'm not sure she's a trustworthy informant. I wonder if her son is involved in the dog-fighting ring, as those big loud dogs in the front of the house seem to be very valuable. Unlike Sarah's pets."

"Ah, the dog-fighting ring. The hypothetical, no evidence for it, cannot talk about it, dog-fighting ring."

The way he said it amused her. "The very same."

"That guy we just saw hits all the stereotypes, right? Big, nasty, leather, scary."

She had to laugh. "Yeah, I guess so. I could be jumping to conclusions. Dog-fighting types could wear suits and have fancy cars for all I know."

"Or just look like your regular folks who can't quite make a living through legal channels."

"Yeah, I guess it could be that." She shook her head. "But dog fighting or not, Sarah's got trouble. She has too many dogs to care for, but they all mean something to her. I figure I can at least supply her with food for them. Or rather, the rescue does that. I just drop it off."

Chad looked thoughtful. "Some of her little dogs are old."

Dorie nodded. "Most of them are old. Old dogs are expensive to keep. Like people, they have medical problems, sometimes need special diets, extra attention. If something happened to Sarah, her dogs would probably be euthanized because it is so hard to place old dogs in adoptive homes. Most people want young, healthy dogs."

"There's a story here, Dorie, and I don't mean about the mad biker-dude-dog-fighting guy in leather. Although that might be a story, too. I mean these old dogs and this old lady, and nobody taking care of them. And Nan, who is old, too, but she does have care, and her dog Frou even had you to take care of him when Nan had to go into the hospital. I don't know the whole picture here, but there is a story."

"This is the watcher in you, isn't it?" Dorie asked curiously. "The part that sees beneath the obvious."

Chad fiddled with something under his jacket. "You don't have to dig too deep here. I probably got some good images." He pulled out a tiny camera.

"Chad. You didn't have permission."

"Yeah, I know. I wouldn't use anything I got that way. But the images help me to think about things."

"It's pretty sad what's going on with Sarah."

"It is. And the whole story feels close to home because Nan is in kind of a similar situation, but different. There's a big contrast."

Dorie thought aloud. "What are the differences? Just because Alice is in her right mind and I'm not so sure about Sarah? Or having family around? Now you've got me thinking."

"What does happen to dogs when their elderly people have to leave them?" Chad asked, his voice thick. "I know Nan would be distraught if she had to leave Frou at the shelter. I'll make sure that never happens."

Frou-Frou sat up in the backseat. Slowly, he stretched his neck over the seat and leaned his chin on Chad's shoulder. Dorie looked over and burst out laughing. "I told you that dog understands English. Look at him. He'll hold you to it."

Chad didn't laugh. He reached up to scratch Frou-Frou's ear. "He means a lot to my Nan. And she means a lot to me. I'll take care of him if she can't."

Dorie was touched. "Besides being important to your Nan, he's a pretty good dog. In answer to your question, I really don't know what happens to the pets of old people. I think it's a good question. My aunt Corinne is a social worker, and she's wondered about that too. It probably is a bigger problem than we know."

Finally, Dorie turned into Alice's driveway, pulling to a stop behind Chad's truck. "Shall I leave Frou with you now?" she asked.

Chad looked at her and at the dog. "I have to go back to the hospital tonight. Now, actually. Do you mind keeping him a little longer?"

"He can come anytime. He's part of the pack now. I'll take him with me, and you can pick him up tomorrow. Do you have any idea when you might pick him up?"

Chad shook his head. "No, not really. But thank you for letting me come with you today. It was good to do something that wasn't hospital stuff."

She chuckled. "No thanks required. I appreciated your company and the help. I even felt a little safer with you there. Frou is a good boy but not much protection."

Frou growled softly.

When Chad and Dorie locked gazes, she saw the fatigue around his eyes, partially hidden by his glasses, but confirmed by a tightness in his jaw. The moment stretched out, and she reached across the seat to put her hand on his shoulder. With a sigh, Chad leaned his face against her hand. His eyes closed.

Dorie's face got warm. "Chad. Chad? You're going to get some sleep tonight, right?"

He startled upright. "Yeah, I hope so. I need to get going, back to the hospital. I, um, I guess I'll go now. See you tomorrow."

He smiled at her then turned away and opened the door. "Good night."

"Good night."

Driving off, Dorie checked in her rearview mirror to see Chad unlocking his truck and getting in. *He's exhausted, but he's still going back. That's a good guy, right there.* She headed for her own home, her father, her dogs, and the never-ending search for supper.

Chapter 12

Early to work again, Dorie sighed as she refiled dusty folders in the BARC archive room. *I guess I'm learning stuff. I understand it's important, but it's also impossibly boring.*

Going to see Sarah, finding resources to help her take care of her animals, checking on hoarding and cruelty and puppy mills, now that was exciting. Unfortunately, it was more like watching television than working. That is, it was fun, but there was no way to make a living from it.

Dorie sat back with relief when the office phone rang. It might be Andrea who was still peculiarly AWOL.

"Andrea Chase, please."

Dorie didn't recognize the male voice. "Andrea isn't in now. May I take a message?"

"Who is this? Do you work for BARC?"

Dorie was nonplussed. "Yes, this is Dorie. I work here. Who is calling?"

"This is Patrick McLannahan from the *Daily Record*. Where is Ms. Chase? I have something to discuss with her."

"She's not here. Can I help you? Are you doing a story about BARC?"

"Sure I am. What do you know about the money grab? Can I come by to see you?"

"What? Money grab?" Shocked, Dorie slammed the phone down, and jumped at a sudden pounding on the front door.

"Coming, I'm coming!" She scooted down the hallway. Since the harassment last week, Dorie had been locking the big main door, as well as the office. Peering through the etched glass, she saw two people, one holding a video camera.

"Ms. Chase! Ms. Chase. Come out." The woman wore a skirt suit and held a microphone. A reporter! It could be that Jeannette, Dorie thought, watching.

"She's not here! Go away!" Dorie shouted from her side of the door, and then peered out again. The reporter turned to look toward the camera and Dorie could hear her voice but not her words.

What the heck? Back in the boardroom, Dorie grabbed her own phone. No relevant breaking news items, but her social feed had a post by a community watchdog group with a picture of Andrea and the headline, "Executive director of non-profit under investigation for embezzlement."

For Pete's sake! More mess for BARC. Quickly she scrolled to see comments piling up. *Wow, the trouble caused by my post on dog fighting is nothing compared to this. Who would do something like this? Was Andrea being set up by those guys I heard in the grocery store?*

What if it was true? Could she have sticky fingers? Or be in some other kind of trouble? Where the heck is she, anyway?

Pacing the boardroom, she called Andrea's cell. No answer. She left a voice mail, asking her to call. Now her multi-day absence felt a little sinister. *What if something bad happened to Andrea? How would I even know?*

Sitting at the table, she tried to work, but it was hard to think. Instead of reading old minutes, she decided to look at more recent records. The office phone rang again. This time she was wary.

"BARC office. Dorie speaking."

"Good morning. This is Constable Doiron of the RCMP. May I speak to Andrea Chase?"

"No, she's not here."

"Are you an employee?"

"Yes, I am," she answered slowly, not sure she wanted to claim it.

"I'm at the door. Please let me in."

She walked slowly back to the front door, Frou-Frou at her side. A uniformed officer held up his identification. Behind him was a uniformed woman putting her phone away. Dorie opened the door a bit.

"What do you want?" she asked unsteadily.

"We need access, Ms...."

"Madison." Dorie held firmly to the door.

"Ms. Madison, we need to enter the premises. Please open the door." She held on for another moment, but the man's foot entered the door and he shouldered his way in. "Thank you," he said, politely.

"What?" Dorie was incredulous. "You just came right in here. My boss isn't even here." Frou uttered a warning growl, but the man headed down the hallway to the open office door. The woman, Constable Doiron, Dorie surmised, followed.

"Now, Ms. Madison, was it? We're going to look around here. You might need to call your boss to let them know, but we're here legally. I'm going to ask you to keep this door locked though, as there were some reporters nosing around and you probably don't want to talk to them."

"No, I probably don't," Dorie agreed, "but why are you here?"

Constable Doiron didn't smile. "I can't talk to you about that, but can you call your supervisor? Someone in charge?" She leaned down to let Frou sniff her hand and gave his head a pat. His wariness subsided.

"Yeah, I guess." Dorie followed the woman down the hall, Frou beside her. "Okay, Frou, you go take a break. Go ahead, lie down in there." He looked back over his shoulder and very slowly walked toward the boardroom. Dorie kept her voice even. "Good dog."

The man was in Andrea's office, poking around in her desk. Dorie didn't like any of this. What was going on? She found the numbers for Young Mr. Barrett and Naomi Snow, the board's counsel. Mr. Barrett's number didn't answer, but Dorie got through to Naomi by being insistent with her office receptionist.

"Naomi, the police are here, right here in Andrea's office. They're taking her laptop and a bunch of files." She followed the police officers around as she reported to Naomi. "Hey, those are the archive files!"

"Where do these belong?" Constable Doiron asked.

"I was working on those this morning," Dorie said. "I didn't get them refiled, not yet. Hey, wait!" she shouted as the woman tossed the old files into a big box. "How am I going to get those back together?"

"Dorie! Dorie," Naomi called, still on the phone. "Do you know why they're there? Do they have a warrant?"

"How would I know? I'm just the help," Dorie snapped. "Hey, police lady, do you guys have a warrant? Our lawyer wants to know."

The woman officer nodded her head toward the man in the other room. "Yes, Jake's holding it. Signed by the judge this morning, Ms. Madison."

The man came through to the boardroom carrying two cardboard boxes. "I've got the relevant files and the computer," he said. "What's left here?" He cast a sharp gaze at the box of file folders Constable Doiron had been assembling.

"Ms. Madison is on the phone with her lawyer," Constable Doiron reported.

Dorie's stomach was doing flips, but she willed her voice to be strong. "Not my lawyer. BARC's lawyer. I don't think I need one, do I?"

The man looked at her with a squint. "How long have you worked here? We might want to interview you. Don't leave town."

She shook her head at the man and turned away, listening to Naomi splutter. "Don't let them intimidate you, Dorie. If they have a warrant, it probably specifies that they can take the files and Andrea's computer. Apparently, there's an investigation into how she was keeping the books. I didn't know it had gone this far. Have you talked to her?"

"No, that's the worrisome thing," Dorie said quietly into the phone. "I haven't seen or heard from her since, oh, Monday at noon. She hasn't come in at all since then, at least not so you'd know. I'm only here in the mornings but there's been no evidence that anyone else has been here at all. She's not taking my calls or returning texts."

"Does Charles know?"

"I don't know what he knows. I didn't think there was anything to be worried about until all this weird stuff this morning. I figured she's the boss, she doesn't have to answer to me. I'm just the social media admin." Dorie peered at the police, still sorting out files.

Naomi made a sound. "Yes, that's right, Dorie. Take the day off. Call Charles and let him know."

"I tried him before you. I think his phone was off."

Naomi sounded brisk. "I don't know what's going on, but you probably shouldn't be at the office today anyway. The board will find Andrea. You just take today off. I'll take responsibility for that."

"Yeah, okay," Dorie agreed, despite her doubts. "I'll lock up after these guys and go home."

The two officers finally completed their collection. Dorie followed them down the hall with their boxes.

"Just so you know, I don't think Andrea's been in the office since Monday," she said, lifting her chin. "You should be looking for her instead of making a mess here."

Constable Doiron turned, her arms full. "Do you want to make a statement? You can come down to the station with us and get that on record."

Dorie waffled. "Uh, no, I guess not."

The constable nodded. "That's what I thought. We'll let you know when we need to talk to you." She turned away, carrying her boxes down the front steps.

Dorie wanted to slam the heavy door behind her, but the thought of the ancient glass shattering stopped her mid-push. Instead, she locked it with a satisfying click.

Back down the hallway, Andrea's office was a disaster. Drawers were askew, cabinets open, and papers scattered on the floor. The archive room looked better, but that was because Dorie had tidied up behind the woman officer. Frou-Frou whined gently at her feet. "Right, Frou. This is a major mess. Naomi said to leave. We're leaving."

Turning off lights, she pulled on her jacket. Before she could walk down the hall, the phone rang again. *I don't want to answer you*, she told the phone. *But what if it's Andrea? Or even Mr. Smith?* With a big sigh, she picked up the receiver. "BARC, Dorie speaking."

"Dorie?" The voice was faint and quavery.

"Hello? This is Dorie, yes."

"Dorie? I'm sick, honey."

"Sarah? Is that you? Sarah?"

"I'm going to the hospital, Dorie. Can you take my babies?"

Dorie strained to hear the voice. "What? Sarah, did you say you're sick?" Suddenly, a man's gruff voice came on the line.

"Hey, you the lady that's been bringing the dog food?"

Unsure of whether it was a good idea to admit it, Dorie said slowly, "Yes. A couple of times."

"Listen, my mam's in a bad way. I gotta take her to the hospital, but she says she won't go unless you take her dogs."

"Me? What about County Rescue?"

"No! No way! I can't have them people out here. Listen, either you come get these mutts or I'm gonna shoot 'em. She's gotta go and I can't have them around here." Dorie heard Sarah's screamed protest in the background.

Incensed, Dorie said, "Don't you dare shoot them. It's not their fault." She looked around for inspiration or support or something. Her gaze fell on Frou-Frou, standing in the doorway, head cocked, looking at her. She could swear he was telling her to step up.

She frowned at the dog and stuck out her chin. "Okay, you tell Sarah I'll come get them."

She grimaced at Frou, who gave a happy tail wag. Yes, Sarah's problem was just like Alice's problem. Only it was bigger, eight dogs bigger. With a threatening, possibly dangerous, gun-toting man involved.

"Tell her not to worry. I'll take care of them. I'll figure out something for them while she's in hospital. How do I get in touch with you? What's your name, anyway?" Dorie grabbed a pencil off Andrea's formerly pristine desk.

"You don't never mind my name. My mam is Sarah Smith and I'm taking her to the hospital in St. Stephen. You can check on her there, but right now, you get these mutts outta here. Don't you go near the front of the house. Don't bring no Animal Control. I'm gonna have someone watching. Make sure you stay in your lane. Just you."

His threats made her wobble. Inside. Outside, she did what her father called "mouthing off."

"Listen, Mr. No-Name, I'm doing you a big favour. Get over yourself." His response was a click as the phone disconnected. "What a blowhard. Forget him though. We've got a job to do." She looked at Frou. "Let's call your daddy or whatever he is and get some help with this job."

"We're doing what? After we raced out of there last night like the hounds of hell were after us? Are you kidding?" Chad stared at her, incredulous.

"Yes, we did, and no, I am not kidding. Sarah called the BARC office looking for me. So we're rescuing dogs. Can you help me or what?"

He sighed. "Yes, of course I'll help you. What are you going to do with all those dogs? Keep them at your dad's house?"

Dorie shrugged. "You know, Chad, I figure that'll sort itself out after we get those dogs into a safe place. Dad likes dogs. How's Alice today?"

"Good. She's really good today, actually. Ida Mae was still there last night when I arrived, and they both told me to go home and sleep, and when I went in early this morning Nan had already eaten breakfast with only a little help."

Dorie smiled at him. "You sound a lot better. More optimistic, too."

He smiled back. "A whole night of sleep makes a big difference. I haven't been that sleep deprived for years, back when I was covering the earthquake in Haiti."

Dorie raised her eyebrows. "You did that? I'd like to hear about that."

"Sometime," Chad said. "Right now, it sounds like we need to figure out how to move a whole bunch of dogs."

"Yes. I haven't even told you about my morning. You know how nothing much ever happens? Since last week, things have been nonstop, and I can't even imagine what will be next. Let's stop at Doc Hartley's vet clinic. They've got crates we can borrow."

"Sure thing."

They sat in the cab of his truck and Frou-Frou sat between them, like a curly-headed child. Chad liked seeing Dorie there, liked her firm voice when she asked him for help. He was a little worried about what they were getting into, but, oh, well. She really cared about those dogs. He sneaked another glance at the curve of her cheek, the way her messy ponytail left strands of hair curling around her face.

"What? What are you looking at?" she demanded.

Chad smiled to himself. Feisty. Determined to be taken seriously. Probably not the time to tell her how cute she looked. *See, I am getting better at this*.

"Just you. Are we all set?"

"Yes. I called the vet clinic already. Do you have any blankets or anything? I've never done this before, except Frou, and it's not really the same thing."

"No, it's different. More of an adventure, right?"

Dorie looked at him with her eyebrows up. "Yeah. Okay, yes. Let's call it an adventure and I won't be scared." She giggled.

"You, scared? I can't believe it," Chad teased.

"Scared like to death by the cops this morning and by that guy threatening to shoot Sarah's dogs. But they aren't gonna know it. So yes, let's have another adventure."

An hour later they arrived at the old house. The back of Chad's truck was filled with dog crates, old blankets, and towels. Dorie had a pile of leashes on the floor of the truck cab in front of her.

A battered black van had followed them into the yard, and Mike Maybee jumped out.

"Hey, Dorie," he said. He held out his hand to Chad. "Mike, with County Rescue."

"Oh, hi. Chad Simmons. I called you last week."

"Oh, right," Mike agreed. "Sorry I didn't get back to you."

"Shh," Dorie warned, shooting a glance toward the front of the house. "Save the small talk. The guy said I couldn't bring you, either of you. But I can't do this alone. Let's go in."

She led the way to the side door of the ell. In full daylight, the house looked even worse than he'd thought. The small porch was rotted through, several windows were repaired with cardboard, and the screen door hung on a single hinge.

"Come on," Dorie gestured.

"Wait," Mike cautioned. "You've only been here with the owner, right? These dogs don't really know you."

"Well, yes, actually, they do. I've been bringing food twice a week. I think I've touched all of them," Dorie admitted. "They're pretty good if you have treats."

Mike grinned and handed her a bagful. "Okay, but I'm right here for support. Our job is to catch these guys and get them crated and out of here. One at a time. Got it?"

Relieved to have someone who apparently knew what he was doing, Chad exhaled. He liked dogs okay, but this place was so filthy and so sad. He wasn't excited to be back, but he had agreed to help and help he would.

Predictably, barking started before they got out of the truck, but it quieted when Dorie cracked the door open and spoke. The big noise in the main house went on, but the dogs in the ell were quiet. Chad watched Dorie drop to one knee, holding out a treat. One of the pugs came right into her hands. She toed the door closed and stood up with the wriggling dog licking her face.

"Oh, does he stink," she moaned. "Here's one. Chad, can you take him?"

"Yes, I've got a crate right here. Let's see if we can get him in." Together they used a combination of enticement and a not-too-gentle push to get the dog in the crate.

"Okay," Mike said. "Well done. One down, how many to go?"

Dorie grimaced. "I know of at least seven all together. It just seems like more."

Mike was cheerful. "Well, we'll do it. It'll be fine."

Chad carried the crated pug to his truck. A motorcycle roared into the yard. His stomach clenched. *What now?*

The bewhiskered man on the big bike parked it and walked over to the truck. Chad wasn't sure, but it could have been the man from last night, Big Guy, in Chad's mind. He looked more agreeable now.

"You getting Sarah's mutts?" he asked. "I thought it was a lady coming."

"Well, it is. It's my truck. I'm helping."

"Need any more help? The old lady, I'm not so sure she's gonna make it. I'd like to get these mutts outta here."

"I heard she was sick," Chad said cautiously. "We've got one mutt so far. Yeah, we can use extra hands."

He walked with the big man around the side of the house where Mike and Dorie were successfully wrestling a ragged-looking Boston terrier into a crate.

"Hey, Dorie, we've got some more, uh, help," Chad said.

Dorie lifted her face after slamming the crate door shut. Chad saw her eyes widen and cheeks go pale, but her voice was strong. "Are you Richie?"

The man shook his head. "No. Richie took the old lady to the hospital. I'm supposed to make sure you get the dogs. I can help."

Dorie gave a quick nod. "Good. This is hard work. More help is good."

Mike was at the door, enticing another small dog out of the kitchen. "We're trying to do this one at a time, keep it manageable. Do you know these dogs?" he asked the big guy.

Big Guy shrugged. "Nope. They're the old lady's mutts. Don't have nothing to do with me. I'll be happy to have 'em gone though. What can I do?"

"Just be ready to grab. We'll get 'em."

After seven dogs were crated and stashed either in Chad's truck or the back of Mike's van, Dorie, Mike, and Chad entered the kitchen. Big Guy stayed outside, smoking a cigarette.

"Let's do a final check. Make sure we got them all." Mike was clear.

Chad covered his nose again. The smell was as overpowering and awful as he recalled from last night.

Dorie headed right for the little bedroom.

"This is where I saw Blackie last night," she said over her shoulder to Chad and Mike. "Oh...oh, no." Her voice dropped.

Chad followed her into the room. A little black dog, clearly dead, lay on the floor. The room was nasty, smelled of urine and feces, and the cot where Sarah had apparently slept had vomit on it, too. The dead dog was part of a whole picture of poverty, illness, and sorrow. Dorie turned to Chad with glistening eyes.

"I should have done something last night," she said in a low voice. "I saw how bad it was. I should have taken him to the clinic or something."

Chad reached toward her. "Come on, Dorie, let's get out of here. No more dogs to rescue here." He slipped an arm around her shoulders to ease her out the door.

Mike had a blanket. "I'll take the body," he said. "We can take care of that."

The three headed out of the house. The big guy was waiting outside. "What you got there?" he asked, nodding at Mike.

Mike stopped to talk to him, but Chad kept Dorie moving toward the truck. He wanted to get away from that awful house, the sadness he felt in there, and he wanted to get her away, too. Dorie was quiet. *She's upset*, Chad thought. *She puts a lot of herself into this*. They reached the truck and Dorie stopped, turning to watch for Mike.

"You okay?" Chad asked.

She looked up at him. Very quietly, she said, "No, not really. But I will be."

Mike carried the small, blanketed bundle toward the County Rescue van. Big Guy trailed behind. The chorus of barking continued, but Chad barely noticed it.

Dorie left Chad's truck to approach the big guy. Lifting her chin, she said loudly, "Okay? I got the dogs. One of them died. More of them might die."

"Yeah."

"You tell Richie, your boss or whatever he is, that the dogs are taken care of. Sarah didn't have any help from anyone. She tried. They don't deserve to live like this."

Big Guy gazed at her without a smile. "Not my business, lady. Wasn't yours either, until Richie asked for your help. I know you've been out here before. You and your boyfriend." His chin indicated Chad.

Dorie kept her gaze on the big guy. "I'm just trying to help an old lady with her dogs."

Big Guy nodded. "Yeah. So thank you from Richie and Sarah. Now from me, an invitation to leave and not come back."

"Gladly," Dorie said. "You and your buddy there left Sarah with those dogs, neglected and underfed, and yet you've got all those barkers in the big house. What's the deal there?" She glared at Big Guy.

Chad's chest tightened. Did she have to keep pushing?

"That is no business of yours. You just get going."

"I need a number. Richie's contact. How can I let Sarah know about her dogs?"

Chad reached for her hand. "Come on, Dorie. We got the dogs. Let's go."

Big Guy looked menacingly in their direction. "Boyfriend's got it right, girl. You got the dogs. Old Sarah wanted that. Nothing else here is your concern."

"What about those other dogs? How do I know they're okay?"

"Dorie." Chad pulled at her arm.

She shook him off and stepped toward Big Guy. "I think we better see those other dogs. How else do I know they're okay?"

She lifted her chin again, but Chad saw it tremble slightly. She's going for broke now, he thought. He slipped one hand into his pocket and found his truck keys. *How fast can we get out of here?*

Mike was in the black van. Now he leaned out of the window to say to Dorie, "It's okay, Dorie. Just get in the truck. Let's take care of what we agreed to take care of."

Big Guy nodded toward Mike, then looked back at Dorie.

"Well, I can see I'm a minority of one here," she said. "Okay. But you..." She lifted her chin again toward the Big Guy, "you tell Sarah where her babies are. Got it?"

Big Guy was still glaring, but he nodded slightly. Chad opened the passenger door for Dorie, barely suppressing his impulse to give her a push, and scooted around to clamber in the driver's seat. The black van passed the truck heading out of the yard, and Chad wasted no time in following.

"Well," he said, looking at Dorie slumped in the passenger seat. Frou-Frou was licking her face. "Well," he tried again. "That was something."

Dorie sniffled and pulled herself upright in the seat. When she swiped her wrist across her nose, Chad found her a tissue and handed it over. She stuck her face in it, then leaned into Frou-Frou's neck. The car was filled with her deep, shuddering sobs.

Chad tried to keep his eyes on the road, but he reached over and awkwardly patted the top of Dorie's head. *Oh, her hair is so soft. This is out of my league, man. I have no idea what to do here.* He recalled a hockey coach telling him once, when you're not sure, just do what you know how to do.

Well, I can drive the car back to town. I can do that.

After a few minutes, Dorie's sobs slowed down and she sniffled some more, then wiped her face with more tissues. Frou sat back upright.

"I'm sorry about that," Dorie said, sounding uncomfortable. "It's just been a super challenging day. That nasty jerk being so mean, right after we found poor Blackie, well, that was the end."

Chad was relieved to hear her sounding more like herself. "Yeah," he managed. It was about the only thing he could think of that couldn't be the wrong thing to say.

Dorie was quiet, perhaps thinking. He stole a look. Her eyes were so brilliant after all her tears. He couldn't help himself. "Green? Are your eyes green?"

"What? Oh, yes, I guess so. Like a cat, my mother used to say." Frou licked her cheek.

Chad was silent. *Stupid question, asking about her eyes. What now? At least the dog knows how to comfort her.*

Dorie let out a gusty sigh. "I'm okay, Chad. It's safe to talk to me again."

"What are we going to do with these animals? What's the next part of the adventure?"

"Mike is taking them at the shelter overnight. He'll treat them for worms and fleas, and Doc Hartley will check them out, then I guess they'll be at my house for a while. Until Sarah gets better."

After a pause, Chad pointed out, "You mean, if Sarah gets better."

"Yeah. I'm also assuming my dad doesn't blow a gasket about more dogs."

"You have high expectations for your father's patience."

Dorie looked down. “I know. Honestly, that’s unrealistic. We can’t take these dogs.”

Silence reigned in the car, then she said, “This whole situation is so messy and sad, isn't it? I mean, all these dogs, and that old lady, and multiply by so many old people without help and their dogs. Everyone getting old and sick, and having to be separated.”

Chad glanced at her. “Yes, that part’s sad, for sure. But there are other parts to the story. Like you and Mike rescuing these dogs. Helpers. The way you’re helping Nan with Frou, and even the part about Nan recovering enough to take care of him herself. Those are parts of the story, too.”

“Yeah. You’re right.”

More silence, then she went on. “When I was a kid, I tried to save every dying animal I ever came across. I found baby robins, out of the nest, and tried to save them. My neighbour's cat had a habit of catching chipmunks. I can't tell you how many chipmunks I tried to rehabilitate. I was so mad at that cat, and at all cats, for catching birds and little animals. I remember my dad saying, Dorie, you can't save them all. You can't change the whole world. But you can change your little part of it.”

Chad’s vision swam. “So that's what you're doing here. Changing things for these dogs. Instead of being taken out in the woods and shot, they're alive in the truck and the van, and they're going to be fed and taken care of.”

She sighed. “I guess that has to be enough. I hoped that working for BARC would give me a broader reach, you know, into changing animals' lives through changing legislation.”

“That sounds good too.”

“I don't think it's working. What was happening at Sarah's house wasn't because the legislation needs to be changed. It was because a lot of old people don't have support to take care of their pets.”

He wasn't sure. "I don't think that's the only thing happening there. Those big dogs and the scary guys... There's more going on."

She shrugged. "Yes, for sure. They could be raising and training dogs for dog fighting. I've been officially warned off from all of that, so I'm keeping out of it."

He scoffed. "I'm not buying that. I just heard you confront that guy about the big dogs. That didn't seem like you were keeping out of it."

She looked out the truck window.

"Dorie?"

"Well, it was worth a shot." She glanced toward him, and he caught the edge of a smile. "But I really am going to stay out of it. Mike's group, they'll investigate. Or the police. Dog fighting is already against the law. Not my problem, and I am trying to remember that. I can't stop thinking about old people and their old dogs though. It seems like this is a problem I can solve."

"A baby robin to save?"

Dorie snickered. "Well, I hope I'm more successful at this. There are a lot of baby birds buried in the backyard at my house."

"You will be," he encouraged. "You already are. Look at what we're doing right now."

Finally he pulled his truck into the shelter parking lot behind Mike's van. The sun was very low in the sky, slanting through the leafless November trees.

"Probably too little, too late, for Sarah, anyway," Dorie murmured.

"You can only do your best. This is our best, right now."

"I guess." Dorie twisted around to gaze into the back of the truck where the crates were stashed. "I just have a lot to think about."

"Me, too. This whole week, since I got the call about Nan, has given me a lot to think about," Chad agreed. "I want to tell you about it sometime. Right now though, it looks like we need to unload these dogs."

Chapter 13

The work wasn't done by simply arriving at the shelter.

By the time Dorie, Chad, and Mike got the small dogs unloaded, moved into a couple of kennel runs at the shelter, fed, and some paperwork managed, her stomach was growling and she could barely keep her eyes open.

"I stink, I'm starving, and I'm tired enough to sleep standing up."

Mike grinned. "Yeah, get out of here. Try to have a good Friday night. We'll get these guys cleaned up and checked out. I'll let you know what I locate for foster homes." He waved them off from his office door.

Dorie stumbled leaving the shelter and let Chad help her into his truck. Frou leaped into the jump seat. "Thanks for coming with me. It was good to have a friend along. This day could not get any weirder. "

"No problem. These little pups sure are a mess."

"We are too, after handling them." Dorie poked around in the dash of the truck. "Have you got any sanitizer? I feel gross."

"No, sorry. Just the tissues."

Dorie groaned. "I can't wait until I can have a shower. Or food. Or sleep. I don't know what I need the most."

He smiled. "Well, at the risk of sounding critical, I think a shower would do us both good."

Frou barked.

Dorie looked over her shoulder at the dog. "You don't get an opinion, buddy. You weren't moving all those stinky, sad little dogs." Frou curled up.

Chad raised an eyebrow as he turned on the ignition. "Want to get some takeout? Pizza? We can take it to Nan's house, if you like."

Oh, that sounds good. But Dad... "Yes. But let's go to my house. Dad's there and I need to help with the dog chores. You can shower there, too," she added. "Dad's probably got some sweats or something you can borrow."

A ringtone sounded. Dorie groaned and dragged her phone out of her pocket. "What now?"

"Hey, Dad. What's up?" She looked at Chad, who was obviously listening.

"Dorie, the police called, looking for you."

"Oh, really? What did they say?" She grimaced at Chad.

"They want you at the station. It was Rene Doiron's girl, you know, but she wouldn't tell me what it's all about. You get in more trouble?

"Dad! No, I'm not in trouble. But I .... listen, they need me like now? Tonight?"

"She was pretty clear, Dore. As soon as possible or they'd be out looking for you."

She closed her eyes. She had almost been able to smell that pizza. "Okay. I don't need to be hauled in by the local constabulary. I'll take care of it. Yeah, thanks. I'll let you know what happens. Bye."

Dorie leaned her head back against the seat, eyes closed. "I can't believe this day hasn't ended yet. Ugh."

"Ugh, like I hate mushrooms?"

"If only. No, ugh, like I have another meeting. Can you take me to the police station? They need to interview me, apparently." Chad's eyes widened.

"Of course. For real though?" He was smiling, but there were lines around his mouth.

He probably thinks I'm some kind of criminal. "Yeah, unfortunately for real. It's probably not a big deal, but Dad says I have to go. So then..."

Chad shook his head. "Okay. I'll take you. Is this about the dogs? Word travels fast."

Dorie shook her head. "No, I expect it's about BARC. I told you about the police at the office this morning." She sighed loudly. "I don't know anything though, so I probably won't be there long." *I hope those aren't my famous last words.*

He pushed up his glasses. "If you're going to be busy, I'll take Frou into St. Stephen. I'm going to try to smuggle him into the hospital. Nan would love to see him."

"That is a great idea. More adventure. It makes me even more sad about having to go see the police," she mourned. "Starving sad."

"Yeah. It's too bad. Sorry you're so hungry."

Her insides were screaming for pizza. Well, honestly, for anything that was food at this point. She rummaged through her jacket pockets looking for something other than dog treats. *No, I'm not desperate enough to eat desiccated liver treats. Not yet.*

"Have you got anything to eat in this truck?" she asked. "I'm way beyond empty."

He opened the glove compartment. "No, not really. You can dig around in here. Sometimes there's an energy bar or something." She poked around but to no avail.

"Well, the cops are going to get the nasty me," she said. "I don't do well with starvation."

"There's a nasty Dorie? I can't imagine," Chad pulled up outside the police station. "Although you were pretty feisty with that Big Guy out at Sarah's house."

"Feisty? I like that. It's better than mouthy, which is the word my father would use."

He grinned at her. "I hope you get out of the pokey fast. How will you get home?"

"Dad will come, no worries." Dorie paused. "Thanks for everything today. I was really looking forward to having a normal Friday night."

"With me?" His face lit up.

"Yes. With you and with food, for certain." When Chad's face fell a bit, she corrected, "Yes, with you. Almost like a date, right?"

"Almost like a date."

His smile was warm, and he looked so hopeful she wanted to hug him. Instead, she said, "After you sneak Frou into the hospital to see his mum, will you call me? I want to hear about it."

"Why don't you call me instead? I'm not the one who's going to get thrown in jail. I might need to be your one phone call."

"Very funny. I hope this is not a big deal, but things are so weird at the office, who knows. If you don't call me, I'll call you. Bye for now."

In front of the district RCMP office in downtown Stella Mare, Dorie waved Chad and Frou-Frou off into their evening. In her imagination, their night was pizza-filled. She sighed deeply as she pulled the heavy door toward her.

Stepping toward the uniformed man behind a heavy clear barricade at the desk, she said, "Dorie Madison. Apparently, somebody here wants to talk to me."

"Have a seat, Ms. Madison."

She didn't wait long on the uncomfortable chair before a familiar woman called for her to come through a heavy door.

"Hi, Dorie," Constable Doiron said. They sat on hard wooden chairs in a room complete with a mirror that was obviously not an actual mirror. Constable Doiron had a clipboard and pen.

Dorie kept her mouth firmly shut. *If she wants to talk to me, she can start.*

"Genevieve Doiron. We met this morning, of course. I'm investigating the allegations of fiscal mismanagement at BARC. I thought you owned the Pampered Pooch. I didn't know you were working at BARC."

"Oh, the Pooch. Yes. Were you a customer?" Dorie looked more closely at Genevieve's face.

"No, but I was planning to give my mother a gift certificate at Christmas," Genevieve admitted. "She's got a shih tzu who needs continual care, and I hate having her drive to St. Stephen in the winter. I'm sorry you closed your business."

Dorie wondered for a moment where this was going. "Yes, I closed in September. Started working for BARC about six weeks ago. I used to volunteer."

Genevieve looked interested. "You got threats last week, right? Was that you?"

"Yes, I guess I shot my mouth off in the wrong place. People don't like it when you call them out, you know?"

"I have heard that. Have you had any other threats?"

Dorie shook her head. "No, not directly. I did overhear a couple of guys in the grocery store talking about dog do-gooders who needed to mind their own business. But that could be anyone, really. Oh, and some guys wrote nasty stuff in the dust on my father's van, in the parking lot at the trailhead. They were trying to break in but didn't mind leaving their handwriting."

"How did you know they were trying to break in?"

"Well, the crowbar was a clue."

Genevieve's lips twitched. "Did you report that?"

"No. They ran off before anything much happened, and ultimately it was just a nasty message written in the dirt."

"In light of the other threats, I would have expected you to take it more seriously," Genevieve commented. "Why didn't you let us know?"

"Well, it didn't seem like a big deal. Except the guys in front of the office, that felt scary. But they told me to just apologize and keep it quiet."

"Who told you to keep it quiet?"

"My boss, Andrea. And her boss, Charles Barrett."

Genevieve's eyes narrowed. "Right. Tell me about your work with BARC. And Andrea Chase."

"Um, what do you want to know? I started volunteering for BARC about eighteen months ago. Mostly I wanted to go out on calls when we had tips about animal cruelty. BARC doesn't do much of that now. I was kind of like Andrea's sidekick for a time. Andrea runs the show. She's been there for years." *Since she was about my age.* Dorie thought uncomfortably of the photo of Andrea draped in Old Mr. Barrett's arm.

Genevieve sat silently. Dorie fidgeted with her jacket. "Um, what else?"

"How do things work at BARC? Who does the banking?"

"Banking? Not me. I assume it's Andrea or Young Mr. Barrett."

"Young Mr. Barrett?" Genevieve was taking notes.

"Yes. The son of Old Mr. Barrett, but he's not young. Only in Stella Mare, right? Mr. Barrett hired me. He's the board chair. I don't do anything about money."

Except try to educate potential donors about the need for BARC's services. And Andrea thinks I should be learning about fundraising. I really hate that stuff.

"Dorie, what computer do you use for your work with BARC?"

"My laptop, mostly, although when things are busy, I'm more likely to use my phone. Why?"

"Can I see your phone now?" Genevieve held out her hand. Dorie suddenly felt wary. She looked at her phone; that seemed a little bit invasive.

"No, I don't think so," she said uncertainly. "Why do you want it?" She remembered with a flush the pictures of her dancing with that long-haired guy at the club last week.

"Dorie, we can get a warrant for your laptop and phone. Don't worry about your social media accounts. We already have access to those. Did you deposit ten thousand dollars into your chequing account on Wednesday morning?"

"What? I wish!" *Ten thousand dollars?* "I don't have one hundred dollars. I can barely buy coffee. I was supposed to get paid yesterday, but I've been so busy I haven't even checked," she said, looking at her phone. "Hold on, I'll show you." She tapped at the home screen and opened up her online banking.

Dorie scrolled back a few days and stopped. She stopped breathing, too.

"Holy cow. Holy cow." She looked up at Genevieve. "Ten thousand dollars. I had no idea."

"Can I see your phone?" Genevieve held out her hand again, and this time Dorie handed her the phone.

"I didn't do that. I didn't even know it was there. I would have had lunch today if I realized there was money. It's been a really weird week, you know."

Genevieve looked at the phone in her hand. "You know how this looks."

Dorie scowled. "It looks like I'm an idiot. If someone is trying to make it look like I've been stealing from BARC, they're assuming I'm a moron, depositing the money in my personal chequing account."

Genevieve laughed. "I can tell you that at the moment, you're not under suspicion of stealing from your employer. But I do need some other information from you."

Ha! The secret to sneaking your grandmother's dog into the hospital is to act like you're not sneaking at all. Chad walked through the hospital halls with Frou proudly by his side. *I deserve an acting award, and Frou too.* Chad pulled open the door of Alice's room.

"Hi, Nan," Chad whispered. Alice turned her head and smiled. "I brought you a surprise."

Frou-Frou began to wiggle from nose to the tip of his tail. "Oh, Frou-Frou!" Alice's voice was a little creaky. "Good boy!" The dog danced around Chad's feet: Chad lifted him up so he could put his paws on the edge of Alice's bed. Frou sniffed her fingers.

"Oh, Chad. Thank you," Alice snuffled. "I can't really move that hand very well. Can you help me?" Chad's chest felt squeezed. She couldn't move her hand? That wasn't good.

Holding Frou in one arm, he reached over to put Alice's hand on top of the dog's curly head. Holding his hand on top of hers, he felt her cool, papery skin. Poor Nan. It was awful that she couldn't yet pet her dog.

Frou-Frou was undisturbed. He hadn't slowed down his wiggling and wagging a bit, despite being gripped between Chad's elbow and chest. Chad would have sworn he was smiling, grinning, really. "I think Frou's pretty happy, Nan."

Alice was also smiling, though her smile wasn't as even as it once was. "He's not the only one," she murmured.

Steps sounded in the hallway, and Chad glanced over his shoulder. "I don't think dogs are allowed to visit here, Nan. We just marched in like we owned the place, but I think we only got away with it because it's night."

"So glad to see you both," Alice said again. "Ida Mae was here, but that woman, what a gossip. All she talks about is what's wrong with everybody in town. Tell me something good."

"I'm not sure good is the word for it, but I did spend most of the day with Dorie Madison."

Alice smiled fondly. "Dorie. Nice girl."

"Messy business though. We rescued a bunch of sick dogs from an old house out in the Settlement." Looking at Nan's face, he could see it was not as mobile as usual, but she still looked interested. "Yep. We picked up seven little mutts. Their owner was sick, going to hospital. We got yelled at by some big guy on a motorcycle."

Alice's eyes widened. "Exciting stuff."

"Dorie called it an adventure. It wasn't what I'd expected."

They were quiet for a moment, while Frou-Frou nuzzled at Alice's cheek. "Frou would like to lie down with you, but maybe he'd better not," Chad said.

"Better not," Alice agreed.

"You're doing better, the doc said."

She gave a half smile, and Chad realized with a start that only half of her face could smile.

Her voice was stronger though, as she said, "I am doing better. I'm getting out of here."

Chad nodded. "That what they told me, too. Monday you go to the rehab center for a week or even less."

"Less."

"Okay. Less depends on how fast you recover, right?"

"Less."

Chad laughed. "I know you're determined. So yes, less than a week. Then we go back home."

"Right."

"I'm staying in Stella Mare until we get you all set up. Right now, I'm heading back and you're going to get some sleep, right?"

"Right," she said, her voice weakening. She was looking pale and fatigued.

Time for me to go. "I'll come back in the morning. I won't be able to bring the dog, but I'll be here." He leaned in to kiss her soft cheek, and Frou licked her hand again. "Good night, Nan."

She smiled, a little wan. "Good night to both of my boys."

"Oh, come on," Chad complained. "Don't I get more credit than the dog?"

Alice brushed him away with her good hand. "Go on with you. Good night."

In the truck before heading out, Chad texted Dorie. *How you doing? Everything okay?*

He wondered how long she'd been at the police station. Sure, it could be about the BARC finances, but they could also be looking into the dog-fighting stuff. Well, he could tell them a thing or two. He wondered if Dorie would be honest about what they'd heard and seen at the house that day. She might be a little scared of those guys. Chad didn't mind admitting he had been put off, but boy, when Dorie got scared, she got feisty. He smiled as he thought about her response that afternoon, sticking up her chin and talking right back to that goon.

No response came to his text, but then the sound of powerful engines caught his attention as four big motorcycles roared into the hospital parking lot. One of the riders jumped off to race toward the entrance. The others were more leisurely as they parked and leaned on their bikes, taking off helmets and chatting. Chad shrunk into his seat and surreptitiously lowered his window. It was cold, but sound traveled. He might be able to hear what they were saying. He was pretty sure he recognized one of the men. In fact, he'd just seen him a few hours before. Beside him, Frou-Frou growled deep in his throat.

"S'okay, Frou," Chad whispered. "Let's just listen."

One of the men lit a cigarette. "How long we gonna hang out here? I got places to go, man."

Another man kicked his boot at the speaker. "Yeah, right. Have some respect. Richie's mother is dying in there."

The third man shook his head. "Happens. Old people die. Young people too, for that matter." *Yep, that's him. The Big Guy from Sarah's house.*

The first man moved restlessly. Chad watched out of the corner of his eye and strained to hear the conversation. "This ain't getting me nowhere. Friday night and nothing going down? I didn't sign up for this." He dropped his cigarette on the pavement and twisted it out with his boot. "You with me, Smitty? This stinks."

The second guy—Smitty, apparently—shrugged. "Let's give Rich a little while. We have plenty of time. Mac's gonna bring the dogs and we'll meet them at the fight. No need to get all worked up. It's early yet."

Chad held his phone in front of his face so it looked like he was scrolling, if anybody should look his way, and peered around the side to see the trio.

A dog fight. Tonight?

This could be a chance to collect evidence against Richie and his buddies for animal cruelty. Catching dog handlers in flagrante delicto was the only way to get convictions. Why wasn't Dorie texting back?

Wouldn't she be impressed if he could get this evidence? Film at eleven, he thought excitedly. *Do I have a decent camera in this truck? I always have a decent camera.* His stomach tightened in anticipation.

Cigarette Guy lit up again. "Okay, I can wait a little while. We just need to meet up at the site, right?"

Big Guy stretched. "I'm gonna go see how things are going with the old lady," he said. "You stick around though. Keep an eye out." He gestured to the street.

Cigarette Guy scoffed. "For what? Nothing going on here."

Big Guy walked closer to Cigarette Guy and dropped his voice. Chad squinted and strained his hearing, but it was just a mumble of irritated voices. He looked at Frou-Frou, whose ears were cocked. "I bet you got all of that," he muttered irritably. "Too bad you can't write it all down." Frou sighed, turned around three times, and settled down on the passenger seat.

Dorie, please respond!

Oh, hey, Chad. I just got my phone back. How's Alice?

Good. But listen, I think I have a line on a dog fight. I'm going to try to follow this up, get video.

What? That's dangerous. Don't even think about it. Call the police.

No, no way. I don't have anything to tell them. I can't believe YOU are saying to call the police.

Can I come with you?

No, no way. I'm at the hospital right now anyway.

He thought for a moment. *I'm going to set it up so you can track my phone location though. Okay?*

Yes, good. Do it.

He suddenly realized what that would mean. Dorie would almost certainly track him down. That wasn't okay. Y*ou are NOT to come after me. Got it?*

Yeah. Got it. How long before I should call out the Mounties?

You know what? Never mind. I'll be okay.

Chad.

Chad!

He turned off his phone, deciding he didn't want her walking into trouble. She was good at finding it. He just didn't know if she was good at getting out of it.

Dorie fumed. This man was going to be the end of her. What was he thinking! Furious, she stomped out of the police station. When she looked up, her father's van was waiting for her.

"Well?"

She clambered in.

"Well, daughter, this is the first time I ever had to pick one of my children up from the police station," James joked. Then he got a good look at her. "Dorie. You look terrible."

"Thanks, Dad. It's exactly how I feel. I smell terrible too, and I'm more tired than I think I've ever been in my life."

Her father turned the van toward home. "Let's get you home. It'll be okay, whatever it is."

She leaned against the back of the seat, feeling the prickle of tears. "Thanks." *Thanks for not giving me the third degree. Thanks for just being here.*

By the time they arrived at the house, she had composed herself. "Dad, I want to tell you about, well, everything, but I have to have a shower first. Can you make me a sandwich or something? Please?"

"I'll do better than that. Go on, get in the shower. You're pretty disgusting right now."

She looked down at her shirt and jeans, covered in dog hair and who knows what else. "I don't even know if these clothes can be redeemed. Thanks."

She grabbed a garbage bag from the kitchen and stripped her clothes directly into it. Climbing into the steamy shower, she finally relaxed for the first time in hours. As her shoulders dropped, her thoughts went straight to Chad. *Why does he have to do this tonight? I'm so freaking tired.*

Hot water, shampoo, soap. *Oh, this feels so good!* By the time she toweled off and pulled on clean clothes, she could even think a little better.

James had reheated pizza. "Oh, my goodness, Dad, what is that? Pepperoni? I don't think anything ever smelled so good."

"Have a seat. There's plenty. No need to wolf it down, daughter. I'm not going to let you starve."

"Dad, you won't believe the day I've had. The week, really. The cops wanted to talk to me about finances at BARC and they've frozen my personal account as well as the BARC accounts."

James frowned. "That's why they wanted to talk to you? You've been a person of interest?"

"Dad! This is not a mystery story. But yes, that's what the cops wanted."

"Hmm," James sounded curious. "Frozen your bank account?"

"Well, that would be because somebody put ten thousand dollars in my account on Wednesday."

"Whoa. I should have made you pay for the pizza. What's going on?"

She shook her head. "No idea. Andrea's been missing for half the week, the police ransacked our office, the board chair doesn't answer the phone, I spent the day rescuing old, sick, dirty dogs, and I think there's fighting dogs being held at the house, too."

"Dog fighting. You mean your speculation might have some facts behind it?"

Dorie shrugged. "No real evidence yet. I mean, there was the site where we got the brindle and lost all those other dogs, but the police apparently didn't link it to anything else."

"How do you know what the police have done? Guesswork?"

"Well, yeah, it is. I haven't seen anything in the news or heard anything on the grapevine. Maybe the police do have some ideas, but I don't know."

"Why would anyone put ten grand in your account, Dorie? I wonder whose money it is." James seemed to be mildly curious. Dorie wondered if she would ever be as calm as her father. She herself was wild with wondering.

"It's crazy. I have no idea. Somebody wanted to make it look like I was stealing so they could get away with it."

James lifted his eyebrows. "Hmm, this is like a movie mystery. That Andrea? She drives a pretty nice car."

"Oh, I hate the idea that Andrea might be a thief. She really, truly wants to take good care of dogs."

"Those things aren't mutually exclusive. She might have good intentions but not be able to help herself. You never know."

You never know, Dorie repeated to herself. "I think Andrea is too smart to try to make me look guilty that way."

James laughed. "I suspect your average criminal isn't too heavy on brains. But I agree. I've talked to Andrea and she's too bright for a dumb cover-up like that."

"The other thing is that she's missing in action. She's not been in the office since Monday, and I can't get any answer from her phone. I think the police are checking into that."

"And you know this because?"

"Well, I told them tonight. Genevieve Doiron."

"Right. Rene's girl. I went to school with her father. Nice family."

"Aren't they all?"

James didn't respond. Then he changed the subject. "That pizza hit the spot?"

She sat back, hand against her stomach. "Oh, yeah. I feel a lot better."

"Are you ready to hear some bad news?" James asked. Dorie's heart sank. *What else?*

"Sure. Whatever." She steeled herself.

"It's the brindle."

"Oh, right. She's been crated all day. Sorry, Dad. I went to work at seven and things just got crazy from there."

James nodded. "I understand that. I did try to take her out for a walk, but she's bad match for a leash. Instead, I just put her out in the backyard for a while with the galoots. When I went out to get them, the brindle was gone. The gates were closed. I saw her try to jump the fence and she couldn't, so I'm pretty sure someone took her."

"Oh, geez, Dad. Stolen?" Dorie felt bits of the story lining up. "Did I tell you about the guys trying to break into your van when she was in it? Yeah, that was on Wednesday. I scared them off. They wrote stupid stuff in the dust, but they were also playing around with a crowbar."

"Could be related."

Dorie scrunched up her face. "I hope they're being decent to her. She's been through a lot. Poor little girl. She was just getting used to living in a family."

"Yep. She was settling in nice here. I put her picture on my social media page and got a lot of unpleasant comments on her breed, but no sightings."

"People can be so ignorant. She could be such a nice dog. I wonder what happened?"

James shook his head. "It's possible the real owners took her, especially if they're trying to stay under the police radar. I don't think the neighbours are too likely to take a dog from our yard. They know that the dog population in this house changes regularly."

"Yeah, plus the brindle is not a breed that appeals to everyone. I'll let Mike know at the rescue center, and I'm pretty sure Animal Control already knew we were fostering her. Darn it. I'm sorry I was gone all day like that, Dad."

"It's your job, I guess, Dorie. How about some sleep?"

Dorie felt her eyes start to close at the very thought. "No, can't do that. Not yet. Chad—you know, Chad? He's out tracking down a dog fight. Gathering evidence, he says."

"I am surprised. I didn't see that boy as overly adventurous," James said. "But good for him."

"Dad! This is dangerous stuff. What do you mean, good for him? You'd hate it if I were out there."

"Correct. That, daughter dear, is the double standard in action. I don't want you in danger, but I like to see your boyfriend willing to step up."

Dorie scowled at him. "Not my boyfriend."

"And why not? He's obviously trying to impress you."

"Dad, do you think I need a boyfriend? I've got the cops breathing down my neck, I have no idea what's up with my job, I've taken on a houseful of rescue dogs (did I tell you that part?) and now my friend—my friend, not my boyfriend—is getting himself in some sort of trouble. I don't have time for a boyfriend."

James sipped his cup of tea.

The silence prompted Dorie to explain. "He helped me all afternoon, getting those dogs. Yesterday, he went out to the Settlement to help me take food to them."

Nodding, James sipped again. Dorie stood up from the table and walked around the kitchen. "He's been pretty worried about his grandmother, but he's still been helping."

"Uh-huh," James agreed. "Kind of a nice guy, would you say?"

She sighed deeply. "Yes, a very nice guy. Only a dumb guy, because he's planning to try to video a dog fight tonight, where there might be organized crime and people with weapons and knives, and all sorts of dangerous stuff."

"Worried?"

"Well, a little. He was going to let me track him with his phone." *But he realized I'd never stay at home if I could follow him. He knows me better than I think.*

"And?"

"Yeah. He changed his mind about that. So, I have no way to find him. It's like the brindle, out there somewhere and probably in danger, and I can't do anything. For either of them." Dorie sighed and sat back down. "Dad, I hate this. I like to be the one in the know, not the one hanging around waiting to find out."

"Sounds like Chad knows this about you. I can appreciate his thinking."

"Oh, Dad. I don't put myself in needless danger. I told Chad he should call the police." She tried to take calming breaths, but her mind refused to settle. “Okay, I just can’t sit here. I'm going to see if I can find him. Them. Either the dog or the guy. I just can't stay here.” She jumped up and hugged James around the neck. “I love you, Dad. Thanks for feeding me.”

“Dorie,” he started.

“No, Dad, I'm going.”

“Okay. You’re an adult. But first, set me up to see your location on the phone. I’m going to call out the cavalry if you don't come back.”

“You mean the RCMP, right?” She grinned at him, already feeling better.

“Somebody. Or I could sic your sisters on you,” he teased. “Stay out of trouble, Dorie. Really.”

“I'll do my best, Dad, but it isn't really something I do naturally.”

Chapter 14

Chad had surreptitiously followed the motorcyclists out of the parking lot. At least, he thought he was surreptitious. He eased out of the parking spot after they exited the lot and turned in the same direction.

Fortunately, the night was cold and quiet, and he could hear the motorcycles even if he didn't follow them closely enough to see them. He followed along a twisty, convoluted route that took him out of town.

Turn off the headlights. They're going to see me on this dark, quiet road. Oops, nope. The moon was bright enough to make shadows, but every shadow looked like a moose or deer with the truck's headlights off. Hitting a large mammal was likely more dangerous than if these guys thought he was behind them. He turned his headlights back on and hoped for the best.

He drove as far behind them as he could while still hearing them. When he suddenly realized the motorcycle engine noises had ceased, he stopped his truck. With all the windows down, Chad and Frou-Frou inched along the country road. *Oh, there was light, over there behind those trees. Yes, a building, an old farm building. No cars though, and no motorcycles.* He pulled the truck over to the side of the road. *Well, at least the police will know I was here*. He patted the truck body. *This might be my last signal*.

Frou jumped out of the truck too. "No, buddy, you have to stay here," he whispered to the dog. "Guard the truck. Bring the Mounties if I need them." Frou appeared to listen carefully. Chad wished the dog really could understand. Why was he doing such a dumb and potentially dangerous thing? To impress Dorie? She wouldn't be impressed if he was dead. But he didn't really think dead was a likely outcome. He was in this far, so he might as well see it through. Checking for his pocket video camera, he set off.

Back in the truck, Frou whined softly. Chad turned to him and held up one finger. *Stay*.

Crunching through dead grass and broken branches, he approached the building. As he got closer, he heard shouting and smelled smoke, cigarettes, and weed. *No music, or it would sound like a party. Like the kind high school kids had when there were no parents around.* Chad tried to remember if he had ever been to such a party. *Well, no time like the present. Gotta start somewhere. I can act like I was invited.*

As he got closer to the building, he lifted his head and straightened his shoulders. *Yep, I belong right here.* He pushed the door open. *Like I own the place.* He stopped suddenly with a catch in his breath.

A very large man blocked his way. His huge forearms were folded across his chest and his massive jaw jutted into Chad's face.

"Hey," Chad offered. No response. He tried again. "Uh, is Richie here? He told me to come."

The man squinted at him. "Richie invited you?"

"Uh, yeah. His mom..."

The big man's face changed. "Yeah, his mom. Okay, yeah. Come on in." He stepped aside. Chad finally took a real breath as he looked around the space.

The space felt huge, larger than it looked from the outside. The ceiling was lost in darkness, and the only light seemed to be concentrated on the right, where there was a noisy crowd. Chad eased toward the left, sliding behind small clusters of people, mostly men. *Take a moment. Figure this out.* Leaning against the wall, he settled his breath and got his camera in place.

A dog whined close by, making him jump. Dog crates, right next to him. Well, at least one big crate. Squatting down, he peered inside. As his eyes adjusted to the dark, he recognized yellow eyes.

Chad whispered to the dog. "Oh, it's you. What the heck? How did you get here?" The brindle Dorie had taken in whined again and tried to lick his fingers.

This is just weird. The crowd roared suddenly, making him jump to his feet. He moved gingerly toward the lighted side.

Nope, no sneaking. Act like I belong here. Like I was invited. He lifted his head and strode with confidence toward the crowd. *It worked at the hospital.*

Look at this. Just like in the movies. Really? Like a boxing ring, only there's dogs in there? He moved closer, checking his camera.

Behind him the brindle barked once, but the sound was swallowed up in the general din. Chad continued to move toward the crowd, cradling his camera. *Hopefully, I look like I broke my arm or something. That way, maybe nobody will break my arm for real.*

As he got closer to the crowd, he realized that he'd just missed a fight. The noise was settling a bit, and men were talking, mingling, in a room full of smoke and harsh smells. Blood dotted the floor, some ropes and hooks on long metal poles slid around, and a couple of guys were dragging away a dog's body. Across the circle, there was a happy-looking crowd, and Chad noticed money changing hands. *Oops! There's the Big Guy from Sarah's house. Looks like he's on the winning side.* Chad ducked away from the circle, turning his face back toward the entrance. The massive dude at the door was still there. *Still ready to beat me up and throw me out. Why am I here?*

Right. Documentation of dog fighting. Too bad I just missed that match, but the gore and the money should be sufficient.

There seemed to be a lull for the moment, so he moved back toward the dusky periphery, staying vigilant and keeping the camera running. The crowd was clearly waiting for another event, and somebody was making announcements near the center of the ring. *This is like prizefighting, or boxing, or something.* He scanned the crowd. *Not all rough. Not all men, either. Some women, some suits. This whole thing, it's weird.*

He felt a little better seeing the mix of people, because he didn't stick out like the proverbial sore thumb. Camera in one hand, he dug his phone out of his pocket with the other. Turning it on, he quickly gave Dorie access to his location, then sent a text. *Your brindle girl is here. Don't answer.*

He looked up from his phone to see the Massive Dude from the door standing over him with his hand out.

"No phones."

"What? What do you mean?" He slipped his phone into his jeans pocket and shrugged deeper into his jacket, covering the camera.

"No phones. Don't use your phone in here. I'll break it if you do. Or I'll break you."

"Yeah, okay. Got it. My first time. No problem."

Massive Dude glared again and headed back to the door. *Whew! It's a good thing he didn't make me take off my jacket. Now I really want to make sure I get some decent film here.*

Chad rearranged his jacket and the camera again. The crowd was gathering around the circle and the noise level increased. Moving in, Chad saw the next contenders coming in. The announcer whipped the crowd into a frenzy. *Hmm, people have favourites.* A tall, dark man came from the darkness into the light of the ring with his heavily muscled Doberman, snapping and snarling at the end of a chain. *Is that dog an actor? Like WWF? Or is that for real?* Chad's stomach turned liquid at the sight of the dog's huge white teeth. *I never saw a dog like that. Dorie would freak.*

The other contender leaped in. The handler was thick and strong, rusty-haired and bearded, holding the chain with both hands. The dog was a reddish, taut, dense bundle of bull terrier aggression, snapping and growling. *Those dogs look like their handlers. Do they do this on purpose?*

This is a show for sure. Chad and his camera watched the crowd, screaming for action. The two handlers were grim-faced, as snarly as their dogs, and the announcer was inciting the crowd. The Doberman leaped to the end of his chain, and the bull terrier leaped back.

What on earth happens to those dogs to make them behave that way? Chad thought of the brindle, tough to like at the beginning, but not aggressive like this. *This isn't normal dog behaviour. I guess Dorie would know. It's going to be ugly.*

At a signal from the announcer, the handlers released their dogs into a snarling, growling, twisting tangle. Horrified, he watched, unable to breathe, until someone grabbed his shoulder and yanked him around. His jacket fell to the floor.

"You! What are you doing here?" Big Guy demanded. "You little..." He smacked Chad's hand and knocked the camera to the floor. Massive Dude from the doorway appeared.

"I thought this one was trouble," Massive Dude said. "I've got him."

"Hold on a minute," Chad squeaked as he was dragged into the darkness. He saw Big Guy pick up his video camera. "Leave that alone!" he tried to shout, but the dude gave him a shake and tossed him against the concrete wall. *Ugh, that hurt.* He slid to the floor.

"You don't listen," the dude said and kicked Chad in the ribs. Lungs on fire, ribs singing in pain, Chad tried to get up and away, but the overhead lights flashed on, and the dude disappeared. Suddenly, there was shouting through a bullhorn and the room was overrun by uniformed police. Chad sighed in relief. *Excellent timing, guys. That was close.*

"Stop! Don't move. Call off those dogs!" A mad scramble ensued. Chad pushed himself to his feet, gasping with the pain, and pulled out his phone to capture the melee. *Any camera is better than no camera.* Beyond the crowd rushing for the exit, the dog handlers were trying to separate the fighters. Massive Dude was being restrained by two uniformed officers, and the air pulsed with sirens.

Chad limped closer to the animal ring, clutching his side, phone pointed toward the action. There were pistol shots, loud, in quick succession. The dogs, still in a death grip and bleeding copiously, went down. The air was thick with the smell of blood and feces. Chad was rapt.

The pistol was held by a woman wearing an Animal Control jacket. The two dog handlers shouted something, and all three moved quickly toward the animals, with Chad close behind. On the way to the ring, his foot kicked something—his camera. He snagged it with one hand and kept his phone camera running with the other.

"You! Hey you, there." A uniformed officer grabbed his arm. "You, there, get over here in this line," the young constable ordered. "Give me that camera. And your phone, too."

"You bet," Chad agreed, handing them over. "Be careful. There's a lot of evidence in that little box."

The constable looked unimpressed. Finally exhaling, Chad allowed himself to be herded toward the cluster of people who were being held by the police. *Arrested. This is excellent.* Chad felt a flicker of satisfaction and a whole lot of relief. *My injuries are probably minor, I got some great footage, and I'm getting arrested. This is a very good night.* He might have been the only person in the place who was smiling. His ribs hurt like crazy, but he was still smiling.

He looked over his shoulder as he was being jostled out of the building. In the ring, the dogs were still on the floor. The Animal Control officer talked with the handlers and a uniformed officer waited for them. The rusty bull mastiff moved a little as the control officer pulled a muzzle over his face. *Oh, good. Tranquilized, not euthanized.* At the far end of the space, the brindle waited in her crate. Animal Control would take care of her for now.

Dorie was in the car heading to St. Stephen when Chad's text arrived. *Don't answer? Who does he think he's talking to?* She started to type her response but paused before hitting send. *Maybe he had a good reason. And what did he mean, the brindle was "there?" Where the heck is "there"?*

She pulled up the location finder and bingo, there was Chad's phone, on the outskirts of St. Stephen. Not time to call in the Mounties yet, she thought. *I'll go check things out first. At least now I have a direction to go in.*

Remembering her promise to her father, she sent James a quick picture of the map location. Then she stepped on the gas. The brindle needed her. Chad might need her, too.

She slowed down as she approached the general location. The winding nature of this road required slowing down, and it was late fall, moose and deer as likely on the road as anywhere else in the long night. Coming into an area of thinning trees, she was startled by a brightly lit building surrounded by police vehicles. But then her attention was caught by something right beside the road. *That truck looks like... It is! It's Chad's truck*. Dorie pulled in behind it, walking warily toward the passenger door. A stick cracked underfoot, and the night exploded with barking inside the truck.

"Frou-Frou!" She tugged on the door handle and it opened easily. Frou leaped out and bounced around her, nuzzling her fingers and exuding joy. "Geez, Frou, it's cold out here. How long were you waiting in that truck?" Dorie looked in to see a woolen blanket piled on the passenger seat. *Good. At least Frou was okay. Chad took care of that.*

Now Frou-Frou had a definite agenda, poking at Dorie's hands and her knees, and trotting toward the building then back to Dorie. "Yeah, I get you, Lassie," Dorie said irritably, "but you need a leash. There's a lot of people over there." Scrambling for a leash in the back of the truck, she looped it around him and they set off through the scant forest.

"Frou! Stop pulling. You never do that!" Dorie protested. Frou was insistent though, and soon Dorie was running to keep up with the poodle. As they broke out of the woods, she saw police cars, a police truck, and clusters of people, managed by uniformed officers. Frou broke loose from Dorie, leash flying behind, and dove into the largest cluster.

"Dorie! Dorie." She heard Chad's voice but couldn't see him in the crowd. She pushed closer. It was hard to sort out the details. A young guy in uniform stopped her.

"Keep back, miss. Where'd you come from, anyway?"

Dorie lifted her chin. "BARC prevention of cruelty to animals."

"Yeah, well, stay back. This is a controlled scene. Step away."

Annoyed, Dorie held back while the constable was watching, but pushed forward as soon as he turned to speak to another person. "Chad? Chad, is that you? Hey, Frou-Frou!"

Peering into the crush of people, she did see his face. Oh, his beautiful face. He was grinning from ear to ear. He pushed his way to the edge of the crowd.

"Dorie! I'm being arrested. Isn't that great?" Frou-Frou leaned on Chad's legs. Chad bent over to scratch his ears and groaned.

"Hey, you didn't even lock your truck. I stole your dog right out of it." She strained to be funny, but she was overcome with feelings. "Wait...are you hurt? Chad?"

He stood back up with effort, holding his side. "Nah, no big deal. Got banged around a little."

"Banged around! Your face is bruised. Your hand is bleeding!" She looked him over. "What else? Holy cow, Chad. What happened?"

Chad scoffed. "It's okay."

"I am so glad to see you." Her voice caught in her throat. Unaccountably, her eyes watered. *Again. When am I going to stop crying at everything? This is embarrassing.*

"Oh, now, everything's fine," Chad's voice grew warm. He reached across the police tape to hold her hand. "I got some really great video, too."

"Chad," Dorie started.

"Scary as anything, Dorie. Big nasty-looking guys and then the dogs, well, I'm glad you weren't there."

"Chad. Why? Why did you do this?" She held on to his hand with both of hers. It felt so good to hold on to him, to feel his warmth and see his excitement about the video. She couldn't believe he'd been out here all alone, getting banged up by bad guys. She didn't want to let go, not ever.

"Well. It's a story that needs to be told, right?" His eyes held hers and she leaned closer, gazing at his lips.

"Break it up." The constable who had spoken to her earlier stepped up. Frou growled mildly. "We're going to the detachment. Get into the truck."

"Hey, Officer," Dorie demanded. "He needs medical assistance."

The officer came closer while Chad scoffed again. "Nah, I'm okay."

The officer scowled. "I'll have the medic look at you over by the truck. Go on." He headed off, herding other people toward the vehicle.

Chad grinned at Dorie and shrugged. "They're taking me to the detachment. I might even have to stay in jail. That's so cool."

"I'm glad you think it's cool. I don't think it's very cool. Don't you want to come home?"

Chad was still grinning. "It's part of the story. The story of getting the story. Don't worry, I'll get home. Can you lock my truck? I'll pick it up when they finish processing me." He handed her the leash, still attached to Frou, and his keys.

Dorie and Frou-Frou watched as he got a cursory look-over by a medic, then loaded into the back of the police wagon along with some others. Chad waved as he climbed aboard. Then the door clanged shut.

She gazed at the mass of vehicles. One ambulance. Police cars, marked and unmarked, yes. And yes, there was the Animal Control van. Maureen was talking to someone nearby. Dorie and Frou trotted over to her.

"Hey, Maureen. Big night?"

Maureen looked surprised. "Dorie. What are you doing here?"

"Hey, Dorie," another voice said. Mike stepped from the side of the van.

"You guys," Dorie said with a laugh. "Animal Control and County Rescue working together. Two of my favourite people. How great is that?"

"We like to think we get along," Mike said with a smile. "But answer Maureen's question. What the heck are you doing here?"

"I had a tip that my foster dog was seen here. She was taken from my yard earlier today."

"Oh, right, you had the female brindle from the last episode," Mike recalled. He turned to Maureen. "I thought I recognized that dog. She's been at Dorie's since we got her from you, three weeks ago."

Maureen nodded. "She's crated and sedated right now, but you can pick her up from Mike in the morning. In the meantime, I've got a few more that have to go into evidence first, and then Mike will get them."

"Are they all okay?" Dorie asked.

"No, of course not. These dogs will probably never be okay. At least one died tonight, but we prevented a couple from killing each other. They're alive, but not really okay."

"So sad."

"Yes. I hope the police got enough evidence this time to shut these people down." Maureen sounded firm. "It's time. It's way past time."

"My friend had his video camera."

"Really? Chad?" Mike was grinning. "Good for him. He's got more going on than I realized. Jumped right in, didn't he?"

Dorie nodded. "Yes, I guess he did. Are you guys all set? Can I do anything?"

Maureen looked at Mike. "I think we've got it managed, thanks."

Mike patted Dorie's shoulder. "You've been doing dog stuff all day. Better get home."

As if given permission, Dorie's fatigue washed over her. "Yeah. Time for me to get home."

Mike answered. "We've got a few things to sort out, you and me, Dorie, so come by the rescue center about noon and I'll have the brindle there."

"Us? What do we have to sort out?" Before she stopped speaking, she remembered. "Oh, all those little dogs. It has been a really, really long day. Okay, Mike, I'll see you tomorrow. Bye, Maureen."

Dorie and Frou headed back toward her car. As police vehicles departed the scene, the light began to dim. Turning away to find her car, Dorie's eyes made a slow adjustment to the darkness of the woods at night. As the excitement faded, her shoulders dropped, her steps grew slow, and she stumbled through the thin woods. Frou, however, was as bouncy as ever.

"Oh, you. You slept all evening in the truck, you dog," she complained. "Come on, let's get home. You might be perky, but I need to sleep."

Chapter 15

When Dorie finally woke, stretched luxuriously, and wandered down the stairs, Frou-Frou greeted her exuberantly. So did her sisters, Corinne and Evie.

"Ah, here she is," Corinne called. "Coffee's here and we want to know everything."

Evie was sitting in the kitchen nursing a big mug, while Corinne was taking scones out of the oven.

Dorie grinned. "Geez, Corinne, you baked. At our house. What's the deal? And boy, do they smell great."

Corinne plopped a basket of warm blueberry scones on the table. "There you go, girls. Evie and I want to hear all about your day yesterday."

Dorie frowned. "Yesterday was the longest day of my life. What do you want to know? And why?" She poured coffee from the carafe on the table, spooned in sugar, and liberally added cream. Taking a sip, she closed her eyes in bliss. "Oh, that is so good. Thank you to whoever saved me some coffee."

Evie scoffed. "Saved it! We made it fresh for you. Now tell us what you were doing at the police station?"

"Oh, is that's what you want to know? Well, let's see if I can remember..." Dorie teased.

"Oh, come on," Evie demanded, and Corinne laughed.

"Where's Dad? He probably told you all this stuff, didn't he?" Dorie looked around for James.

"James got a call from your feller and went to pick him up in St. Stephen."

"Really? Chad?" Dorie felt a little shocked, but she retorted automatically, "He's not my feller. Why's he calling Dad?"

"He called the house line, Dore. That's all. Dad didn't want to wake you, so he went to pick him up."

"Oh, shoot." Dorie thought hard. "I've got the keys to his truck. I wish Dad had told me."

"No, actually, James has them," Corinne corrected. "Chad told him to check your coat pockets."

"Huh. All this going on while I'm asleep. Imagine." Dorie shrugged and bit into a scone. Okay for them. Chad didn't need her at all. He and Dad could just be buddies.

Evie laughed at her expression. "I swear you're jealous of Dad. That's hysterical."

"I am not!" Dorie protested. "Well, maybe I am a little. I would have liked to, you know, rescue him from the police."

"Oh, Dorie," Corinne said. "You'll probably have another chance. Well, not the police but something else."

"I guess." She applied herself to her food. "Oh, my gosh, what time is it? I've got somewhere to be at noon." She looked at the old clock ticking on the wall. "Thanks, you guys. I've got to get dressed and go." After tossing a kiss to Corinne, she headed back up the stairs at top speed.

"Wait! We want to know if you embezzled from BARC!" Evie shouted.

"Or if you are part of the organized crime ring that runs dog fights! Hey, Dorie! Inquiring minds want to know." Corinne was laughing so hard she could barely get the words out.

In her room, Dorie grinned as she threw on jeans and a sweatshirt. What a pair of goofs. But here they were, in her corner, more or less. Scones and coffee, at least. Tearing down the stairs, she grabbed jacket, keys, and a leash for Frou-Frou.

"You don't have to take the dog. I'm going to be here for a while," Evie said. "At least until Dad is back."

"No, I have to bring home the foster and Frou keeps her calm. Thanks though. Tell Dad I'll be home later in the afternoon."

She could have walked to the rescue center if she'd had more time, but the car would be easier with two dogs on the way back. Mike's dark van was no longer the only vehicle in the parking lot. Saturday mornings were biggest time for visitors and potential adoptive pet parents. Dorie went in through the front door with Frou-Frou, waved to the receptionist, and slipped through another door to Mike's office.

Reclined in his chair, feet on the desk, Mike sat with a shih tzu perched on his midsection. Dog and man were eye to eye, but both had their eyes closed. Dorie was very quiet, but Frou snuffled, and Mike's eyes opened.

"Dorie," he said. "Ah, sorry. Late night."

She grinned. "Yeah, I know. Only, unlike you, I didn't have to work this morning. I'm here to pick up the brindle, like you said."

Mike tucked the little dog under his arm and sat up in his chair. "Have a seat. We've got a couple things to talk about."

"Sure. Like what?"

"We're at capacity here, and that pack you and Chad picked up from the Settlement yesterday is pushing us over the edge. Doc Hadley checked them out, and of the seven we recovered, four have some severe health needs, even beyond malnutrition. Three are in pretty good shape, and could be traditionally adopted, but I hate to separate the pack."

"What are the options?"

"We don't have many. I don't have a foster home that will take seven dogs, even small dogs. Four of those dogs are going to require ongoing medical attention, and funds for that are, as you know, limited. Beyond that, Maureen has those dogs from last night. Some of them are likely to come our way."

"What will happen to them. Can they be rehabilitated?"

Mike shrugged. "Not by me, and not by anyone on our volunteer list. There are people who work with dogs that have been trained and treated that way, but we don't have a local connection. Besides that, they're evidence in a criminal case. We can't place them anywhere, even for rehab, unless and until their owners are convicted. Those dogs have owners."

"That doesn't sound good at all."

"It isn't. Those dogs could be euthanized as dangerous dogs, and that probably will happen to them. I sure wish there was a way to give them a chance."

"Is it funding? Is that the problem?"

Mike shook his head. "Not the only problem. Funds would help, but they wouldn't solve it. We need resources, human resources. We need places for old, unadoptable dogs, and we need places for poorly trained, poorly treated dogs, and we just don't have them."

"What's this got to do with me?" Dorie was curious.

"Well, you've had good results with that brindle. And you work for BARC. Andrea has sometimes found grant funds to help us with our special projects."

Dorie was stricken. "I'm not so sure I still work for BARC," she said slowly. "Have you talked to Andrea? Lately?"

"She's not answering. I thought you might know something."

"There's some mess going on at BARC. I don't get it, but there's shady money stuff and the police are involved. Now we've got a verified dog-fighting ring, and then there's those little sad mutts from Sarah's house. I almost can't keep track of everything going on. I know for sure that I haven't heard from Andrea since last Monday."

"A mystery, I guess," he said. "BARC's financial stuff is none of my business, but Andrea could be helpful to us. It's unfortunate she's unavailable."

"I'm kind of concerned. Something bad could have happened."

He shrugged. "You told the police. We just have to find some other sources of help for the dogs."

"Aren't you even curious about what's going on?" she asked.

"Not my business." He shook his head. "If there was something I could do, I would do it. But right now I have a responsibility to these dogs."

"Right. Okay, I'll try to curb my nosey nature and focus on the dogs. I don't know what to do about Sarah's dogs. I wish I did." She hung her head. "I feel responsible for them. In a way, I was enabling the medical neglect by trying to help her feed them."

"No, I disagree. You couldn't do nothing, so you did what you could do. But it is a problem we see often. We've talked about this before. If you can come up with a solution for that, I want to know about it right away." He grinned at her, but she could tell it was a bit forced.

"I'd like to believe I can take them home, but we already have a houseful."

"Okay. I didn't think you'd be taking them home. But let's go get your foster dog. You can look in on Sarah's pack, too, if you like." He led the way down the hall. "Keep thinking about what we can do. We may just need to get very creative about this."

Getting the brindle leashed was easy with Frou-Frou beside her. Dorie got both dogs into the car, gave them chew toys to entertain them, and headed back home. Her mind swirled. So much information. So many unrelated and peculiar circumstances. Her mind wanted to make them all fit together like a neat puzzle, but that just didn't work. Alice having a stroke wasn't related to Sarah having to leave her home and dogs. Fostering the brindle wasn't related to somebody putting money in her bank account. Andrea missing wasn't related to goons threatening her and BARC online and at the office. Or was it? None of it made any sense.

The one thing that did make sense in the whole catastrophe was Chad. Chad who put himself on the line for dogs and maybe even for her. *I hope he's really okay. He could have been hurt badly.*

Driving home, she recalled his loyalty to his grandmother, his excitement of last night, the way his T-shirt fit snugly over his shoulders. *He's been such a good guy, all along. Well, except that first date.* She tried to put that unfortunate experience out of her mind. *He's pretty cute, too, and now the cops might finally end dog fighting. Because of Chad.*

She was shocked to realize it had only been six weeks since that catastrophic first date. *So long ago, but not really long at all. But I feel so different now.* Dorie wondered if she would even recognize herself if that pampering pooches party girl showed up today.

While that girl might think Chad was awkward and boring and maybe even predictable, this woman, she realized now, knew better.

Predictably reliable. That was a good kind of predictable. Nobody else in her life ever showed up for her the way Chad had done last night. She got a little weepy when she remembered his excitement about having the video evidence to end the dog-fighting ring. Of course, whether that was true wasn't up to them. Chad took her seriously, took her concerns seriously. Plus, his grandmother was the sweetest lady, and Frou-Frou had become like part of Dorie's family. Frou-Frou and the brindle, along with Mallow and Custard.

Hmm. Dorie wondered whether James could tolerate a few more dogs. Sarah's pack really did need a caring home. She imagined her father's face, then imagined telling her sisters that she'd just added seven more dogs to the mix. Seven geriatric dogs. No, there would have to be another solution. She was grateful that Mike understood her father's limits.

When she got home, James's truck was in the yard and Corinne's car was gone. The brindle took a little while to sniff her way around in the kitchen, but soon enough she located her dog bed and settled down. She'd only been gone about twenty-four hours, Dorie calculated, but it could have been a very hard time. The poor pup had been through lots in her young life.

"Hi, Dad." Frou bounded from the kitchen to James's side in the living room.

"Frou-Frou!" James was happy to see the dog, who made himself at home at James's feet. He was now a dog of many homes, Dorie thought fondly.

"Yes, say hi to Frou. And Dorie," she prompted her father.

James smiled at her. "Hi, Dorie. Big night last night."

"You saw Chad." She tried not to sound plaintive. "Those goons hurt him. How was he?"

"Fine, I guess. Nobody roughed him up in the clinker, if that's your worry," he teased.

"Dad!"

"No, really, he's tired, but okay. Said they didn't think his rib was broken, and no concussion. The RCMP understand he's not involved in the betting, so they're not pressing charges, but they kept his camera. I took him out to his truck. That was quite the crime scene. You got there after the Mounties, right?"

"I know that means you love me, Dad. Yes, the Mounties were already handling everything when I got there. Animal Control picked up our brindle girl there, but now she's home where she belongs."

"And so are you. For at least half an hour, I guess." James looked at her.

"Well, I was at home asleep for a long time. Evie and Corinne fed me, but I had to go downtown to get the dog."

James looked at her consideringly.

"What? You look like you want to say something. Go ahead," Dorie said. "I can take it."

James snickered. "It's not even about you. You know, your Chad is a good feller. The police might be able to put those nasty ones away for a long time, and hopefully it will end dog fighting entirely in this area."

Dorie nodded. *He's not my Chad. But I wish he were.*

James wasn't finished. "That boy is a good grandson, too. When I dropped him off, he was headed to the hospital to see Alice. He seems to have his head on straight."

She smiled at her father. "Yes, Dad, I like him too. He's a good one."

"Seems to be. Too bad he's in Saint Jacques, but you know."

Dorie frowned. "What do you mean, 'you know'?"

"Love finds a way. That's what I mean."

She wore a full-on scowl now. "Nobody's talking about love. Just keep that idea to yourself, Dad."

His little half-smile irritated Dorie. "Why are you so prickly about this? It's not a sign of weakness to love somebody." He snickered. "Oh, I see by your expression that this conversation is over."

She tried to smooth her forehead. "I'm going to take Custard and Mallow out for a walk. A little everyday chore seems like the right thing for now. Some fresh air. Frou-Frou?"

Frou gave her a glance but settled in closer to James's feet. When she rattled the leashes, the big galoots meandered to the kitchen door, and the three of them jostled out into the cold, clear afternoon.

While driving from the hospital back to Stella Mare, Chad hummed a little tune. He had a lot to think about. His grandmother getting better, for one. The fact that he'd busted into a dog-fighting event and only got arrested. Well, that and a few bruises, like a badge of honour. The way the police were talking about his video footage, like it could bust the dog-fighting ring. The prizes his imagined documentary could win.

But the constant in all his thinking was one woman. Her grin, her quick retorts, her commitment to making life better for dogs. Most of all, though, was her face last night, seen through the filter of his own adrenaline excitement, and the glistening of her eyes as she looked at him, the feeling of her two hands holding his so tightly. Her willingness to jump in and take Frou, come and find him. To do whatever was needed. Dorie. It was the most beautiful name he'd ever heard.

His grandmother must have agreed because the topic of Dorie kept coming up in their conversation. Finally, Chad had to get firm. "Nan, we really need to talk about you. Can we stop talking about Dorie and dogs for a little while?"

"Oh, Chad. She's a nice girl. Got some edges, but who doesn't?"

"Nan," he had warned.

"Oh, okay. What do you want to talk about?" Alice sounded agreeable.

"Well, you. The physiotherapist said you're going to need some help getting around, even after rehab. Did you hear that?"

"Oh, fluff. I'm going to be fine." Alice looked out the window.

He leaned toward her and took her hand. "I know you're going to be fine, Nan. But you can be fine and need some help getting around."

She looked at him, and for the first time, he could see she was scared. "I'm fine, Chad."

He nodded. "Yes, I know, but you can't get to the bathroom by yourself yet. Getting groceries and cooking meals might be a little hard." She looked at him suspiciously, then grabbed his hand more tightly.

"Chaddie, I can't go into one of them homes. Not now. Not until I really need to."

He shook his head. "Nobody said anything about a home. You have a home."

She had relaxed her grip slightly. "Yes, I do. Only, you said..."

"You need some help. That's all I said. What if I move back to Stella Mare to live? Would you let me live with you?"

Alice smiled. "Silly goose. You can always live with me. Why do you think I keep your bed made up?"

He smiled in return. "Okay. It's a plan."

"What about your job, Chad? Your work?"

"That's not your problem, Nan. I'll handle that part. You handle doing the hard work in rehab, okay?"

Yup, I've got a lot to think about. Dorie, figuring out work, and Nan. Who knows how much better she's going to get? There's a lot of unknowns. But he understood that. Sometimes you had to make a commitment even before the ramifications were clear. When it was your grandmother, your only living relative, being there was the only option.

The details though. He sighed and set aside the details. Instead, he thought about Dorie's hair, the soft curve of her cheek, her green eyes. Even her father was a plus. James had collected him from the St. Stephen police station, had driven him to his truck out in the middle of howling nowhere, and was just as nice as he could be about it all. James had allowed Frou-Frou to live at their house for the last week. This man seemed like an all-around good guy. *I think he likes me okay, too. Not that I have to impress her father, but it can't hurt.*

Back at Alice's place near midafternoon, Chad showered and flopped on the Chesterfield. Uncomfortable, he gave that up for his bed, where the soft mattress cradled his sore ribs. It was the middle of the day, but his night had been nearly sleepless.

He crashed so hard that he didn't hear the knocking at the door, didn't hear the footsteps coming up the stairs, or the voice calling his name. What he did notice was when somebody sat on the side of his bed, sinking it down so that he slid across the old mattress toward the person.

"Wha–what? What?" he spluttered, waking suddenly.

"Hi," Dorie said, looking at him directly.

"Oh, uh, hi," Chad uttered, profoundly grateful that he was fully dressed. He rubbed at his eyes. "Am I awake?"

She smiled at him. "I think so. Do you think you're awake?" There was a click of nails and Frou-Frou came into the room.

Chad leaned over to see the dog. "Oh, now I know I'm awake. What are you doing here? On my bed?"

"Do you want me to get up?" she asked. "I can leave, you know."

"No, wait, hold on," Chad sputtered. "Awkward moment. Hold on. I can recover." She giggled at that, and he smiled a little. "See, I'm recovering already." He hiked himself up to a sit, pillows behind his head. He picked up Dorie's hand, conveniently resting on his coverlet.

"Hello. Welcome to my room. Did you knock?"

She nodded. "Yes, I did, and rang the bell, and stomped up the stairs and I even brought a dog, as you can see. I think you were well and truly asleep."

"I think you are correct about that. I'm awake now. Can we get out of my room and go downstairs?"

"Sure," Dorie agreed. "I'll go first, shall I?" She headed downstairs with Frou behind her. Chad tossed off his covers, shook out his clothes, and brushed a hand through his hair. *She is here. The woman is here, in my house, and I didn't even invite her. She was sitting on my bed.*

Dorie was sitting on the Chesterfield, smiling up at him. He sat beside her, and then she slid closer. *What the heck? Has she been reading my mind?*

"Listen, Chad, I'm still blown away by what you did last night. Are you sure you're okay? That was some scary stuff. Thank you so much."

He shifted uncomfortably. "Yeah, I'm okay, but you're right, it was scary. Thinking about getting the story kept me going. I've done a few things the past week that I would never have tried before."

She was looking right at him, eyes glistening, and her lips looked so soft and slightly open. He could imagine kissing her, but then he could easily imagine missing her lips, falling off the couch, accidentally biting—too many possible things to go wrong.

But wait. She was leaning into him. He stayed still, barely breathing, while she gently kissed his lips.

"That's something I've never tried before," Dorie said with an arch look.

"Very nice," Chad said. "We should keep trying new things."

She giggled. "It's been a week, hasn't it?" She leaned closer.

He nodded his agreement but pulled back. "Listen, Dorie, I need to talk to you."

"Oh?" She sat back too.

He sighed. "Sorry to spoil the moment, but this can't wait. Nan is not going to be a hundred percent, not ever, I think."

"Oh, no. I'm so sorry."

"Yeah, well, she's pretty good and she's going to get better. She'll be at the rehab starting on Monday. I've decided something. I'm not going back. I'm staying here in Stella Mare."

"For real?" Dorie's face lit up. "You're really staying?"

Wow, she's happy about that.

"Yes, I am. I have a lot of details to figure out, of course, but this is one sure thing. Nan is here and she's my family, and I'm not leaving her alone here."

"You're very certain." Dorie's smile deepened.

"I am. I hope that means we'll get to spend more time together, too."

She looked up. "You and your Nan?"

He scoffed. "No, Dorie. You and me. Always giving me a hard time, right?"

She laughed. "Yeah. But I just wanted to hear you say it right out loud."

"Say what? That I like you and I want to spend more time with you?" He reached over to brush the hair out of her eyes.

"Yes. That."

His hand cupped her cheek and they leaned closer. This time Chad took the lead. Her lips were warm, soft, pliant. For a feisty woman, she sure tasted sweet. He was leaning in for more when she pulled away.

"Sorry to spoil the moment, but I have a problem, or more than one."

"With me?"

She dropped her jaw and scoffed. "No, not with you. A dog problem."

He relaxed and grinned. "Imagine. Dorie Madison with a dog problem."

She smiled, looking a bit self-conscious. "Yeah, imagine that. But the problem is Sarah's dogs. Mike's place is overfull. They can't be fostered just anywhere, and besides, nobody has room. When I think about adding seven more very needy pooches to the menagerie at home, I can imagine my father fainting."

"Fainting? James might faint?"

She flopped back onto the Chesterfield. "No, I meant that metaphorically. But we are all a little worried about Dad, and I don't want to cause him any more stress than usual. Adding dogs to the pack at home is probably not a great idea right now."

"The problem is too many dogs, and not enough dog homes."

"I overestimated my capacities. I was worried that Richie guy would shoot her dogs, so I told Sarah that I'd take care of her babies. I have no way to do that. I hate this feeling."

Dorie fell silent and Chad didn't know what to say.

Seeming to talk aloud, not particularly to him, but working out her problem, Dorie said, "They are a pack, you know. Dogs are pack animals, and that bunch has been together for who knows how long."

An idea tugged at Chad, but he couldn't make it take shape. Something that could happen but hadn't happened yet. Like when he had an idea for a film or a story. It would start like a little itch but over time would develop into something more.

"What's happening now with the pack?" he asked, waiting for the idea to expand.

She shrugged. "Mike's getting them checked over by our vet, and then we'll know a little more. There are also the dogs from the fight last night. I got the brindle back, but of course we still don't know who owns her. The other dogs, the fighters, they're with Animal Control. Their fate is unknown, too."

"There's a lot of unknowns." *I was just thinking that about my life. Guess it is bigger than just me.*

Dorie nodded vigorously. "Not just about the dogs. Like, what about Sarah?"

"When I was eavesdropping on those motorcycle guys, they thought she was dying."

"Not a great source of information, right?"

He laughed. She had a point. "Listen, when I'm trying to figure out how to tell a story in a documentary, I lay everything out graphically. That's how I keep information straight. We should try that."

"Sure. If it's going to help me figure out what to do with these dogs, I'm open to it."

They went to the kitchen table and Chad produced a big pad of paper.

"Okay. What we know and what we don't." He drew a line down the middle of the page.

Dorie looked at him blankly.

"So, what do you know?" he prompted.

"Well, Sarah's in hospital and her dogs need care."

"Right." Chad scribbled a note on the left side of the page. "And what else?"

"Andrea is missing. For days, now. It's probably unrelated."

"Related, unrelated, we don't assume anything in this process. So yes, we'll add Andrea."

"There really is dog fighting going on here in the province."

Chad nodded as he wrote. "We know that for sure."

Dorie's voice grew stronger. "But we don't know who is behind it, or if there's some larger criminal element involved."

"Correct," Chad agreed as he scribbled on the right side of the page. "We don't know how Sarah is, either."

"We know somebody's been cooking the books at BARC, and they put money in my account for some reason."

Chad stared. "Really? Somebody put money in your account? A lot?"

"Yes, that's what the police wanted to discuss with me."

"Oh my gosh!" He smacked his forehead. "I forgot you were called in to the station. You must think I'm so insensitive. How could I forget that?"

She frowned. "You were out chasing down criminals and getting beaten up and arrested. That's how you could forget. Don't sweat it."

"What did happen?" He felt terrible, despite her reassurance.

"They had questions, mostly about Andrea and Young Mr. Barrett, and then they told me that they were watching my bank account and there was a big deposit. I've been so busy I didn't even know."

"How big?"

"Ten thousand bucks. They have frozen my account while they investigate, so I can't even pay my phone bill. And with Andrea gone, I didn't get paid this week."

He was gobsmacked. "Ten thousand dollars? What were they thinking?"

"I can't imagine," she said dryly. "Or I can imagine. I imagine that somebody wanted to implicate me, but it was a stupid way to do it."

"No kidding. They should have hidden cash in your car or something." He grinned at her.

"Yeah. That would have been more suspicious. Even the police don't think I have anything to do with this mess."

Chad gazed at their worksheet. "What else?"

Dorie pondered. "I don't know if it belongs on here, but it's something I keep thinking about. Old people's dogs. We know that there's a problem when old people have to go into care or can't take care of their pets. That's a known, and it's been bothering me for weeks. It keeps showing up. With Alice, and Sarah, and my aunt the social worker has talked about it, and my sister Rett who works in long-term care."

"Okay, it's an unknown. I'll write it down. Any idea how it relates to all of this?" Chad gestured across the page.

"Well, Sarah's dogs. Obviously. But otherwise, maybe nothing. Just another problem without a solution."

"Frou-Frou is a lucky dog," he said soberly.

"Yup."

Shoulder to shoulder, they gazed at the sheet of paper.

"See anything?" Dorie asked. "You're the one who uses this method."

"What's most pressing? Most important?" He turned to look at her. Oh, her face was so close. He watched the little wrinkles form in her forehead as she considered. The place where his shoulder touched hers was so warm. With an effort, he turned his attention to her words.

"Some of this mess has nothing to do with me," she declared at length. "I do feel responsible for Sarah's dogs. The BARC mess might put me out of work again. Darn it!"

"Yeah, that stinks."

"Naomi, the BARC lawyer, told me to go home on Friday morning when the police came with their warrant. Andrea's got to show up sometime, but..." Dorie trailed off. "I feel kind of selfish, worrying about my job when all this other stuff is happening, but it's not been a great fall for my so-called career."

She turned to look at him. "Oh, well." She turned her hands palm up.

He let his gaze linger on her shiny hair, her little frown, her expressive hands. The sound of her voice stayed in his ears.

"You're right, of course. For those things we can't control, 'oh well' is the only response. But..." Abruptly his vague idea became an image in his mind. Oh, yes. There it was. Crystallized. "Instead, let's think about what we might be able to do."

"We?" Dorie's eyes searched his face. Feeling his cheeks warm, he looked back at their worksheet.

"Yeah, so I'm going to be right here. Where Nan has a barn."

"A barn, yes. So what?"

"You might have an unfortunate amount of free time, until you find another job." Chad's mind was tumbling with his vision, but Dorie looked puzzled.

She shook her head. "You're going too fast for me. I don't see how all those things are related."

Frou-Frou put his chin on Chad's knee and whined a little.

"Right," Chad said to the dog. "We have to show her." He got up and grabbed his jacket. "Come on. Let's go look at the barn."

Chapter 16

Dorie went back to work at the BARC office on Monday, after a conversation with Naomi. She could at least clear up the mess left after the execution of the search warrant.

She snickered internally. Execution. That was the word. Someone had tried to do a hatchet job on her reputation, but they were so ham-handed it had backfired. The mess in Andrea's office was daunting, but she turned on some music and worked to tidy and organize the materials that were left. Who knew how long the full investigation might take?

Being in Andrea's office felt a little strange. She'd never been in here without Andrea, except last Friday with those officers. Where was Andrea? Even though she expected nothing, she pulled up Andrea's number and called. Clearly the phone was off, going straight to voicemail.

Oh, well. She surveyed the damage and decided where to begin.

By ten, she was more than ready for her morning coffee, and headed to the Sunshine. Cassandra was there, as usual, and curious, as usual.

"Still no Andrea? And where's Frou?"

Dorie shook her head. "Just me." Cassandra busied herself at the espresso machine, lips pressed together.

After another moment of silence, Dorie prompted, "Go ahead. I can see your curiosity is killing you. Ask away. I'll tell you what I know, but it isn't much."

Cass gave her a guilty grin. "There's so much going on and nobody knows anything. I don't gossip, but I sure like to know what's happening. Got time to sit for a minute?"

She looked around the empty diner. "Yeah, okay. Let's sit."

Cassandra brought two coffees to the table. "So, dog fighting? Embezzlement? What's going on here?"

She shook her head. "I'm going to disappoint you. I don't know anything really. Yes, you heard about the dog fighting on Friday night. One of my fosters was taken from my dad's yard on Friday and she showed up at the dog fight. But not fighting, just there in a crate. Andrea's missing and the cops did question me, but I honestly know nothing about the financial affairs at BARC."

"Do you still have a job?" Cassandra asked, glancing at Dorie's coffee.

"Nobody has told me different," she said, thinking uncomfortably of Naomi sending her home last Friday. "I didn't get paid last week, but don't worry. If BARC isn't paying the coffee bill, I'll pay it."

Cassandra scoffed. "I'm sure Sonny won't go bankrupt from a couple of coffees. But this whole situation is wild. Nothing exciting happens in Stella Mare, and now there are two big stories at the same time."

"That's the truth. But I'm more worried about a little story, really."

Cassandra raised her eyebrows.

"Remember we were talking about old people and their dogs? On Friday we got a bunch of them from one house. Mike has them but can't keep them. They all need to be fostered and preferably together. You don't want a houseful of foster dogs, do you?"

"No way. I'd volunteer my mother, but she'd kill me. How many?"

"Eight. No, seven," Dorie said, thinking about Blackie's stiffening body. "They're old, some of them, and sick, some of them, and she may not be coming home."

"That's an ongoing story, isn't it? So sad."

"Yes, very sad." Dorie sipped her latte. "So, that's all I know. I probably need to get back to the office, though I'm not sure why. I guess I just feel responsible." She shrugged on her coat and bid Cassandra good-bye.

The office phone was ringing. She hurriedly unlocked the door and grabbed for the handset on Andrea's desk.

"Hello?" Dorie was wary, but the last call had been from Sarah and it was a good thing she'd answered.

"Dorie? Is that you?"

"Oh, my goodness, Andrea. Yes, it's me. Where are you?"

Andrea's voice was quiet, almost as if she didn't want to be overheard. "It doesn't matter. I'm going to the police, and I might not get to talk to you once I do that, so I wanted to call."

The office line? Why not my cell?

"Yeah, good. Are you okay?"

"I'm not hurt, if that's what you mean. I just, well, I think you got caught up in something. Actually, I got caught up in something and you by association, and I'm sorry about that. Listen, I don't know what's going to happen, but I'm pretty sure that BARC will be no more. You keep in touch with Naomi, she's a good person and really on the outside of the mess, and, well, I don't think you need to be at work anymore. I have to go, Dorie. I'm really sorry." The line went quiet as Andrea hung up.

Dorie remained standing at the desk holding the handset to her ear. "Andrea?" No good. What had she said? *I'm going to the police*. Wow.

Slowly replacing the handset, Dorie looked around the still messy office. As if in a dream, she stacked papers and put files in drawers. *You don't need to be at work anymore*. She really was out of a job once again.

Moving slowly, Dorie tidied as much as she could, hung the skeleton key to the archive room in its place, and took a final look around. *I might not be back.*

Not just me. Andrea might not be back. She briefly imagined Andrea, holed up somewhere, or trying to get to the police. She could be in danger, but at least she was able to call. Dorie sent Constable Doiron a brief text, telling her than Andrea had called to say she was going to the police. *Hopefully that will have them looking out for her. If they weren't already.*

Well, Andrea was okay, at least for the moment. That was a good thing, and one that could be checked off the list she'd made with Chad. Thinking of the list reminded her that she needed to talk to Mike. She turned left toward County Rescue. It was a brilliant late fall morning, frost everywhere still glistening despite being almost noon. Her brisk walk felt good too, cold, clean, salty air pulled into her lungs. *I should feel worse. I just lost another job. But I don't feel too bad at all.*

Mike was in his office, feet on the desk as usual, staring down a spreadsheet. A couple of dogs sprawled on the floor.

"Hey." He put his feet down.

"Yeah. Big goings on, right?"

Mike sighed. "Your buddy Chad there, he did a great job of getting footage that the Crown Prosecutor can use to nail at least some of the bad guys. He's a pretty good one." He gave Dorie an arch look.

"Yep," she agreed. *He is a pretty good one.* Despite her best efforts, her mind drifted to their kiss in Alice's living room. She said, "He had an idea that might help us."

"Go ahead. We need all the help we can get."

"Yeah, I know. Sarah's dogs, the fighting dogs, plus all the usual stuff."

Mike nodded.

"Chad's moving here to help his grandmother. She had a stroke and probably is going to need another person in her house."

"That poodle, right?"

Dorie grinned. Dog people always remembered humans by their canine companions. "Yes. I had him for a while because she was ill, and Chad was taking care of her. But anyway, he's going to be in Stella Mare, and she's got a barn she's not using."

Mike's eyebrows asked a question.

"I looked at it Saturday with Chad. It looks like it's in pretty good shape, and there's even heat in part of it, and it isn't being used for anything. It could be a temporary place for Sarah's dogs."

"Wow, Dorie, there's an idea. Space at least."

"Yeah. BARC is probably closing, so I don't have a job again. I could take care of them out there."

"Temporarily," Mike filled in.

"Yes, temporarily. I have to get a job."

"Okay. So we have temporary space and temporary help. That's a good start. What we don't have is the funds to take care of them. They need medical care, at least three of them. Doc Hartley discounts his fees for us, and there's plenty of food donations, but it's still expensive." Mike steepled his fingers. "Now there might be sources of support for a project like that though. Especially if you were to take in other dogs, not just Sarah's."

"Other dogs?"

"Old people's dogs. I bet there are funding agencies that would help a project like that."

"Funding agencies. Like pounding the pavement for money, right? That sounds a lot like my last job," Dorie sighed. "Grant writing. Fundraising. Except I never got to do any of that."

"Well, you think about it. In the meantime, your guy had a good idea. I'll take a trip out and check out the space, and we can talk about what you might need to make it work for this little pack."

Dorie nodded. "Okay. You have Chad's number. It's a good temporary solution. But emphasis on temporary."

****

Mike called Dorie on Monday evening. "Strangest thing," he said.

Dorie's hands were full of dog bowls, and the kitchen full of attentive canines. Juggling the phone, she said, "What's that?"

"Something I've never seen before," he said bemusedly. "We got a donation."

Dorie scowled as she pushed the brindle toward her own bowl. "You always get donations."

"Yeah, not like this. This was in a manila envelope, slipped under the door."

Now he had her interest. "Really? From who?"

"Anonymous, I guess. But the note said it was for Sarah's dogs." She could almost hear Mike's smile.

"Really? Cash in an envelope for the pack. Maybe that Richie came through for his mum. That's great."

"Yes. Want to know how much?"

"Well, sure. Any amount is helpful. What was it, fifty bucks?"

"Nope. Get ready."

"Yeah?"

"Five thousand. In small bills."

Chad had never felt so busy in his entire life. He was talking with staff at the rehab hospital about Nan's future, checking in three times a day with Alice, and editing a film project that was consuming a lot of time. *I'm not even working and I'm working harder than ever.*

Thank goodness the police returned his camera after downloading and erasing his video from Friday night. He was glad he had a habit of making daily backups, so his other nuggets were not lost, but the dog-fighting video apparently was not going to be returned, at least not until after a trial.

A couple of new projects were very exciting though. Mike had checked out the barn, and he'd sent a couple of guys to make some changes that would help turn it into a good place for a pack of small homeless dogs. The plan involved the best possible use of the anonymous donation and preserving funds for dog food and medical care. But the barn was being transformed, fast.

What Chad liked best about the whole barn-as-dog-shelter was that Dorie, his Dorie, would be working on the property. He could hardly wait until everything was done and the pack moved in. At the same time, he hoped it would take a few days because he was making something special for Dorie to celebrate the event.

She called him Friday. "I haven't seen you all week. What are you doing?" she asked plaintively. "Want to take the dogs out with me?"

His gut wrenched. *There's nothing I'd like more, really, but I have to get this work done. How can I say that?* "I'd like to but I, uh, I have a lot to do."

He could almost imagine her frown. "Yeah, okay. I'll be busy too, when the pack moves into the barn, but right now I'm at loose ends, kind of."

Sympathetically, he said, "I know. I'm not, unfortunately. I've got guys working in the barn, and there's a guy here putting grab bars in the bathrooms and other stuff so Nan can come home, and I have a project I'm working on too."

"A project?" Dorie perked up. He could hear her interest in her voice. *Uh-oh. It's a surprise for her. Don't want to ruin it.*

"It's for work," he prevaricated. He didn't like lying but he didn't want to spoil his surprise. Dorie let out one of her gusty sighs.

"I'm sorry," he said. "Can you come for supper? Tomorrow?"

"Not tonight?" She sounded disappointed.

"I just can't tonight. I wish I could," he said.

She sighed. "Tomorrow, then. Actually, that's a nice invitation. You can show me the new stuff."

The new stuff? His surprise? Oh, no, in the barn and the house. "Yes, for sure. You'll have some ideas about the barn, too. See you later."

She clicked off. He fought the desire to call her right back, tell her to come over right now. *You're in deep, buddy. Never been like this before. Now get a grip and get your work done.* He returned to editing video.

Dorie stood in front of her closet on Saturday evening, with Evie sitting on the bed.

"Thanks for coming over tonight," she said over her shoulder. "It's nice that Jase doesn't mind you spending so much time in Stella Mare."

"Well, Jase is pretty busy with work. He's got a huge show in the spring, plus teaching a couple of classes. He's not that much fun right now, so coming home, well, it works out for both of us," Evie explained.

"I can't imagine being that busy. Even with the little I have going on I've been worse than usual at the dinner thing. I imagine Dad will be grateful for a real meal."

Evie scoffed. "I know I'm welcome whenever I bring food, but I think we're going to go out. I masquerade as a cook, but I really only do it when I must."

"Still more than me." She held a sweater up to her chest. "What do you think?"

"Good colour for you," Evie said. "But dressy. It's only supper."

She tossed it on the floor. "Yeah, I can see that. How about this one?"

"Why are you all worked up? You're going to Chad's grandmother's house, right? Not out on the town."

"Yeah, I know." Dorie gazed into her closet. "How about this dress?"

"Oh, my goodness," Evie exclaimed. "I get it. You like him."

She scowled. "Of course I like him."

"No, no, no. You really like him. Ha! I thought that would never happen to you." Evie was chortling. "Dorie never met a guy she couldn't dump, but wow, you really like him."

She sighed. "Darn it, Evie, why do you have to make everything hard? That's it." Pulling on her jeans, she then picked up a sweatshirt from the floor.

Evie stifled a laugh. "It's normal, you know, to like a guy, especially one who's taken on your projects and helped you out, and who appreciates you. You don't have to be embarrassed."

I'm not embarrassed. Dorie sat on the bed with a thump. *Well, yes, I guess I am embarrassed.* "I don't know why I'm like that. Yes, I do kind of like him, and why not?"

Evie reached around and gave her a side hug. "There you go. Emotional maturity. Put that pretty dress on and don't let your mean big sister get to you."

She considered. “Nah, I think I’ll stay in my jeans. But I could put on a clean shirt.”

She arrived at Alice’s house to find the back porch well lit and the fragrance of woodsmoke in the air. After a quick rap at the door, she let herself into the kitchen. Frou-Frou wiggled his pleasure as she scratched his ears and called out to Chad.

She looked up from the dog to see him standing in the living room doorway, gazing at her. “Hi. I let myself in.”

His smile wrapped around her. “Yes, you did. Dinner’s almost ready. Do you want to take a look at the barn?”

“Oh, yes, please. I can’t wait to see what’s been happening.”

Frou-Frou led the way as they walked from the back of the house to the barn. There was a new light by the door so Chad could see to unlock it. He looked at Dorie. “I’ve been locking up since we’ve put materials and time in here, plus I need to get in the habit if we’re going to have dogs. Watch your step. It’s a construction site.”

He entered and clicked on the lights with a new switch by the door. Dorie peered in as she stepped over the threshold. “Oh, look at this! Wow, you’ve made a place for paperwork, and, oh, look, separate rooms with dog beds for the pups.”

“Mike thought we needed some separate spaces, but each space has plenty of room for three dogs, even more if one wanted to sleep on the floor.” Each room had little cots for the dogs, and Dorie could see that there was an access panel so the dogs could go outside on their own. “I can’t believe how fast this work is going.”

She wandered around, marveling.

“What about outdoors? It was dark when I got here, so I didn’t see anything.”

“Not much to see yet, but the fences are going in Monday. We’ll have two separate areas in case we get some incompatible pups, or someone is having a bad day.”

"Wow, Chad. This looks like more than just temporary housing for a few desperate mutts."

"Maybe," he said, but he looked as if he wanted to say more. Then he turned away. "We better get back to the house. I don't want to overheat dinner."

"I'm with you on that! Dinner is important." They laughed as Frou led the way back to the kitchen door.

"Can I hang up your jacket?"

"Sure you can. How's your rib?' Her heart squeezed when she thought about Chad getting beaten up. "All healed?"

He shook his head. "Not completely, but I'm okay. Doing well."

"That's good." She peered curiously toward the stove. "What did you make? It smells incredible."

He brought her a glass of wine. "I made takeout, to tell the absolute truth. But it's warming in the oven. I have something I want to show you before we eat." He pushed up his glasses and gave her a quick glance. "If that's okay, I mean. Are you starving?"

"Are you worried about nasty Dorie when she gets hungry?" She grinned at him. He was so sweet. "No problem. I'm good. I am looking forward to whatever you've got in that oven, but I won't bite off your arm if I don't eat right now."

"Okay, then. Come on into the living room."

He showed her to the Chesterfield. *This is where we kissed. I sure hope we can do that a little more.* A shiver of anticipation made it a little hard to settle, but she tucked a pillow behind her back. Frou curled up her feet.

Chad was messing around with a laptop and the television. "Did you get Alice a new TV? I don't remember that one."

"It was time. I think hers was made in 1990. If I'm going to live here, I need a good screen. I hope she doesn't mind," he added.

"I don't think she minds anything you do, Chad. She's probably over the moon that you're staying." *I know I am. Oops, did I say that out loud?* Relieved to note that her filter was working, she watched him fiddle with cables.

"Okay, I think we're ready." Chad sat next to her. He turned to Dorie. "This is...well, this is what I've been working on. I hope you like it." He looked away quickly, and she noted his face was flushed.

She patted his leg, so close to hers. "I'll like it. I'm sure I'll like it."

"You never know. Anyway, here goes." He clicked on a remote. Music started, maritime fiddle music. Immediately Dorie was captivated by layered landscapes opening to the title, Our Best Friends. Frou-Frou jumped into the scene with a bark. The real Frou-Frou stretched out on the floor by Dorie's feet.

"Look! There's Frou. You're a star, buddy!" Dorie suddenly stopped talking when she saw herself on the screen. She was talking about dogs. And again, taking care of the lunks, and then Frou. Chad had shot footage of her shop. Absorbed, she watched the story unfold.

Sarah's place, and old sick dogs. Mike Maybee talking about old dogs. Chad's grandmother Alice greeting Frou-Frou in the hospital. Oh, that was touching, how much it meant to her to see her dog. And Dorie again, this time arms full of Sarah's dogs, covered in hair and who knows what, but her face glowing.

She was barely aware of Chad sitting next to her, looking at her face, as she watched. Oh, look, there was Alice's barn. And wait, Corinne? Corinne had talked to Chad? What was that about? Oh, there she was shouting at the big guy about it not being the dog's fault. Wow, she had taken a big risk there.

Further on there was footage showing the modifications to the barn. Now Mike again, talking about old people and their dogs, and finally, a closeup of Dorie, saying "Dogs are better people than some people."

The final screen showed Frou-Frou looking as cute as possible, with the narration giving statistics on old people and old dogs in the province. The music swelled and dropped, then the screen went blank.

Dorie was speechless.

"You don't like it. Oh, I'm so sorry, this was a mistake. I didn't, I mean...."

Chad looked at her with concern. Dorie shook her head very fast. "No, no, Chad, I like it. I do like it. I just never saw myself that way. I can't believe you had all that footage, and what you made with it."

"Well, I do have a camera all the time. Sometimes it comes in pretty handy."

"I just don't know what to say. I have never seen myself, you know, like that."

He relaxed a bit. "Like what?"

"On film. And so, kind of, determined."

He laughed and nodded. "I think determined is a good word. This work, taking care of dogs who are losing their homes and families, this lights you up. I told you that before. It's your work."

"I remember what you said about being lit up, but I didn't know what you were seeing. I guess now I do."

"This is the Dorie I know," he said emphatically. "She's the woman who takes on the bad guys, doesn't shy away from the messy stuff, and who will move mountains to take care of dogs."

Dorie felt her eyebrows shoot up, but there was no retort she could make. She could only listen.

Chad went on, "Plus she's sweet and funny and cares about her family. She's cute and a terrible cook." He was looking right into her eyes now. "I just want to be around her. She makes my days better."

Dorie finally caught a breath. "I really like you, too, Chad. That was an amazing gift. I didn't know what kind of filmmaker you were, but now I have an idea."

Chad picked up her hand. "I wanted to make this for you. You needed to see yourself the way I see you. Your family shows you a different image, but this is the Dorie I see. This is the person I want to be with." His forehead wrinkled, and he pushed his glasses up with his free hand.

Feeling like her heart might burst, Dorie gripped his hand. "Don't look so worried, Chad. I'm right here. I don't want to go anywhere. Except to move a little closer."

His warm shoulder pressed into hers, and she could suddenly smell his fragrance: woodsmoke, a clean smell of soap, and a hint of pine. When she leaned toward him, he cupped the back of her head with his free hand, threading his fingers through her hair.

"Those green eyes," he murmured. "I love those green eyes." His eyes were roving around her face and settled on her lips.

Dorie felt herself falling into his look, leaning into his kiss. It was so sweet, so soft. Then it became more urgent and searching. She was just starting to feel lost in the sensations, the heat of his body, taste of his mouth, and the feel of his hand in her hair, when a buzzer went off in the kitchen, startling them both.

Reluctantly they pulled apart, gazing at each other. "Well," Dorie said. "I wonder if I'm smiling as much as you are?"

Chad nodded. "You do have a big smile. That was lovely. I hope we get to do that again."

"Again and again," she agreed. "But I think that was your timer for dinner."

"Yes. What do you think? Should we eat dinner? Or I can just get it out of the oven, and we can have dinner a little later?"

"What a great idea. Let's have dinner later. I think we have more pressing things to do right now."

Chapter 17

Chad was so busy throughout the fall, he almost didn't realize he wasn't working. Well, he was working, but he didn't go to work anymore. He did repairs on the barn and house, filled the woodshed with logs he split for the woodstove, outfitted his truck with a snowplow. He fell into bed, sleeping instantly, almost every night. In early January, howling winds woke him early.

The air was cold, but he moved with purpose to pile kindling and fuel into the woodstove in the living room. Soon the house would be warm. Chad sighed with enjoyment. These early morning moments were his. Peaceful. Quiet. Frou-Frou nosed him as he squatted in front of the stove.

"Okay, okay. Your turn's coming. But first I have to make the coffee."

Frou whined a little, then sat beside the kitchen door. When the coffeemaker was bubbling, Chad shrugged into his coat and peered out the window toward the barn. "That's a lot of snow, buddy," he said to the dog. "Don't get lost." He cracked open the door and Frou dashed out.

Pulling on boots and gloves, Chad followed. It was like heading into a different world; howling wind, icy snow pellets blowing horizontally, and the drifts beside the porch were already two feet high. The barn was barely visible through the screen of falling snow.

He grabbed a shovel and headed toward the barn door. The place was full of dogs who needed care no matter what the weather, and Dorie wouldn't be coming until the roads were plowed.

It took twenty minutes to clear a narrow path from the porch to the barn door, and the snow filled it in behind him almost as fast as he shoveled it. Frou was at his heels, and they squeezed through the narrow opening of the barn door. *Snow blower. We need a snow blower.* Chad put another item on his mental wish list for the dog sanctuary.

The interior was dim, but it wasn't quiet. The inhabitants were lively and loud, letting Chad know that they heard him. Frou trotted from pen to pen, trading nose touches and occasional whines with the sanctuary dogs.

Chad flipped on the lights and peered at the thermostat next to the light switches. This place was a barn, but the part that held the dogs did have heat, at least a rudimentary heating system of baseboards. He tapped at the device on the wall, clicking it on and off. Nothing happened.

He groaned. What now? The dog runs were full of snow, the dog doors impassable. The heating system was off, and it was getting colder in the barn. Dorie was stuck in town, and he was here with dogs, lots of dogs, a shovel, and an infirm grandmother. As if reading his mind, Frou gave a sharp bark. "Right, Frou. I appreciate the support, but you're not a lot of help with these practical things."

First things first, but what should be first? These dogs had to go outside, but how to do that? Chad couldn't imagine, so he did what he knew how to do. He looked for the electrical panel to see if the heating problem was just a flipped breaker. He headed out of the friendly space warmed by dog bodies into the dark further reaches of the barn, trying to recall the location of the breaker panel. Using his phone as a flashlight, he headed deeper into the belly of the barn.

"Frou, you stay out there," Chad told him. "Keep an eye on things." Frou obediently sat down.

Picking his way through the dark barn, stepping over old feedbags, garden tools, and a lot of unknown items, he pointed his light to the far wall where he vaguely remembered seeing the panel. A sudden resurgence of barking out front startled him, and he tripped over something and fell, hard. "Ow!"

Lying on the floor, he took stock. Just his elbow; he'd tripped over a garden rake. Those teeth looked lethal; it was a good thing he missed it with his head. A sudden light came from behind him as the sanctuary door opened.

"Chad? Are you okay?"

He struggled to his feet, turning his light toward the voice. "Dorie? What are you doing here?"

She walked in the path of light from his phone. "I came late last night when I saw the forecast. I just bunked into the spare room. I figured you and Alice wouldn't mind."

He ignored the pain in his elbow to give her a hug. "I am so glad to see you. The heat's not working, and I don't have a clue how to get these dogs out with all the snow. Wow, you were really thinking ahead."

She smiled modestly. "Yep, that's what I do. Think ahead." Then she grinned and said, "Dumb luck, or maybe it was Dad. He pointed out that the plows won't get us cleared out until after the snow stops, and maybe you'd need a hand out here."

"I don't care whose idea it was, I'm just glad you're here. Can you hold this light while I try to figure out the circuit board?"

"Sure."

It took almost two hours to get all of the dogs outside to use the small space that Chad managed to clear. Dorie took them out, two by two, leashed, to do their business, while Chad filled water and food dishes for everyone.

Dorie came in with the last pair. She and the dogs, an old golden retriever with three legs and a blind Boston terrier, looked like they were made of snow.

"Still coming down hard, I see," Chad commented, looking at them.

The big dog shook the snow from his fur, and Dorie pulled off her toque and shook it, too. "Yep. It's a humdinger, as Dad would say. How's the feeding going? I could use a little breakfast myself."

Chad shook a bag of kibble. "Is this the last one? I couldn't find any more in the storeroom."

"Yeah, that's it. Mike has a couple of bags for us, but they're in town. Is everyone fed?"

Chad looked around the pens. "Yeah, I got them all. It'll have to do for today, I guess."

Dorie shrugged. "You ready? I'm in big need of some coffee and food."

"Yeah, I'm coming. It's cold in here, too."

Dorie looked appraisingly at the pens. "Well, everybody's got a blanket and most of them have fur, right? And it's warmer in here with all these dogs than it would be if they were outside somewhere." She herded her charges into their home and watched as they went directly to their food bowls.

"Let's go, Chad. We've got some stuff to figure out." She pulled her toque back on and pulled her collar up. "And Alice will be looking for us."

She grabbed the shovel just outside the door and headed back toward the house, moving snow out of the way. Chad followed, elbowing her aside and taking the shovel. They stumbled together, laughing, up the porch steps and through to the warm smell of coffee.

"Hi, Nan," Chad greeted, taking off his snowy outer clothes. Alice sat at the table, newspaper folded in front of her. "What's new in Stella Mare?"

"Nothing new, Chad. This is yesterday's paper. No paper delivery today. But I can still do the crossword."

Dorie bent down to give Alice a kiss on the cheek. "Oh, my, your face is cold!" Alice exclaimed. "What a day."

Dorie poured a mug of coffee and sat across from her. "Yeah. This might be the best coffee I have ever tasted." She sighed with pleasure.

"Eggs? What do you guys want? Chef Chad is in the house."

Alice perked up. "Pancakes?"

"You bet. Pancakes coming up." There was a scratch at the door and Chad let Frou in. "I thought you were staying out with your friends. Changed your mind, huh?"

Dorie frowned. "How'd he get out? Is that door open?" She went to the sink to peer into the storm. Now that it was daylight, it was possible to see the barn, but the door seemed to be closed. "Oh, you're just a mystery dog, Frou," Dorie commented. "Too smart for me." She sat back down.

After the plates were emptied and Dorie piled them in the sink, Chad stretched out his legs. "We've got a couple of problems to solve, pretty soon," he said.

"Only a couple?" Dorie asked sardonically. "Seems like everyday there's another one."

"Yeah. Well, we're new to this, and making it up as we go. This is our first big snowstorm. We learn stuff."

"I knew we were almost out of food, but I figured I'd get to Mike's today or tomorrow." Dorie said, a little shamefaced. "I should have gone earlier, but I was in St. Stephen with those grooming jobs."

"Yeah, and we need you to have paid work so we can pay for dog food. It's not about blaming. I should have realized that dogs can't get out of their dog doors into the runs when we have two feet of snow. I should have come up with a Plan B."

"Why you? Why not me? And how could anyone know that the heat would stop working?"

"What?" Alice was startled. "The heat in the barn?"

"Yeah. I'm going to look again, but I think we'll need an electrician."

"Chad, how are we going to pay for that? We've gone through the money from Richie's donation, and you and I have been supporting this project for weeks now."

Chad nodded. "Yes, I know we have. But we just got a cheque from the Elderdog people, and you've got that social media funding call going on. The blizzard will give us interesting footage to use with our patrons, and I'll make an extra video to ask for donations."

Dorie sighed. "This is harder than I thought. It's a lot more than just the physical work of caring for old dogs."

"And old people," Alice added. "You two do a lot for me, too. Can I contribute to the project?"

Dorie scoffed. "Alice, you're contributing the space. And you feed both of us a lot of the time, plus whoever we have working out here."

Chad pulled his legs back under his chair. "Nan, we're a family. This is just what we do."

"Hm. Okay," Alice conceded. "But if I have a good idea, I'm going to say it."

"Of course! We want to hear all the ideas." Dorie was certain.

"Dorie, you were pretty smart to show up last night ahead of the storm."

Dorie preened. "I think so, too. But to be truthful, it was Dad's suggestion."

Alice pressed on. "I think you should consider moving in here. You're here at the crack of dawn seven days a week to see to the dogs anyway." She gave Dorie an arch look. "Think of the gas money you'll save."

Dorie looked at her appraisingly. "Do you have an ulterior motive, Alice?"

"Moi? What on earth are you thinking, Dorie?" Alice gave her a coy sidewise glance.

Chad stood up. "It's a really good idea, Nan. But I think Dorie and I are the ones to make a decision about living together."

Alice raised her eyebrows. "Oh, living together. Right."

Dorie hurried to say, "I'm sure Alice meant in the spare room."

Chad's jaw tightened. "Let's talk about this a little later. Right now, we have to get the heat going, find out if Mike can deliver dog food, and move some more snow around." He headed out of the kitchen and Dorie looked at Alice.

Alice whispered, "I don't care whose bedroom you sleep in, Dorie. You and Chad are a good couple and I am happy you're here."

Dorie giggled and got up to wash the breakfast dishes.

By St. Patrick's Day, Dorie had settled into life at the farm, taking a couple of shifts of dog grooming each week in St. Stephen for a little cash, maintaining their social media sites, cultivating sources of support for old dogs in town and in nearby towns. Chad did some freelance work for his old employer and supplied video material for Best Friends' fundraising efforts.

"Here's another one," Dorie called out to Alice who was in the kitchen. "This one is two little guys, been together since puppyhood, and their dad just died unexpectedly. They're twelve years old."

Alice came in, wiping her hands on a dishtowel. "Let me see," she said. "Oh, they are cute. Won't somebody adopt them?"

"Probably not," Dorie admitted. "Look, the rescue agency even lists their medical problems. Not a lot of people want to take that responsibility."

Alice sat on the Chesterfield beside her. "This is good work you and Chaddie do," she said seriously. "I wish someone could see it."

Dorie smiled ruefully. "Yeah, see it and fund it. We're doing well on getting seen. Chad's working on a news item and the next documentary. I really feel like we just have to get through this beginning phase and things will lighten up."

Alice patted her hand. "That's a good attitude."

"Yeah, I think so. My dad thinks I'm unrealistic, but even he agrees that the work is valuable."

Chad came in, holding the newspaper gingerly.

"What's up?" Dorie demanded.

He shook his head. "Look at this." He handed the paper to his grandmother who shared it with Dorie.

Dorie's eyes grew wide. "Oh, my goodness! Look at this! Charles Barrett was convicted of money laundering. What?" She looked up at Chad. "I don't get it."

"He was using BARC. He had money coming in from illegal sources, including—look, it's in there—dog fighting. He put that through like it was donations to BARC and then he took it for himself. So embezzlement too."

Dorie was gazing at the page. "Andrea Chase has also been charged but her trial is pending. Oh, my gosh." She looked up at Chad, mouth open.

"Amazing, huh?" He dropped onto a chair by the woodstove. "Those motorcycle guys with the fighting dogs, that trial happened last month, but this is deeper. I don't know who else was working with Barrett. He certainly wasn't with BARC to help dogs."

Dorie pondered. "Poor Andrea."

"I don't know about that," Chad said.

"No wonder things were so weird last fall," Dorie said. "There was a lot more going on than I knew anything about." She shivered. "I'm glad to be out of that mess."

"Me, too," agreed Chad, rubbing his side.

Alice nodded her agreement. "You two are doing better things on your own."

"Listen, Chad, we've got two new dogs maybe," Dorie changed the subject.

Chad's head was shaking already. "We just can't, Dorie. We don't have kennel room and we can't feed them or pay the vet bills we already have. I ran up my credit card to get the electrical done in January, we don't have the water heater installed yet, and we're so crowded in the barn that we could lose our permit before I have time and money to build the new pens."

"Chad, look at them," she picked up the laptop to show him. "I can't bear to think of them being euthanized for no good reason."

He sighed. "I know it's not my call, Dorie, but I think you need to consider our real resources. We're both working ourselves as hard as we can. Every month we fall further behind."

"Yes, and every month these dogs have a home and someone to care for them," she said vehemently, sitting back down.

"There comes a point where taking on more dogs means not having enough for the ones you're already committed to," Chad said slowly. "I don't know if we're at that point."

Steaming, Dorie spluttered, "But, but..."

Alice patted Dorie's leg. "I'll leave you two to your discussion," she said and headed out of the room.

Dorie watched her walk away, taking a moment to breathe. Then she began again. "I don't think I can say no to this request.

It's coming from a social service agency that has helped us out with emergency dog food before. We have to be available for their needs too."

Chad's jaw tightened. "I know you'll make the best decision you can, but I have to say I don't recommend taking any more dogs. This is a financial hole we're in, and I'm having trouble seeing any kind of future for us or the dog sanctuary. It looks grim from here."

Dorie felt stung. "What do you mean, no future for us?" Her stomach plummeted.

He shook his head. "It just feels like all too much. That's all." He stood heavily and headed for the back door.

Wordless, she stared after him.

Easter came late in April, and the sun was brilliant on Easter morning. Dorie put a pretty bow on Frou-Frou's neck, and she and Chad dressed up to accompany Alice to church at her request. Frou traveled with them but had to wait in the car. After church they would all go to Dorie's family home for Easter dinner, hosted by James with Corinne. Evie and Jase, Rett and Harry, and the kids were all expected. But first, church.

Dorie liked the sunshine pouring through stained glass, the lilies on the altar, and the message of hope. She hadn't been to church for a long time, but the ritual was a familiar one from childhood. She sat, rapt, with Chad's fingers holding hers. When the final waves of organ music fell away, she shook herself as if awakening from a trance. *Last time was probably when Mum died. Maybe I should come back. This is beautiful.*

Ida Mae Maybee monopolized Alice during the after-church coffee hour, leaving Chad and Dorie to wander, hand in hand, through the happy crowd. A tall woman stopped them. "Are you Dorie?" she asked. "Alice told me about what you're doing. I think it's a blessing for dogs and their older people. And my book club does too. We want to make a donation."

"Oh, my gosh, that would be wonderful!" Dorie was breathless. "That's so kind of your book club."

"Well, most of us are dog lovers, and we're all going to be old someday," the woman said with a smile. "It's so nice to meet you. Where shall I send the money?"

Dorie whipped out a business card, adorned with Frou looking his cutest. *Low tech but effective.*

"May I take a few to share?" the woman asked.

"Please do," Dorie agreed. "Thank you. We need all the help we can get." They waved goodbye, gathered Alice, and headed out.

"Well, that was interesting," Dorie commented as they headed to the car. "I didn't expect support like that."

Chad opened the door for Alice, while Dorie let herself into the backseat. "People like to help," Alice said. "Sometimes they just need to be told how to do it."

"You don't seem very surprised," Dorie said suspiciously. "Have you been telling people how to help?"

Alice hummed to herself.

"Okay, then. I won't ask any more," Dorie noted. "But thank you."

Alice looked over her shoulder. "Maybe you two might want to go to church? Regularly?"

Dorie burst out laughing. "You're unstoppable, Alice."

Chad grinned, too, as he took the wheel. "Yeah, Nan, nothing subtle about you."

Alice looked self-satisfied. "I like to get the job done."

Later, at her father's house, Corinne asked Dorie how things were going.

"We're not in great shape financially," she admitted to her aunt. "But for some reason I feel more optimistic than I have all winter."

Corinne smiled. "Spring can have that effect."

"Maybe that's all it is. We've gotten through our first winter and it was lean. We still don't have any way forward, but we keep on going anyway."

"I heard about a social work initiative around pets and elders that has some funding attached. Do you want me to put you in touch with the planners?"

"Do you even have to ask? Yes, please. I've learned more about funding and budgets than I ever thought possible."

"Are you and Chad doing okay? Financial stress is real stress on a relationship," Corinne observed.

Dorie wasn't sure she wanted to talk about her relationship with Corinne. "We're fine, thanks." Then she relented. "I think everything would be easier if we weren't struggling to make ends meet all the time. We're in debt, we squeeze every penny, and both of us scramble to find the occasional paying job that we can fit in with our other responsibilities. But I love what we're doing."

Corinne's smile deepened. "You do love it. I can see that on your face. And I can see that you love him, too."

Dorie felt her face warm. "He makes it all possible," she admitted. "And worth doing."

Corinne hugged her. "Good for you. That's what it's all about. The money stuff, that's going to work out."

Dorie laughed. "Oh, thank you, psychic Corinne. Do you know something I don't?"

"No. But you might as well be optimistic. You can always cry later."

Chapter 18

By early June, summer was more than in the air. It was in the garden and the apple trees, and out on the salt flats, too. Dorie took deep breaths as she released Custard and Mallow from the backseat, and they all headed toward Alice's barn. She'd spent the night at her father's house in town but coming home to the farm felt good.

The rustic wooden sign over the door still made Dorie feel warm inside. Chad had commissioned it as a gift. It read, Best Friends – A Home for Dogs, and had been hand carved by one of the locals best known for making seagull sculptures for the tourists. Before she could open the barn door, Alice called to her from the house.

"Dorie. Come on over when you can. I've got coffee and I made some muffins."

"Thanks, Alice. I'll be there in half an hour. Gotta feed and water the troops."

She entered to a cacophony of barking, but it was all friendly and familiar. Frou trotted over from the house to offer his greeting, and Custard settled down on the rug near the desk. Studiously ignoring the pile of bills under a Labrador-shaped paperweight, she opened the gates to the runs and started cleaning pens and preparing to feed the pack, now grown to nearly a dozen.

Chad appeared in the doorway. "Hi," he said. "Need any help?"

"Always," she said. "But first I need a kiss."

She grinned at the light flush that overtook him. "Still exciting, even after all these months?"

"You bet." He laughed, held her firmly, and kissed her again. "Especially when you spend the night away. How about you?"

She dropped the dustpan to settle into his embrace. "Very exciting. I miss you, you know, when we're not together."

"You just miss my cooking," he gibed. "Or my help with the dogs."

"No, it's your manly charm." Dorie smiled. "And how delicious you smell. And how sweet your neck is." She buried her face in his neck.

"Ahem."

Dorie and Chad turned as one to the door, where a thin woman in a suit leaned against the doorframe.

"Sorry to interrupt. I'm Naomi Snow. Are you Dorie?"

"Naomi! Welcome to Best Friends," Dorie exclaimed and stepped forward with her hand out. "We never met, not really. Come on in. This is my partner, Chad Simmons. Chad, this is Naomi, who is, well, who used to be the lawyer for BARC."

"Hi, Chad. You're the filmmaker, right?"

Dorie watched a slow flush slide up Chad's face as he nodded. "Among other things."

Naomi smiled tightly. "I'm still a lawyer, but as you know, there is no BARC. That's what I wanted to talk about with you. Both of you."

Talk to us? What now?

"Sure. Uh, do you think we can go to the house, Chad? There's not a lot of places to sit here." She looked pointedly around the barn.

"Actually, I want to see this place. What do you call it? A sanctuary, right?"

"Right. It's a place for dogs who can't be fostered or adopted but who are able to live with other dogs."

"Is it like an old folks' home for dogs?"

"Well, something like that. Let me give you the tour," Dorie offered.

They walked through the barn. Dorie was especially proud of the intake area, where new dogs stayed while they were getting used to the group. They wrapped up the tour in the yard, standing under Alice's old apple trees and watching dogs play in the bright sunshine.

"As you can see, we have more dogs than space. The need just keeps growing. We're not willing to just warehouse them here. This is their home. They've lost their human families, so we become their pack. I think Best Friends is the only old dog sanctuary around here."

"This seems like valuable work."

Dorie smiled. "We think so. But there's more. This place helps old dogs, but we're trying hard to help old people too."

Naomi raised her eyebrows. "How?"

"We have dogs here who aren't necessarily old, but their owners have gone into residential care. Dogs and people miss each other, so we're trying to create a program where the dogs still visit with their owners. I've been trying to get funding from social service and animal welfare groups to support the different parts of this project."

"I saw the spread on the news," Naomi commented. "Was that your doing, Chad?"

He reddened further and pushed up his glasses. "Sort of. I used to work for the Maritime News Network. Now I freelance."

"You have an impressive vision. I saw the documentary you did on dog fighting, too. You really know how to tell a story."

He nodded. "Thanks. That one was satisfying."

Dorie jumped in. "He won an award for it, too, did you know that?" She gazed proudly at him as he bent down to pet Frou. *Sweet man. Still prefers being behind the camera. Doesn't enjoy the gaze of the audience.*

Naomi wasn't finished. "You've got a nice place here, and you two seem to have some big ideas."

"Well, we have ideas but they're in response to problems. We're trying to solve problems, along with our community partners, like County Rescue."

Naomi nodded. "What you're doing here looks wonderful, and your future plans sound good too."

"Thanks." She took a breath. "You know better than anyone how hard it is to fund these kinds of programs. These guys need food, obviously, and medical care. Chad and I have squeezed every drop out of any donations we receive, but every month I wonder if I'm going to be able to pay the kibble bill. I love this place, and I love my work, but we're always in need of funds." She saw Chad look in her direction. Yes, she was on her soapbox, but somebody had to do it. To her surprise, he picked up the ball.

"Dorie does the work here," Chad said. "She does the daily rounds, feeding, grooming, cleaning up, playing with the dogs, and managing our communication, fundraising, and new referrals that come in.

"We get referrals every week, and right now we're so full we have to turn them away. We've been turning them away for weeks. We have space to expand but no funds, and we've gone into personal debt to try to keep the lights on and the dogs fed."

Dorie felt her eyes swim. *He does know how hard this is. Maybe it's hard for him too.*

"That's the problem with non-profits," Naomi said. "The work you do can be priceless, but it all comes at a real cost in dollars and time and energy." She turned to look around the barn again.

"I do know how hard it is. There's a danger of burning out, too, when you throw yourself into something like this work."

She gazed quietly out the window at the dogs that were cavorting in the play yard. As if coming to a decision, she turned back to them and said, "I have some information that might be good news."

Biting her lip, Dorie glanced at Chad, gazing at Naomi.

"You know BARC is disbanded, but you may not realize that there is money left in the foundation. There is a substantial investment account, plus Young Mr. Barrett has been required to pay back what he stole."

Dorie shook her head. "No, I never thought about it."

Naomi said, "Well, now is a good time to consider it. BARC is no more, but the remaining board members have been tasked to develop a plan for the use of those funds. We have decided to donate this money to a cause that is consistent with Miranda Barrett's original vision."

Dorie's heart started to pound. She could see, clear as day, the document with Mrs. Barrett's signature on it, the one that first created BARC. "Mrs. Barrett wanted dogs to be safe, especially from people who might harm them."

"That's right," Naomi agreed. "You got caught in the cross fire last fall. I've always felt a little bad about that. All that nonsense with Charles and Andrea, and then them trying to implicate you, that was terrible. Clearly you rose above though, and you're doing something that helps dogs and people. Helps dogs to be safe from harm."

"Trying," Dorie corrected. "Not really doing, not yet. We got some donations to do the initial renovations to the barn, but money only trickles in. Right now, we're holding on by our fingernails."

"I think the BARC bequest could be your answer," Naomi replied thoughtfully, looking first at Dorie and then at Chad. "If you come up with a compelling way to show the problem and your vision for solving it, the board will be delighted to donate their funds to Best Friends dog sanctuary. It will have to go to a vote, of course, but I think you should apply."

Eyes wide, Dorie looked at Chad. "Well?"

"I think we're in, Naomi," he said firmly. "I've already got a film that does the first part and we've been working on a business plan to try to get the bank to lend us some money, but this would be a lifesaver."

"That's what I hoped you would say." Naomi smiled wider. "The board wants to get this sorted out by the end of the month. Do you think you can make a proposal by then?"

Dorie and Chad locked eyes. Turning to Naomi, Dorie stated, "Absolutely."

Over the next two weeks, Dorie was in consultation with Naomi, Mike, and Chad almost continuously. Naomi was full of suggestions about how best to approach the board, and Dorie and Chad listened closely and took advice. She worked feverishly on the presentation whenever she wasn't caring directly for dogs, and she and Chad had nightly meetings to assess their progress. The nights were short and the days were long, but a lot was happening.

The Friday before they were to present to the board, Dorie had a late afternoon meeting with Naomi, who shared new information about the funds. Dorie walked out of the meeting as if she was in a bubble. She was almost afraid to draw a deep breath. Could this be real?

Bubbling excitement threatened to overtake her, but she had an idea. Coming out onto the street, she sent a text to Chad.

"Dinner tonight? On me? How about a picnic on the beach?"

"Sure. Who's cooking?"

"Don't worry. I'll get takeout. No food poisoning tonight."

She smiled to herself. *Good job, Dorie. Just the right tone of casual. He's going to be blown away.*

The long June days stretched well into the evenings now. Waiting for Chad in the parking lot near the beach, she paced, barely containing her excitement. *Too bad the days are so long. No romantic moonlit evening here, but maybe the sunset will be pretty. Romantic sunset beach picnic.* She started to unload her car.

Chad arrived in the parking lot just after her, Frou-Frou dancing in attendance. "He left Alice to come with you!" Dorie noted. "You must be growing on him."

Chad grinned. "I hate to admit it, but he's a great dog. Now that I know more dogs, I get what you and Nan have been saying all along. He's pretty special."

So are you. "Can you help me carry this stuff? I brought a blanket and some wine and the food."

"Sure. You went all out. Is this a special occasion?"

"Well, kind of. The presentation is finished, put to bed. We've been busting our butts with work, probably since last fall. It's time to take a break. We deserve a nice night out."

"I like the way you think," he smiled at her. Laying out the blanket, Dorie served the picnic dinner while Chad shooed away the ever-vigilant gulls. Putting their leftovers in a basket discouraged the noisy flock. Finally settling back with a glass of wine, Dorie noted the sun was edging closer to the horizon. The sky was a radiant rose colour. She was keeping the lid on her excitement, but it threatened to bubble over.

"It's after nine. The sun sets so late in June. Beautiful, isn't it?"

"It sure is," Chad agreed, looking into his camera. He finally put it away and picked up his glass. "This is so nice. We haven't done this, like, ever, have we?"

Dorie shook her head. "No. First time. I wanted to do something special because I learned something today that, well, means something special." Her heart started racing.

"Are you being mysterious on purpose? I didn't follow any of that."

"Chad, Naomi finally told me how much money is likely to come from this BARC donation." She looked at him meaningfully but felt like she could burst any moment.

"And? Will we be able to get the van?"

Her eyes filled as she broke the news. "Ten vans, Chad. And add a building. And hire staff. Pay me a salary, and even pay for the video work you've been doing to try to keep the sanctuary afloat. Pay off the debt we've accrued." She sniffled. "It's so good." Then, irritably, "I don't know why I'm crying. It's all good news."

Chad looked thunderstruck and sympathetic all at once. "Wow. No wonder we're celebrating. That's great. Amazing!" Chad ran his hand through his hair and laughed out loud. "I know why you're crying. We really need this good news." He stood up and waved his hands around. "Think about it! Running the sanctuary will be a real job. A career."

"Yeah. I'm sure there will be lots of administrative stuff that I don't like doing, but it will be worth it to see the dogs cared for and connected to their owners."

Chad started pacing. Frou-Frou leaped up and barked. "Dorie, do you know what this means? There's a real future here. No more holding on by the fingernails, trying to scrape together money for food and gas."

She grinned through her tears. "You look like I felt this afternoon when I heard the news."

"Oh, this is great. I had no idea BARC was sitting on that kind of money."

"Me either."

"And they want to give it to you."

"No. To the Sanctuary. To Best Friends."

"Yeah, but that means you. A job for you."

"Us. The sanctuary is us. We still have to get through the presentation on Monday, but there's no competition and Naomi wants to help us. It's so exciting."

Chad waved his arms and Frou barked. "This is wonderful news. I can't believe you kept it to yourself all evening." He paced around the blanket, laughing and shaking his head.

"Chad." She reached toward him. "Could you come and sit by me for a minute? There's something else."

"Anytime. I'm yours." He took her hand and sat back down on the blanket, still smiling. He reached over and knuckled away a tear she didn't know was on her cheek.

She reached for his other hand and gazed at their four hands, clutched together. She took a breath and looked up to see his eyes were on her.

"What is it, Dorie?" he asked, suddenly serious.

Her head felt light, and her heart was pounding. "Now that we have a future for Best Friends, I was thinking about our future." She looked at his kind eyes, hidden as they were behind those glasses, the concern on his face, the tousled hair.

"Chad, will you..." She cleared her throat. "Will you marry me?"

His eyes suddenly took on a glaze, like a scared rabbit, and he pulled his hands out from hers. She rapidly backpedalled. "Never mind, it's okay. Maybe I was just kidding. You know."

"Hold on, Dorie. Can you just hold that thought, just for a minute?" He held up a hand. "Stay right there. Don't move." He took off across the beach toward the parking lot.

Dorie's tears were full on now. Sobs threatened to overtake her. *Darn, darn, darn it. It was too soon. When will I ever learn to keep my mouth shut?* Frou-Frou nuzzled her cheek and whined. She hugged the dog and sniffled.

In a heartbeat Chad was back, panting after his run. He threw himself down on the blanket, and then looked at Dorie holding the dog.

"Oh, no," he said. "Don't cry. There's no reason to cry. I'm sorry. Just me being awkward as usual."

"It's okay, Chad. We're good. I just got carried away." She couldn't look at him.

"Dorie. Did you mean it? Do you want to marry me?" His tone was gentle.

She braved a glance. His kind eyes were back. "Well, yes, but I don't need to push you on something you're not ready for. I, uh...." Her voice trailed off.

"You said what I was thinking. The last few months have been a struggle. I've been trying to get the freelancing going and you haven't been able to work for pay because you're so busy working for nothing, and so there didn't seem to be a future that we could count on."

She gulped. "I know. It's been hard."

"Every time we turned around there were more expenses, more dogs that needed a home. But our future had to open up sometime. I knew it was coming. I've been ready." He reached into a pocket and pulled out a small box. He pushed up his glasses and looked at her.

Dorie stared at the box, and then at Chad. "How long have you been ready?"

He chuckled. "I bought this ring right after I was arrested at the dog fight. I knew right then that I wanted you forever. I just didn't know how we were going to make it happen."

"Way back then?"

"I can't tell you how many times I wondered if I should sell it to pay some bill. But that would be giving up."

Her smile came slowly. "You don't give up, do you?"

"If you give up, you don't get to see how the story ends. I like to see things through."

Yes, that's you. That's one of the things I love about you. She could only nod.

"I'm stubborn, Nan says. When I decide on something, I don't waffle. Like deciding to come home to Stella Mare. Getting a ring for you, same thing."

Wide-eyed and silent, Dorie processed everything. *He knew long before I did. But I remember how I felt when he was driving off to that dog fight, and finally hearing his voice that night. If I had been paying attention, I would have known then, too.*

"In answer to your question, Miss Dorie Madison, yes. I will marry you. Will you wear this ring?" He opened the box.

"It's beautiful." Tears fell again but they felt different. "I most certainly will."

Chad plucked the diamond-encrusted band from the box and slid it on her finger, Frou-Frou watching every move.

The end

Preview: Domestic Arts

...

A door slammed downstairs, and running footsteps heralded her sister Dorie.

"Evie? Evie, where are you?" she called out, leaping up the stairs. Evelyn stuck her head out the bedroom doorway. *Great. Just what I need. Youthful enthusiasm. I never felt older.*

"Here. I'm in here," she said, turning back to the pile of clothes.

With a gust of energy, her baby sister flung herself into the room and grabbed her for a hug.

"What?" Evie laughed in spite of herself. "What's this?"

"Dad said you were coming, and I just couldn't wait to show you," Dorie pulled back and looked in Evie's face. Suddenly serious, she said, "Hey, are you okay? What's up?"

Evie turned away from the look of concern. "I'm fine. I'm always fine, you know that." She looked back at her sister, glowing skin, bright green eyes, long light hair. "You look wonderful. What's with you?"

"Thanks!" Dorie bounced over to sit on the edge of the bed. "I kind of feel wonderful. You know Chad and I are getting a big grant for the old dogs home, right?

"Yeah, I heard that from Dad. I'm happy for you. That's wonderful."

"So, because we're going to have jobs and not be scrambling to try to feed a pack of old dogs and pay for their vet bills and barely having enough money to feed ourselves, we decided..." Dorie stopped suddenly. "Just look." She held out her left hand. Sunlight sparkled off the diamond ring.

Oh, no. Not this. Not today. She suppressed tears.

"Oh, my," Evie said reverently, as she took her sister's fingers in her hand. "What a beautiful vintage piece. You're buying jewelry now?" She raised her eyebrows.

"Evie!" Dorie protested. "Don't play dumb. We're engaged!"

With an effort, Evie laughed. "Congratulations. I'm sorry to tease you. That's wonderful. When did that all happen?"

"Well, really just last night. We just found out about the grant. So that's why you didn't know yet about being engaged. We only told Dad and Alice, and we're going to make a more general family announcement on a Sunday video chat. But you're here so I get to tell you in person!"

Evie felt that pain in her chest again. She pushed it away and said, "Chad's such a good guy. I'm very happy for both of you."

Dorie smiled happily on the bed. "I really didn't think it would happen so soon, but things change and then, you know, things change." She held out her hand and gazed at it admiringly. Then she looked back at Evie. "And what about you and Jase? I imagine you'll be making an announcement soon, too. Right?"

Evie's breath caught in her throat. "I'm not thinking that, no." She looked away from Dorie's puzzled stare. "But let's talk about you. Do you have a date or anything?"

Dorie laughed. "Nah. I'm not in a rush, but the change in status makes Alice happier to have me and Chad living together in her house." Alice was Chad's grandmother, his only family.

"She's a little old fashioned, I guess, " Evie suggested. "I bet that applies to Dad too."

"Maybe. But he hasn't said so, and I've been mostly living there since last fall. Only now we have a real plan." Dorie sounded jubilant.

There it was again, that feeling. Not jealousy, but a pang, nevertheless. Who knew emotional pain could be physical?

"How long are you staying?" Dorie asked, surveying the pile of clothes on the bed.

"The weekend or maybe more," Evie said vaguely.

"More? Don't you have to work?"

"Yeah, well, you know, work. One perk, maybe the only perk, of the artsy-fartsy life is that you have some flexibility about work."

"That's what Mum used to call it, right? Evelyn lives the artsy-fartsy life."

Evie gave her a dark glance. "I hated it when she said that. But now I kind of get it. Making a living in the arts isn't easy but when you can pull it off, you get to do the thing you love best every single day."

"I get it," Dorie said, getting up off the bed. "I get living from grant to grant, after this past year with the dog sanctuary. If the work is your calling, you don't have a choice but sometimes eating would be good, too."

Evie chuckled. "My, my, how my baby sister has grown up." She slung an arm across Dorie's shoulders, and they headed downstairs.

...

About Annie

Annie M. Ballard writes about women and family ties in the small villages that feel like home. With one foot in the Canadian Maritimes and the other in New England, she digs deep into the lives of her characters. When she's not writing, she's happily baking, gardening, powerlifting and trying to make friends with every dog in her neighbourhood.

Annie's stories include strong women living real lives, good men trying to do better, and always a happy ending.

Did you like this book? Please let others know, and consider posting a review on Goodreads, Amazon, Kobo, or another site. Thank you so much!

Find Annie at her webpage, anniemballard.com, or email Annie@anniemballard.com.